John Oates

The Teaching of Tennyson

John Oates

The Teaching of Tennyson

ISBN/EAN: 9783337001636

Printed in Europe, USA, Canada, Australia, Japan

Cover: Foto ©Andreas Hilbeck / pixelio.de

More available books at **www.hansebooks.com**

THE TEACHING
OF TENNYSON

By JOHN OATES, Author
of "*The Sorrow of God,*" etc.

" *We only feel, whate'er he uttereth,*
This savours not of death,
This hath a relish of eternity."
William Watson

New and Revised Edition

LONDON JAMES BOWDEN
10 HENRIETTA STREET
COVENT GARDEN W.C. 1898

First Edition, ✢ ✢ ✢ *January* 1895.
Second Edition, Revised and Enlarged, December 1898.

TO

MY WIFE AND CHILDREN

THIS BOOK

IS

LOVINGLY DEDICATED.

PREFACE.

HAS Tennyson any message, or is he merely "an idle singer of an empty day"? Is he content to leave us in admiration of his beautiful art without a guiding gleam for the conduct of life? Does he give us any great verities upon which we may stand, as upon rock, in the midst of the surging voices of doubt? Does he sing of the ultimate man—the·final triumph of the race; or does he wail a requiem over lost ideals, and a creed out-worn?

By careful classification of the related poems I have striven, in the following pages, to extract the teaching of the poet. We shall find that he not only gives an ethical law for the guidance of life, but an answer to those deeper questions that utter their tremulous voices in the shrine of the soul.

The Ethical Poems naturally fall into two groups, and as they delineate the victory and the defeat

of the soul I have called them Poems of Life and
Poems of Death. The ethical law, which is the
pivot of the groups, may be thus formulated—
*the soul must rule the senses and not the senses rule
the soul, while the soul itself must be ruled not by
self but by that higher love that finds its deepest life
in sacrifice.*

I have placed "In Memoriam" among the
Ethical Poems—though it is partly a religious epic
—for the reason that it affords a powerful illustration
of the conflict of soul with subtle doubt.

The second division deals with the Emotional
Poems. The first group falls under the classification
of the Sanctity of Love, and reveals the poet both
as a perfect artist and a pure moralist. The second
group I have called the Degradation of Love in
which the passion of his indignation burns like
flame.

The third division comprises the Religious Poems,
in which will be found Tennyson's threefold message of immanence and immortality and evolution,
along with side-lights, indicating the relation of
the poet to certain creeds—*viz.* Mysticism,
Calvinism, Latitudinarianism, and Spiritism.

The poet is reported to have said that the
English people positively hated poetry and would

not read it. Doubtless there is a popular dislike of poetry, but the reason lies in its almost enforced obscurity. When the meaning is clear, the most prosaic yield to its charm.

I hope it may be found that I have done something towards drawing out the teaching of Tennyson, and that this book may be of service as an introductory study to students, who should, however, carefully read the original poems in the order in which they are classified, along with the delightful "Memoir" by Hallam, Lord Tennyson, to which I am indebted for some explanatory foot-notes. I may, also, be allowed to thank Lord Tennyson for a kind letter in reference to my book, an extract from which, on the next page, I am permitted to publish.

Facsimile of Letter from Lord Tennyson.

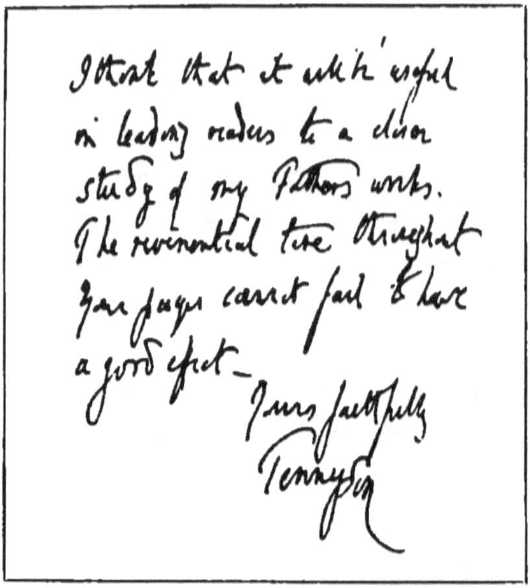

I think that it will be useful in leading readers to a closer study of my Father's works. The reverential tone throughout your pages cannot fail to have a good effect —

Yours faithfully
Tennyson

CONTENTS

THE ETHICAL POEMS

POEMS OF LIFE; OR, THE VICTORY OF SOUL

POEMS OF DEATH; OR, THE VICTORY OF SENSE

12 CONTENTS.

THE EMOTIONAL POEMS

THE SANCTITY OF LOVE

THE DEGRADATION OF LOVE

POEMS OF LIFE; OR, THE
VICTORY OF, SOUL.

The Lady of Shalott. The Palace of Art. The Two Voices. Locksley Hall. The Sailor Boy. Ulysses. In Memoriam. Idylls of the King (in part).

The Lady of Shalott. IN "The Lady of Shalott" we have a lovely isle pictured with such realism that "nowhere are the vivid pictures of the pre-Raphaelite school more brilliantly forecast than in this extraordinary lyric." We see the white willows, the quivering aspen, the pure lilies, the ever-flowing wave, and, in the centre of the wooded isle, a hoary castle. We see the heavy barges towed by patient horses, and the silken-sailed boats, with swift white wings, flitting down to Camelot.

In this sequestered spot lives a Lady. She is never seen at the casement looking out on the flowers, or waving a hand to the passing boatmen ; but the reapers tell how in the early morn, when cutting the golden grain, a sweet song came floating down the wave, and at noon it came again, and they whispered, "'Tis the fairy Lady of Shalott." Why does she live in solitude? How does she spend her time? She weaves a magic web, sitting before a mirror.

> "She has heard a whisper say,
> A curse is on her if she stay
> To look down to Camelot.
> * * *
> And moving thro' a mirror clear
> That hangs before her all the year,
> Shadows of the world appear."

" The mirror into which the Lady gazes is, in the first place, the mirror which always stood behind the tapestry, whose face was turned to the glass, so that the worker could see the effect of her stitches without moving from her seat. But it has another use. Each view which the earlier part of the poem presents is cast upon the mirror. Scene follows scene as in a *camera lucida*, vivid, detailed, delicate."

She sees the highway and the river, the village churls and the market girls, an abbot, a shepherd boy, a page, a mounted knight, a funeral, and two young lovers.

> "Came two young lovers lately wed;
> 'I am half sick of shadows,' said
> The Lady of Shalott."

She is waking out of the world of unrealities. She had seen in her magic mirror the pictures of

death and love, and the latter had made the deeper
impression. She is "half sick of shadows," and
longs for realities. Hitherto she had lived in her
fairy world of dreams, but now the awakening comes
with a shock that dispels the unreal by revealing
the actual. Sir Lancelot appears riding gaily down
to Camelot. The effect upon the Lady is instan-
taneous and complete : she leaps out of the sleep
of fancy ; she is in love with Lancelot ; she looks
after him down to Camelot.

> "The mirror crack'd from side to side ;
> ' The curse is come upon me,' cried,
> The Lady of Shalott."

What, then, was the curse ? Why, that if she turned
from dreams to doing, from shadows to realities, she
should become involved in the passions of mortals
and suffer their fate. But is it not better to know
the actual and take the risk of pain and loss than
live in idle dreams ? The Lady awakes to the
passion of love, and is brave enough to take the
consequence.

She comes to the river, where she finds a boat ;
and, as if in expectation of a tragic end, she writes
her name about the prow, and is carried by the
stream down to Camelot, singing her last song
as she glides through "willowy hills," while the
reapers pause to listen to her mournful carol.

She floats down the wave between the houses,

and knights and burghers read her name upon
the prow and cross themselves in fear.

> "But Lancelot mused a little space;
> He said, 'She has a lovely face.'"

The ethical meaning of the lyric is the emptiness
of life lived in fancy. The soul, roused by realities,
turns from shadows, and is satisfied with the reward
of feeling and knowing. Was it not better that
she should love and be lost than not know love?
Was not such a reality, to herself, worth infinitely
more than the weary life of unreality? The poet
teaches here, and always, that the soul must awake to
actualities, and be willing to suffer the curse involved
in mortal passions, that it may win its highest life
of sacrifice.

The Palace of Art. THIS is a characteristic poem. All the archi-
tectural details of the palace are sharply and
accurately defined. It is no cloud-wreathed
"castle in the air," vague and filmy. If we were to
paint it, we could not omit a single detail without
spoiling the effect of the whole. It affords the best
illustration of the descriptive imagination of the
poet. Suddenly rising out of a meadow-land, where
the green grass waves, is a high crag-platform,
scaling the light, and difficult of ascent—a great
lonely, lordly pile of rocks, that laughs at the storm,
and from its smooth, burnished platform mirrors

the sun.   Upon this isolated crag, looking down
in regal splendour upon the little hills that nestle
at its feet, the poet builds his stately palace.   We
see the gleaming pile, which is the " pleasure-house "
of the soul, and the four courts, and the squared
lawns, and the golden-dragons spouting " a flood of
fountain-foam," the cloisters running round the courts,
through which the flood sends its sonorous music.
We see encircling the palace-roof a gilded gallery,
looking far away o'er hill and dale to the glistening
sands and the creaming sea.   We hear the
splashing of the fourfold cascades as they fall over
the crags, and far up on every peak we see a
statue holding a golden cup, from which perfumed
clouds of incense rise, while deep-set windows all
around the palace, stained and traced, glow with
crimson fires.

Within the palace art has lavished beauty with
prodigal hand.

There are long-sounding corridors, and many-
sized rooms.

> " Full of great rooms and small the palace stood,
>   All various, each a perfect whole
> From living Nature, fit for every mood
>   And change of my still soul."

The artistic rooms are filled with selected pictures
to fit the fancy of the changing mood.   The
subjects are carefully delineated.   We have various
scenes from nature and domestic life touched with

shadow and with light. We look upon faces and forms of classic loveliness. We are charmed with choice paintings of seraphic Milton, or bland Shakespeare, or world-worn Dante. We see the ceiling made celestial with angels ascending and descending, and the floor all mosaic " with cycles of the human tale of this wide world." In the towers great bells swing out their silver sounds. Thus the palace rises in sublime and solitary grandeur on the far-off crag, filled with forms of beauty and rich with glow of colour. But for whom is the palace built? *It is the home of a human soul*— a soul withdrawn from the stern realities of life, with an ambition to live for sensuous pleasure in its purest form. She will in solitude seek to realise her own ideal, and live for art and all things lovely. For a while we learn of her seraphic bliss; she has solved the riddle of life, and is steeped in its sensuous delights. The spirit of art charms her into sweet dreams and mystic worlds, but the effect upon the moral nature is seen in her selfish egoism.

> " ' O God-like isolation which art mine,
>   I can but count thee perfect gain,
>   What time I watch the darkening droves of swine
>   That range on yonder plain.' "

Living in selfish solitude she becomes self-centred. From the height of her isolation she looks down upon humanity with the disdain of fancied superiority

and the contempt of irreligion, and speaks of men
as " droves of swine ! "

Thus she loses touch with human life and with
the great questions that move the world. She can
look with satisfaction upon the human herd, driven
by devils into the raging deep !

This is unnatural and immoral. The process
of degeneracy is subtle and sure. What is the
cause ? Is the poem a condemnation of pure art ?
Is it possible that love of the beautiful can spoil the
soul ? Does not beauty inspire and elevate ? Is
not it the ideal of true art to realise the mystic
beauty of nature which lies around us, and give our
mortal eyes some glimpse of immortal loveliness ?
It is evident that art, flooding the palace with
beauty, was not the cause of her loss of pity. Her
degeneracy lies in the fact that she did not use
beauty to refine and gladden other lives. She
appropriated art as if she alone were selected, and
seated on an oriel throne to receive the homage
of sculpture and painting and song ! True art is
cosmopolitan and teaches its own sublime truths.
The poet does not condemn pure art, but the use
to which art is put by this self-centred soul. Her
selfishness lies in the egoism that claims beauty
for herself alone. Living with such surroundings,
she conceives herself the elect of heaven. Hence
the pride and cynicism that can speak of human
beings as " darkening droves of swine." She might

have used her palace for the people, but she abused
it in her isolation. Thus the soul turned a blessing
into a curse, and shrank into the littleness of self.
She can even prate of the moral instinct and her
right of rising from the dead, and at last she vaults
on to a throne of pure egoism !

> " 'I sit as God holding no form of creed,
> But contemplating all. ' "

The sharp transition from this life of rapt ecstasy,
makes the contrast clear and the teaching impressive.
The soul passes swiftly from heights of rapture to
depths of remorse. The cause of transition lies in
the ever-living problem of the meaning of life—
whence ? whither ?

> " Full oft the riddle of the painful earth
> Flash'd thro' her as she sat alone."

The pain that throbs with burning pulse through
creation strikes into her heart. The sobbing as
of a troubled sea, that breaks out of the deep of
personality, makes discord in her music. The sun
of life, that seems to set in final night over the glad
laughter of the young world, flings a shadow across
her sensuous soul. Is there a God ? Does God
smile behind the curtain at the tragedies of life ?
Does He like to watch the contortions of creation
as the fire burns out its heart ? What is man ?
Spray flung up from the deep to catch the gleam

of higher worlds, then sink into the wild, hungry
sea ?   Thus,

> "Lest she should fail and perish utterly
> God before whom ever lie bare
> The abysmal deeps of Personality,
> Plagued her with sore despair."

Then she awakes to the sense of loneliness. She
is face to face with tragic problems, and longs for
sympathy and the sound of a human voice. She
had chosen solitude and disdained sympathy in her
selfish, æsthetic love ; but now that she is waking to
the realities of being she hates solitude, and craves
sympathy.

> "Deep dread and loathing of her solitude
> Fell on her, from which mood was born
> Scorn of herself."

Her sense of loneliness becomes a terror. The
beautiful palace is filled with phantoms weeping
tears of blood, and with ghosts bearing hearts of
flame, and with corpses standing against the wall.
Are not they the shadows of realities falling on her
wakeful vision ? She begins to realise her hateful
self and lonely isolation. Now she is like a fixed
spot amid infinite motion, and now she is like a pool
on the shore listening to the music of the sea, and
now she is like a star that watches the starry dance,
itself motionless. Nature thus aids art in impress-
ing the terror of loneliness.

"Back on herself her serpent pride had curl'd.
'No voice,' she shriek'd in that lone hall,
'No voice breaks thro' the stillness of this world :
    One deep, deep silence all !"

Then despair enters. In her slothful shame she
feels exiled from God, and hates death and life,
time and eternity.

"She finds no comfort anywhere."

Is there no satisfaction to be found in her beautiful
palace ? None ! Her crime is selfishness. She has
lost her pity for the world, and her penalty is to
crave the sympathy denied to others. Fierce is
her torment, her own self is her hell, and it blurs
the palace and blots out the face of beauty. Now
she seems to hear the sound of " human footsteps."
Her humanity is returning ; she will be selfish no
more, and will seek the lowly lives in their innocence and purity. The soul had lived in the pride of
voluptuous enjoyment of nature and art and culture,
only to find that these cannot solve "the riddle of
the painful earth," nor give peace amid the surging
problems of time.

"'Make me a cottage in the vale,' she said,
    'Where I may mourn and pray.'"

She learns to pray ! She comes now to God and
duty; and, giving the right place to religion, she may
go back to her palace *with others,* to make art and
culture aids to religion and humanity.

The poem teaches that the meaning of life cannot be found in selfish solitude and sensuous enjoyment. Love of beauty in itself is noble, but love of beauty all for self is fatal to religious life. Nature and art and culture may not take the place of religion. We may love the beautiful without feeling any pulse of pity for the world; but to love God and man is to feel the pain of creation, and to awake out of self and the sensuous to a life of pure sacrifice and helpful service.

The Two Voices.* To mingle imagination with philosophy, and write the purest poetical diction while engaged in metaphysical analysis, is the problem of the poet. Tennyson, in "The Two Voices," has solved the problem by giving us in a philosophical poem sublime poetry. While sounding the deeps of personality, and showing the conflict of soul with direst doubt and tormenting fear, his music never falters, but flows on until it falls into peaceful triumph.

Two voices are represented as speaking within the soul. The one voice stands for faith, and the other voice stands for doubt. DOUBT sees no way out of the "curse," nor how to solve "the riddle of the painful earth," but thinks death is the end

* "When I wrote 'The Two Voices,' I was so utterly miserable, a burden to myself and to my family, that I said, 'Is life worth anything'?"—TENNYSON, *A Memoir*, i., p. 193.

of all being, and truth a phantom on far-off hills alluring the soul into blinding mist. It urges self-destruction as giving instant relief to the agony of being. FAITH relies chiefly on the " inner evidence " of soul against sense, on its hunger for God and immortality, which is ever the protest from within against the doubt that would make God the fiction of fancy and immortality the dream of delusion.

Listen to the discussion. DOUBT, in view of the miseries of the soul, urges suicide.

" Were it not better not to be ? "

FAITH replies that personality, with its wonders of reason and will and consciousness, is of too great worth to be flung away on the voids of death. DOUBT will not concede the value claimed for personality, and draws an illustration from the dragon-fly as it leaves its husk. What could be more beautiful than this bright creature, with its gleaming plates of sapphire mail flashing on its winged way ? Are you of greater worth than the dragon-fly, that you should live ? FAITH will not grant the equality, but claims supremacy for personality in power of mind and heart over the dragon-fly with its fading beauty. DOUBT cynically charges the soul with the blindness of self-pride, and alleges, what it does not prove, that in the boundless universe are beings of vast superiority.

Granted you are superior to the dragon-fly, there are many beings superior to you.

FAITH replies that there are no two things alike, but there is great diversity, and so a specific value attaches to the unit. DOUBT, while conceding the argument, scoffs at the conceit of the soul that thinks it will be missed, or that any one will weep, or that any beam of light will be less radiant.

This is not argument, but cynicism, in which FAITH is silenced by satire.

DOUBT, mistaking silence for consent, again urges self-destruction, and draws a vivid picture of the soul's anguish—sleepless nights and impaired reason. FAITH answers that life is full of possibilities, and to end it is to destroy its " happier chance." Life is an evolution, and it is instructive to watch the unfolding.

> "And men, thro' novel spheres of thought
> Still moving after truth long sought,
> Will learn new things when I am not."

DOUBT replies that the end must come sooner or later, and the man cannot remain to witness the evolution of all " new things."

FAITH affirms that the process is constant, and every month shows some new feature of growth. And so it would be folly to commit suicide, and not see

> " How grows the day of human power."

DOUBT will not be held too closely to the line of argument, and from the limited strikes off at a tangent to speak of the limitless ; draws a picture of the far-off silent summit of truth, with the sacred morning spreading overhead ; tells how the " highest-mounted mind " (the mind that has scaled the heights) sees only the dawn and not the day, and asks if the soul can expect, in the years of its natural term, to see plainly all the light of knowledge,

> " Or make that morn, from his cold crown
> And crystal silence creeping down,
> Flood with full daylight glebe and town ? "

Or should the soul be winged into knowledge, not yet realised, the heights would still be above.

> " Nor art thou nearer to the light,
> Because the scale is infinite."

This is not fair argument, for the soul pleaded to live, not with the hope of finding here the absolute, but with the wish of watching the growth of the finite towards the infinite. FAITH seems to waver, and the argument takes another turn. The soul, almost tempted to self-destruction, is restrained by fear of public opinion. Men will say, " He dared not tarry," he was afraid to face life !

DOUBT replies that to live and be wretched is worse than to commit suicide and be called a coward ; besides, when the soul goes into dust, it cannot be vexed by what men may say.

"The right ear, that is fill'd with dust,
Hears little of the false or just."

And men will forget, is the cynical taunt of Doubt.

FAITH, stirred by the possibility of being forgotten, recalls the "resolve" of its young life to immortalise itself by noble deeds, to war with falsehood, to fight for liberty of thought, to search for hidden causes, to sow generous seeds, and die in some good cause "wept for, honour'd, known." Surely it is better to live an d recall,and strive to realise such a resolve? DOUBT answers, The dream was good, but it was caused by the hot blood of youth, a passing pulse of a generous heart, which cannot be realised in later life, when the heart-fires burn low.

"Then comes the check, the change, and fall."

And should the soul realise its noblest ideal, it would be little worth in solving the riddle of the earth ; every man, like a worm, spins out his own cocoon, and cannot tell the meaning of life, nor scale the height of truth. Truth is unattainable, gleams for a moment upon the mist, and shoots its golden ray along the gloomy crag ; and should Faith leap forward, it would only be to find the "fold is on her brow," and the shadows gird the hills. If so,

"Cease to wail and brawl !
Why inch by inch to darkness crawl ?
There is one remedy for all."

3

FAITH answers triumphantly by appealing to the experience of the many who did not find Truth a mocking phantom, nor life a curse, nor heaven a fiction, but who found "the joy that mixes man with heaven," saw the gates of Eden gleam, heard in the vaults of death the murmur of life, and died, like Stephen, touched with glory.

DOUBT, growing sullen, replies that all this is purely a matter of organism, the mere phantasies of a soul in which "the elements were kindlier mix'd."

Then the argument changes. FAITH suggests that death might result in worse evils and in greater suffering. DOUBT, in reply, calls the soul to look on one dead, the face without passion, the hands folded, the lips sealed, deaf to every call, blind to every sight, placid and peaceful, with naught to suggest suffering after death. Tragedies of shame are wrought in his own home, "but he is chill to praise or blame." There lies the dead apparently without will or consciousness or power, crumbling away into dust and darkness. It does look so. It would seem as if death seized all of being, and flung it into the grave of never-broken silence. How will FAITH meet this argument? Can the soul deny its own senses? There is no motion in the dead man, not a sign of life. FAITH replies, How do you know that the man is dead? The evidence of the senses is in your favour, but

the evidence of soul is against you. I have known
all this from youth, have seen the shadow creep
from grave to grave, and the daisy die beneath the
touch of death. Men have always seen it, and
yet refused to believe that death ends all. They have
clung to the belief of their immortality, and have
felt a something which death cannot kill, and
FAITH asks—

> "Who forged that other influence,
> That heat of inward evidence,
> By which he doubts against the sense?"

The "inward evidence" is this—Man has the idea
of eternity : whence came it ? He has a type of perfection in his mind not realised in nature : whence
is it ? He seems to hear a heavenly voice, and he
sees the evolution of beauty and order : who is it
that evolves ? He feels a power within, that wars
with lower things : what is it ? DOUBT does not
answer, but changes the argument—You came
from nothing, and to nothing may return. FAITH
replies—How do you know my birth was my
beginning ? I may have had a pre-existence, and,
as in trances men forget, I may have forgotten my
pre-natal life ; or I may have fallen from a nobler
place, which would account for my "vague emotion
of delight" in the presence of alpine splendours ;
or I may have come up out of lower lives which
I have forgotten, even as we now forget our first
years of childhood ; or I may have been "naked

essence," and, if so, incompetent of memory, yet, at times, I seem to recall some experience of a pre-natal life—

> "Like glimpses of forgotten dreams."

DOUBT ridicules the dreams and reminds him of the reality of pain. FAITH will not be allured into suicide by false issues, and shows that the universal longing is always for life, and not death.

> " 'Tis life, whereof our nerves are scant,
> Oh life, not death, for which we pant;
> More life, and fuller, that I want."

Thus, by appealing to the " inner evidence " of soul against sense, DOUBT is silenced. Still the man sits as one forlorn, for victory has not brought peace. Reason by argument has triumphed over doubt, but his moral and emotional nature are not satisfied. The satisfaction comes in a symbol. He looks out upon a domestic picture—father and mother and a little child between them going to church—and it becomes to him the symbol of the unity of love.

> " These three made unity so sweet
> My frozen heart began to beat,
> Remembering its ancient heat.
> *   *   *   *
> The dull and bitter voice was gone!"

He could no longer question the existence of God and immortality in presence of such love.

The close of the poem relates the final victory of faith over doubt.

> "'What is it thou knowest, sweet voice?' I cried.
> 'A hidden hope,' the voice replied."

He finds fellowship with God through love, and, filled with peace, finds also a glory in nature, while her varied life quickens the pulse of hope, and he marvels

> "How the mind was brought
> To anchor by one gloomy thought."

ley   WE have thus far illustrated (the central truth of the poet's teaching, that the soul only comes to its best life through strenuous conflict with the dream of selfish solitude, as it cherishes the egoism of æsthetic culture, and with the despair of materialism, as it wrestles with faith.) These Poems of Life portray the different phases of the war waged by the soul with the forces of spiritual death.

(In "Locksley Hall" the same truth finds fresh illustration. In the hall down by the sea, looking over the sandy tracks, within sound of the roaring waters, there lived a sentimental youth fond of star-gazing and fairy tales of science and mystic musing on the unknown.

Such a youth would be sensitive to love, and

soon he finds "all the current of his being" setting towards his cousin Amy. They become engaged. There is much beauty in the incidental references to the sublime effect of pure love,—how in its hands the moments of time, like golden sands, slipped all too quickly through the hour-glass ; or how self, touched by the hand of love, found no place, but yielded itself gladly and died away as if in music ; or how, in the morning on the moorlands, love found its song in the "ring of the copses," or in the evening, by the sea, watching the stately ships,

"Our spirits rush'd together at the touching of the lips."

And so the poet sings of the sacredness of love, its power to touch life with tender grace, and transfigure nature with subtle beauty.

But the scene quickly changes.

Amy, utterly weak, yields to the tyranny of her father, is false to her lover, and marries a man of lower character, with the prospect of his coarser nature rudely crushing out the fineness of her own. If the jilted lover had wished for revenge, he might have found it in the degeneracy of the fickle Amy ; but we have to trace the influence of disappointment upon the man. Love had created for him new light and beauty : will he lose both, since Amy has been false ? He had nourished a youth sublime, with great self-esteem, and he writhes beneath the wrong! Will he allow his life to be spoiled? Will he yield to the weakness of senti- mental crooning over the " tender grace of the day that is dead," or will he gird himself to noble action, and in earnest doing triumph over fruitless sentiment?

The evolution of character is interesting. At first he is cynical. He pictures the husband with coarse sensibility coming home with heavy eyes, and the duty of Amy to soothe her weary lord with his overwrought brain by her finer fancies and lighter thoughts.

Then he finds relief in cursing. He curses most eloquently the " social wants that sin," and " the social lies that warp," and " the sickly forms that err," and " the gold that gilds." He has been dis- appointed in love, and blames the whole social system.

Now he becomes introspective. He begins to think that he is mad for cherishing the seed of bitterness, and resolves to pluck it from his bosom ; but to forget seems impossible, and he asks, " Where is comfort?" Can he find it in thinking only of the Amy he first knew, loving and kind?

Can he think of her as dead? And since death sanctifies and sweetens the memory of the dead, may not he think only of her love? No! for she did not love him truly. Then there is no comfort in memory.

> "This is truth the poet sings,
> That a sorrow's crown of sorrow is remembering happier things."

The memory that torments him may have its vision of pain for Amy as well ; though, for her, nature will bring solace in the purer life of her little child.

But what of himself? He finds that in cursing the social system, in sentimental introspection, in analysis of memory, there is no compensation. He begins to see there is only one remedy, if he would save himself.

> "Wherefore should I care?
> I myself must *mix with action*, lest I wither by despair."

He must find some noble work, and fling himself into action, if he would redeem his manhood from sentimental misery ; but he knows not where to turn, for "every gate is throng'd with suitors." Then comes the vision of his boyhood, with its "wild pulsation" and yearning for the "large excitement" of the coming years, its glimpse of the flaring lamps of London and its never-resting sea of life. The vision inspires him, and he seems to see the great end towards which the mighty masses are moving.

> "Till the war-drum throbb'd no longer, and the battle-flags were furl'd
> In the Parliament of man, the Federation of the world."

He sees "men the workers," shaping the glorious

future of the world, and he will be a man among men.

"So I triumph'd ere my passion . . .
  Left me with the palsied heart, and left me with the jaundiced eye."

Then he shows how to the "jaundiced eye" all things seem out of joint. Science only creeps along. Feudalism, as it "nods and winks behind a slowly dying fire," dreads the power of the people.

Suddenly, with the call of his comrades, another life opens to him, that would tempt him from the life of energy and effort into sensuous delights and mystic dreams, "in yonder shining orient."

"There to wander far away,
On from island unto island at the gateways of the day."

It is the temptation which comes to many—the softness and sweetness of a life of self-indulgence, in exchange for the life of strenuous effort. But the hero of "Locksley Hall" resists the temptation by choosing the life of action, and heals the wounds of his heart by mingling with the progress of humanity.

"For the mighty wind arises, roaring seaward, and I go."

The Sailor Boy. THE lesson that the soul only finds its true life in noble effort, with its sacrifice of selfish ease, rings again in the bright voice of "The Sailor Boy," who, tempted to renounce the calls of duty and danger, and accept the life of indolence, bravely answers,—

> "God help me! save I take my part
> Of danger on the roaring sea,
> A devil rises in my heart,
> Far worse than any death to me."

Ulysses. THE same truth, like a battle-cry, is heard clear and strong in the war-song of "Ulysses." * The old king had travelled far and seen many lands, had held his soul in red battle with its clash of arms, and found manhood in strife and action; but now he feels his strength is being sapped by an indolent, self-indulgent life.

> "It little profits that an idle king,
> By this still hearth, among these barren crags,
> Match'd with an aged wife, I mete and dole
> Unequal laws unto a savage race."

Caged like some bird with strong pinions, he would break from his prison and beat his way through the storm, and gaze in the face of the sun. He will leave his sceptre to his son, and go again upon the dark, broad seas with the old mariners.

> "Souls that have toil'd, and wrought, and thought with me."

---

* Ulysses was written soon after Arthur Hallam's death, and gave my feeling about the need of going forward and braving the struggle of life perhaps more simply than anything in "In Memoriam."—TENNYSON, *A Memoir*, i., p. 196.

the Bristol Channel and the far-away waters where the ships come and go. A fitting prelude to " In Memoriam " is the pathetic song—

" Break, break, break,
   On thy cold gray stones, O Sea !
   And I would that my tongue could utter
   The thoughts that arise in me."

Throughout his grief verges on despair. There is no line of light upon the weary face. The poem is ethically dark, and might have been written by an agnostic. It is a pathetic wail of unredeemed tragedy, out of which no music of hope flows. The fisher boy will shout, and the sailor will sing, and the ships will sail to their haven—life going on and ever, but not life for him, now that his love lies buried.

"But the tender grace of a day that is dead
   Will never come back to me."

Is this, then, the teaching of the poet—death, darkness, oblivion ? No ; it is only the mood of his wild grief. Sorrow has so stunned him that he does not feel the good of life. Doubt has so blinded him that he does not see as yet the dawn of " boundless day." He stumbles through chaos and rushing darkness, where God is not and death seems everywhere. Study this picture of despair before passing into the gallery of " In Memoriam " ; then pass on and watch the face of grief

revealed in the poem—how it changes, until
doubt brightens into faith, and sorrow into joy,
and despair into hope, when darkness vanishes in
the light of God ! Look first at those pictures
which speak of Hallam, and describe the moods
of the poet as the body of his friend is brought
across the sea, and up the Severn, and laid in
its grave on the lonely hill looking over the waste
waters.

The epic may be divided into three main sections.

**First
Section—
Grief.**
I. IN the first picture we see that mingling
of love which saves the soul from utter loss
and death. If in its sacred sorrow it is to
find a gain in loss, and "grasp the far-off
interest of tears," it can only be by wedding grief
to love. When they are united, the soul soars over
death and its darkness ; but when love dies, the
" victor hours " triumph.

II. Grief turns to the yew tree, curtained by
endless night. The summer suns had shone, but no
bright beams had pierced the " thousand years of
gloom." In the dark winter's foliage, the stricken
soul sees the symbol of its own grief shadowing all
things.

III. The soul awakes to the consciousness that
sorrow has " lying lips " when she declares that the
whole course of nature is determined by blind force,

or that the face of the sky is a delusion, or that
the music of the many voices of the world is but
mocking sound, and asks whether sorrow is to be
trusted when she casts such a tragic gloom over
the bright sky, and kills the music of the glad
creation. Shall he accept her as a guide ?

> "Embrace her as my natural good;
> Or crush her, like a vice of blood?"

VI. His grief refuses to be comforted by the
kindly meant letters of condolence with the stereo-
typed phrases, "other friends remain," and " loss is
common to the race."

> "And common is the commonplace,
> And vacant chaff well meant for grain."

He rejects the proffered consolation. If his love
for Hallam were forgotten in the sorrow of others,
it would be a loss to himself. Whatever destroys
pure love is a curse, not a blessing. God would
not have us forget but cherish our sacred loves, that
we may find them in Him, or else " what to me
remains of good ? "

VII. He is thinking of the dead friend and the
dark house in the loveless street where the hand of
Hallam grasped his. He is unable to sleep, and,
rising in the " earliest morning," creeps along like
a stricken deer to the well-known door, as if once
again to see the radiant face and clasp the
outstretched hand of his friend ; but, alas !

> " He is not here ; but far away
>   The noise of life begins again,
>   And ghastly thro' the drizzling rain
> On the bald street breaks the blank day."

What a picture is portrayed in the dreary words, " the drizzling rain," " the bald street," " the blank day " ! We look through them into the soul of grief, and see utter desolation within.

VIII. He states the reason for " In Memoriam." As a happy lover returns to look upon the face of his love, and rings the bell only to find her gone, and with her light and music, and then wanders into the deserted walks to find and cherish a flower that she had reared, so the poet, knowing his friend had been pleased with his poems, would take his " poor flower of poesy " and plant it on his tomb.

IX. We have a beautiful prayer for the safe arrival of the ship bearing the " loved remains " from Vienna. He would have her come quickly : " Ruffle thy mirror'd mast." Speed creates agitation ; the reflection in the mirror of the waters is " ruffled." He would draw all nature into sympathy with his sacred wish for the safety of the " holy urn." At night he would have all the lights above ensphered, and the " gentle heavens " sleep " before the prow," even as the man he loved sleeps.

> " My Arthur, whom I shall not see
>   Till all my widow'd race be run."

X. Chastened Grief still lingers about the vessel,

and seems to hear the noise of the keel and the striking of the bell at night, to see a light in the cabin window and the sailor at his watch. The feelings of sorrow thus find expression in the sounds and sights which fill imagination, and in the freight conveyed by the coming vessel ; while the poet contrasts the awful thought of a body buried at sea in the " roaring wells," with the happier thought of burial on shore in some spot blessed of nature.

> "To rest beneath the clover sod,
> That takes the sunshine and the rains,"

or, in the chancel of the church,

> "where the kneeling hamlet drains
> The chalice of the grapes of God."

XI. His grief looks out upon nature across the wolds, to the sleeping sea beyond, where peace seems to have fallen. It was nature's Sabbath ; but the calm without serves to remind him of " the dead calm in that noble breast " of his sleeping friend, and of the calm in his own stunned heart, only

> " If any calm, *a calm despair.*"

XII. Grief becomes impatient, and takes wings of love and flies to the ship at sea, and hovers about it like a bird.

> "And circle moaning in the air:
> 'Is this the end? Is this the end?'"

How restless !—coming and going, wanting to be where the body of Hallam is, who was

> "More than my brothers are to me."

4

Such is grief clasping love—restless until it find the object loved, lingering about the mortal shell, once the dwelling of the noble spirit that had left its subtle impress on the calm face.

XIV. The bereaved soul cannot realise its loss. If some one came and told him the vessel was lying in the port, and he went down to see the passengers, and the man he loved "as half-divine" suddenly struck a hand with his, and asked "a thousand things of home," he says,—

> "I should not feel it to be strange."

How true! Death seizes our friend, and still we look for him. We seem to hear his footfall in the hall, and turn to see him enter as of old. √ XV. A storm has risen. The winds are roaring from out the western sky; the leaves are whirled before the tempest; the rooks are driven; great trees are torn from their roots; the sea is white with foam; the cattle huddle in fear. He is concerned for the safety of the vessel.

> "And but for fancies, which aver
> That all thy motions gently pass
> Athwart a plane of molten glass,
> I scarce could brook the strain and stir."

XVII. The ship arrives, and he craves the blessing of Heaven on her, for she bears

> "The dust of him I shall not see
> Till all my widow'd race be run."

XVIII. The poet finds some little solace in the
thought that his friend will be buried in English
earth, among the sacred places of home and youth,
while those who bear the body to the last sleeping-
place must have " pure hands." Then in the
longing of pathetic sorrow he would fain cast
himself upon the lifeless form, and breathe his own
almost dying life into the frozen lips of the dead,
but now he can only treasure the look and the
words of the sacred past.

XIX. The ship sails up the Severn, bearing " the
darken'd heart that beat no more," when his grief
is like the flowing of the tide and the hushing of
the Wye.   The rising tide meets the incoming
stream, and by its mightier volume hushes its
babbling.   So with the coming of the body a
greater sea of sorrow floods his being, and his song,
like the stream, is hushed.

> "I brim with sorrow drowning song."

Presently the tides of sorrow fall, and the speechless
soul finds voice.

> "My deeper anguish also falls,
> And I can speak a little then."

XXII—XXVII.   The poet recalls the past, his
tender recollections of all his friend had been, and
how the burdens of life were halved by love.   In
XXVI he cannot bear the thought of love ever
forgetting or becoming indifferent—he thinks this

more awful than death, and would welcome "that shadow"; while in the next canto he does not envy the linnet "that never knew the summer woods," nor "the heart that never plighted troth," for the power to love lifts us far above the beasts, though the object loved be lost.

> "'Tis better to have loved and lost
> Than never to have loved at all."

XXVIII—XXX. We have the coming of Christmas and the changing moods of grief. At first there is gloomy sorrow, as they recall the days when Hallam was with them. How can they be glad when he is not there? They try to be merry.

> "with an awful sense
> Of one mute Shadow watching all."

It is the shadow of death, not the shade of Hallam. But see how the face of grief is changing: a new light plays upon it—the light of hope.

> "Our voices took a higher range;
> Once more we sang: 'They do not die.'"

This ends the first section of "In Memoriam." Grief continues, but is rising, transfigured by love— the love that refuses to believe that death breaks the continuity of life, and that the grave is the tomb of the spirit. He now would rise "as if on stepping-stones" of dead regrets, and with straining eyes look into the sacred mysteries of the world where Hallam is with God. He sees that grief,

cherished alone, means death to love and joy ; but
should chastened love, true to its deepest instinct,
be allowed to take wing and soar, it may find some
light on the problems that darken the soul. Amen.

ond   HIS grief, sustained by love, is now face to
tion—   face with the mystery of the future. Out
ibt.   upon the trackless way, as if searching for
        his friend, he is startled by the mystic pro-
blems that rise out of the deep, and so shape
themselves as to cast a shadow of doubt upon his
spirit.

Is immortality a dream, and death extinction?
or is death unconscious sleep, waiting for the touch
of the finger of God? or is it swift transition into
life eternal? Does that life possess memory, or is
the past buried deep in Lethe? Will friendship
here win fellowship there, or does identity change?
Such are the troubled questions that cannot be swept
out of the way of the bereaved spirit as it passes
into the cloud of the mystery of God and immortality and death. Most of the great souls have
gone into this solemn shadow of Eternity to wrestle
with doubt through the lone night, until the dawn
broke and grew into the " boundless day."

XXXI. The poet begins to face the question of
immortality* and the problems that circle round it.

* The Odes relating to immortality are xxxi-ii-iv-v. xli-ii-iii-iv-v-vi.

He is troubled by the secrets that have drawn a veil over the mouth of the grave. He would fain learn from the experience of Lazarus the meaning of death. Did Lazarus yearn to hear his sister "weeping by his grave"? If asked of all that happened "those four days," the only answer is,—

> "He told it not; or something seal'd
> The lips of that Evangelist."

Our dead do not come back to tell us of the life beyónd, or what they found death to be. When they pass into the house of the Eternal Life, the door is shut on us, and we are left wondering without; but if permitted to visit us and to speak, the poet thinks they "had surely added praise to praise."

XXXII. The human note of this praise is sounded in the home at Bethany, when Mary, looking upon Lazarus, turns her ardent gaze upon Christ, "the Life indeed," and her spiritual love for Him supersedes her natural love for her brother.

> "She bows, she bathes the Saviour's feet
> With costly spikenard and with tears."

The love that raised Lazarus opens for her the gate into spiritual life. She too has her resurrection, and begins to feel the pulse of Life, and know a little of the bliss of which her brother might not speak. To love the highest is to be raised to the highest, and to love the lowest is to sink to the lowest.

> " Thrice blest whose lives are faithful prayers,
>   Whose loves in higher love endure."

But here comes the doubt, casting a darkling shadow upon the spirit—Is there any such thing as immortality ? Does not death strangle life ? Is not the grave like some extinct volcano—the burnt-out cinder of all human hopes and aspirations ? Is not spirit a mode of matter, destined to disintegrate and dissolve ? If thought is identical with cerebral changes which an accident may end, then what becomes of the ego ? Such questions pass like a procession of mocking phantoms through the solemn shadow of the great doubt. This is the problem—Is mind identical with matter ? Is thought one and the same with motion ? The materialist says it is. If he is right, then immortality is a delusion, and dust and ashes are our destiny ; but the answer to the problem given by the greatest scientists is that it cannot be proved !

They do not regard mind and matter, feeling and motion, as identical.* Their testimony, though

* "That a unit of feeling has nothing in common with a unit of motion becomes more than ever manifest when we bring the two into juxtaposition."—*Herbert Spencer.*

"Granted that a definite thought and a definite molecular action in the brain occur simultaneously, we do not possess the organ, nor, apparently, any rudiment of the organ, which would enable us to pass by a process of reasoning from one

negative, is against the materialist, and favours the
Christian belief that the ego is distinct from matter,
and that matter is only the vehicle.   Hence the
poet appeals to the voice of the ego, "the dim
life" within, as suggesting reasonable ground for
cherishing the hope of immortality—a hope central
to the human spirit all the world over.   In all
ages and under all conditions, man has steadfastly
refused to believe that death extinguishes the flame
of life, or that all of his wondrous being, with its
glowing splendours, is only a flash, meteor-like, into
the oblivion of endless night.   This fact of the
human consciousness has never been explained by
philosophy, nor is the philosophy complete which
does not take it into account.   There it stands, as if
a palpitating thing of life, within the house of the
body, with piercing eyes that seem to see "Him
who is invisible," and with boundless energy of
conviction, defying death to touch the spirit, and
showing itself superior to matter by thinking sunlit
thoughts when the darkness deepens.   How explain
this spirit-life that refuses to be circumscribed by
matter, that leaps the bounds of time, and feels at
home only within the spiritual and eternal ?   Is not

phenomenon to the other.   They appear together, but we do
not know why."—*Professor Tyndall.*
   "The materialistic assumption that . . . the life of the soul
accordingly ends with the life of the body, is perhaps the most
baseless assumption that is known to the history of philosophy."
—*The Destiny of Man.*

the very nature of the restless spirit an argument
for a life that death cannot dissolve nor the grave
imprison ?   Yes, and the poet makes his appeal to
the inner consciousness.

XXXIV.

> "My own dim life should teach me this,
>   That life shall live for evermore,
>   Else earth is darkness at the core,
> And dust and ashes all that is."

If life is not immortal, its aspirations are a mockery.
The " dim life " that rises in dawn never grows
into day.   Robbed of immortality, all the world
becomes meaningless.   Nature, as if in sympathy
with the deluded spirit, reveals only " darkness at
the core."   The beautiful world of order and
adaptation becomes only "fantastic beauty," as if
wrought by some wild poet " without a conscience
or an aim."   God ceases to be the object of love
and adoration.   For how can the human spirit
love and worship a God who formed it to aspire
towards Him only to mock its aspirations, or gave
it the dim dawn only with cruel hand to blot out
the sun, or let it see " the distant gates of Eden
gleam" only to bar the gates for ever ?

> "What then were God to such as I?"

He could not be an object of love and desire, if
thus He made a toy of the human soul, or let its
aspirations grow like tender flowers, only to blight
them in the chilling night of death, or trample them

in sportive mood of ridicule. Such a God would be cruel and hateful indeed. A human soul might well lose all "patience," and welcome the jaws of death and darkness as an escape from infinite tyranny.

> "'Twere best at once to sink to peace,
> Like birds the charming serpent draws."

Observe, it is not merely a question of immortality or continued existence beyond the grave apart from God. Such a life, without an object of love, without noble motive or final cause, would be the greatest curse, a very horror of anticipation to make the spirit shudder! Life is only real life when it is found in union with God. Immortality, without conscious knowledge of the absolute good, must be a living death, or an awful void for ever unfilled, through which wander the winds of darkness. Always to look up to the infinite sky, and never to see the face of an all-loving Father, would be the tragedy of immortality; and thus the poet by implication not only assumes the existence of God, but that life can never be complete, even though immortal, without the eternal life of God.

XXXV. But conceding immortality to be a myth, and that the " jaws of vacant darkness " seize all of being, then another question rises to shadow the soul.

> "Might I not say? 'Yet even here,
> But for one hour, O Love, I strive

To keep so sweet a thing alive:'
But I should turn mine ears and hear
The moanings of the homeless sea."

He would hear the work of devastation going on tearing down the hills, while love itself would see in all an image of her own destruction, and languish in

"The sound of that forgetful shore."

Thus, apart from immortality, the love we cherish would become our pain. The thought that death might put a chilling finger on the warm pulse would eat out the heart of life. But the case is idly put. The poet thinks that love, seeing only death and no immortality, would not have been, or else being, would have run in so narrow a channel as to have left man a mere brute that "wallow'd in the woods." Love linked to death could not be spiritual, must be animal, and would leave man in "coarsest Satyr-shape." In purest human love we find an intimation of immortality. Strike out immortality, and love becomes a mocking phantom, revealing the "narrow house," where hope lies dead for ever. Thus the poet finds in love, lived in the faith and life of God, the possibility of the reunion of lives and an evidence

"That life shall live for evermore."

XLI. Now another doubt rises. The question of immortality is settled ; but what of the vanished

life, what of its growth and glory lifted to a height
to which he (the poet) cannot soar ? Must not
that interfere with their sacred friendship and
exchange of thought and feeling ever ?

> "My paths are in the fields I know,
> And thine in undiscover'd lands."

While together on earth, though the spirit of Hallam
ever rose like "heavenward altar-fire," it was possible to have companionship ; but now that the
earthly links are broken he can no longer watch
the growth of his friend, and fain wishes

> "To leap the grades of life and light,"

that he may be with him in fellowship of intellect
and soul. He fears lest, in that other and spiritual
life, his friend may soar beyond his own power to
attain, and thus the doubt shadows his heart,—

> "A spectral doubt which makes me cold,
> That I shall be thy mate no more."

As the eternal years roll on, he grieves lest he
may be "evermore a life behind" that of his friend
who lives with God.

XLII. But he lays the "spectral doubt," as he
reasons that his friend when here still soared above
him, and it was only their being together—"unity
of place"—that made him think he ranked with
Hallam. If here, why not there ? May not unity
of place there bring again friendship and fellowship,

when his friend, now "a lord of large experience,"
would be able to train his mind and will ?

> "And what delights can equal those
> That stir the spirit's inner deeps,
> When one that loves but knows not, reaps
> A truth from one that loves and knows."

The ode suggests not only eternal life in God,
but growing knowledge. If growth in knowledge
add to the sum of human happiness, may we not
infer the same of the life of heaven ? Will not
the bliss of the immortals consist in their ever-
widening vision of the mystery of God ?.

XLIII. But what is death ? Suppose it to be
unconscious sleep, in which, as if in a trance, the
spirit slumbers, folded like a flower at night, bearing
traces of the past ? Would not there be in the
resurrection, with the unfolding spirits of the dead,
a complete record of life ?

> " So then were nothing lost to man ;
> So that still garden of the souls
> In many a figured leaf enrolls
> The total world since life began."

The idea is beautiful—death unconscious sleep.
Our "loved and lost awhile" folding within their
passive memories the sacred scenes and fond
friendships of life, fresh as when they fell asleep,
now waiting like flowers for the dawn to open and
reveal "the traces of the past." If such be death
—a sleep into richer life in which the loves born

in time appear in eternity—then the grief of the
poet is consoled.

> " And love will last as pure and whole
>   As when he loved me here in Time,
>   And at the spiritual prime
>   Rewaken with the dawning soul."

It is a subject which does not admit of dogmatic
statement.   Our knowledge of consciousness in
relation to the body is too limited for us to define
how far the one is dependent on the other, or
whether the spirit has consciousness apart from the
body. As far as science has penetrated it would seem
as if consciousness and organism were correlated.
If the body perish, we may conceive the " ego "
sleeping and waiting unconsciously for the new
organism.   " There are also celestial bodies and
bodies terrestrial."   With the new body the
consciousness may awake with memories and
affections vivid as the unfolding flower. Few are
the gleams that pierce the veil of that silent world
where our dead ones may be sleeping.

XLIV. The subject is continued and viewed from
another point. As man grows in knowledge here
he forgets the experiences of his infant life when

> " God shut the doorways of his head,"

but still dim memories seem to float up to him out
of the mists of those early days,

> " A little flash, a mystic hint."

Then is it not possible that the spirit of the departed, "If Death so taste Lethean springs,"* may be touched with the memory of earthly things? So he prays that his tormenting doubt may be solved.

> "If such a dreamy touch should fall,
> O turn thee round, resolve the doubt."

XLV. But if the departed have knowledge of us and the past, shall we know them again?

The question of personal identity after death is suggested. It may have shaped itself thus—Shall I know my friend again in that other world? Can I be sure that identity will remain unchanged? It is the shadow that creeps over many hearts, the doubt that they may not recognise the vanished face.

The poem shows how conscious identity is formed in childhood—the child grows to distinguish between " I " and " not I." It wins that knowledge through the senses.

> "So rounds he to a separate mind."

But if after death we must begin again to distinguish personal identity,

> "Had man to learn himself anew
> Beyond the second birth of Death,"

---

* Lethe has a double power—to call to remembrance as well as to obliterate.

then the knowledge gained in the body must be lost, which seems incredible. That our identity once realised does not change with the changes of the body seems clear from the fact that every particle of the body is changed while identity remains, and we know one another. Identity must thus lie in the spirit and not in the body, which is only the fading veil of the spirit. If so, then recognitions hereafter become a certainty. Not to know the vanished face again would break the human heart, and reveal a gulf of darkness in the hills of Life !

XLVI. But all is to be made clear. Upon the retrospect of our chequered life the shadows of forgetfulness fall and veil

> "The path we came by, thorn and flower."

But in the life of God the shadows are sunned away. The past lies in His light, and we shall see the meaning of thorn and flower.

> "So be it: there no shade can last
> In that deep dawn behind the tomb."

The "richest field" of restrospect will be those five years of tender human friendship. But love will not be limited by time and sense. It can only be satisfied with the infinite as the field of pure delights—

> "Love, a brooding star,
> A rosy warmth from marge to marge."

Thus in the odes relating to immortality we have seen not only the sanctuary where grief with folded wings sat weeping, but the darkness that dimmed the light on the altar. Will a hand come to wipe away the brimming tears, and the light glow again in the holy place of sorrow?

d   LXXVIII. WE have the coming of another
ion—   Christmas, and, when contrasted with cantos
ory.   xxix., xxx., we find a healthier condition.
Then excessive grief made the festive games a
" vain pretence " ; now

> " Who show'd a token or distress?
> No single tear, no mark of pain."

There are no tears nor marks of pain nor shadow of death. Is grief dead? No, but death does not seem so awful. A new element, as yet undefined, gives colour and warmth to grief.

> " Her deep relations are the same,
> But with long use her tears are dry."

LXXX. The poet imagines himself to be dead and Hallam living, and pictures the grief of his friend sustained by religious faith and life—

> "A grief as deep as life or thought,
> But stay'd in peace with God and man."

He thinks how in his case sorrow would have been sanctified, and seeming loss turned to gain, and the thought of such endurance and progress,

5

gives consolation. That "picture in the brain" of sustaining power is transferred to his own spirit.

"Unused example from the grave
Reach out dead hands to comfort me."

LXXXI. He is still looking back upon the past, thinking of his vanished friend, when he is haunted with the thought

"More years had made me love thee more";

but that would be selfish—to wish him back ; and he finds some joy in the sunnier thought that his loss and pain are Hallam's gain and peace.

" My sudden frost was sudden gain,
And gave all ripeness to the grain,
It might have drawn from after-heat."

Grain and fruit are ripened by a sudden frost. In the thought of the fruition of his friend, ripened by the frost of death, he finds some compensation. Thus grief, that had looked back into the grave with its blighted hopes, now begins to lift longing eyes to the future. The gaze is turning slowly from the grave. This forward look means the coming of health and hope. Note how he speaks of the gain to Hallam. So long as grief sits over against the sepulchre weeping it is night, but when it sees the angel it hastens to speak of the risen life.

LXXXII He has no feud with death on account of the changes wrought upon the body—

"And these are but the shatter'd stalks."

Nor does he blame death for transplanting his friend, who

> "Will bloom to profit, otherwhere."

It is not of the body he thinks, but of the progress of the spirit.

> "From state to state the spirit walks."

But he is angry with death because their lives are separated.

> "He put our lives so far apart
> We cannot hear each other speak."

The mood is human, but not healthy. The longing is natural, but not spiritual. Note this thought of the separation, for it will make vivid the contrast when he sings of the finding of his friend and the meeting of their spirits.

LXXXIV. He draws a picture of what might have been had Hallam lived. The more tender the scene, the crueller the blighting hand that

> "Made cypress of her orange flower,*
> Despair of Hope, and earth of thee."

Or he thinks of his friend growing with him until

> "Arrive at last the blessed goal,
> And He that died in Holy Land
> Would reach us out the shining hand,
> And take us as a single soul."

---

* Hallam was engaged to Miss Emily Tennyson.

But he realises that in this backward look of possibilities extinguished by death there cannot be health and hope.

> " Ah, backward fancy, wherefore wake
> The old bitterness again, and break
> The low beginnings of content."

LXXXV. We have a poem of exquisite music and deeper spiritual mood with the outward and forward look of the soul. In the first stanzas he repeats the assurance of canto XXVII.

> " 'Tis better to have loved and lost,
> Than never to have loved at all."

Then he addresses a friend * who wished to know what effect sorrow had upon his "trust in things above," and whether his love for Hallam had drained his love. The poet in reply suggests that, when the news first came

> " That in Vienna's fatal walls
> God's finger touch'd him, and he slept,"

the even tenor of his life was broken. Now he seems to see how the risen spirit of Hallam was welcomed by

> " The great Intelligences fair
> That range above our mortal state,"

and was led to the " fountain fresh " of the streams of knowledge. Then came reaction with the faded

* E. L. Lushington.

vision, and he tells how lonely he felt in his sorrow
with only a memory left. But the poem relates—
and this is the transition from sickness to health,
from despair to hope—how the sacred memory
became a power infusing comfort and strength.

> "And so my passion hath not swerved
> To works of weakness, but I find
> An image comforting the mind,
> And in my grief a strength reserved."

He begins to find the secret of victory over grief
and doubt. At present the experience is fitful, but
in the end it becomes fixed.

The second question he answers thus :—

> "I woo your love : I count it crime
> To mourn for any overmuch."

But he cannot love him as he loved Hallam. His
love had outlived time, and was eternal. Their
converse was not in human speech, but by spirit
contact. Yet for him he has "the primrose of the
later year."

XCV. We have an illustration of spirit communion.
It marks a crisis in the struggle of the soul through
grief and doubt on to joy and victory. It is the
meeting of the spirits. Tennyson finds Hallam.
There was a family gathering on a warm summer's
evening, so calm that the tapers burned upon the
lawn, and so still that afar off was heard the music
of the stream ; night moths "with ermine capes"

were flitting through the dark, and songs were
pealing through the knoll.   The poet was left alone
and read

> " In those fall'n leaves which kept their green,
> *The noble letters of the dead.*"

Mark the result.   The letters seemed vocal.   The
spirit of Hallam breathed in them.   The fire of
his intellect glowed in every line,

> "And all at once it seem'd at last
> The living soul was flash'd on mine,
> And mine in this was wound."

Thus the poet finds his friend, and their spirits rush
together in the ecstasy of communion.   It is the
first meeting, and is short-lived—a gleam telling
of light, a broken chord prophetic of the rhythmic
whole ; but soon the sweet light and mellow music
die away.

> "At length my trance
> Was cancell'd, stricken thro' with doubt."

And he comes back to earth to the old familiar
scenes ; but though his spirit is still touched with
doubt, he has fulfilled the conditions of XCIV, and
won

> "An hour's communion with the dead."

It is the way of communion with God and the
good—a pure heart, a peaceful spirit, and a hushed
being.

CVIII.   We have a healthy moral resolve giving

tone and colour to the sequel. He resolves no
longer to be misanthropic and "stiffen into stone,"
nor will he eat out "his heart alone." He recognises
that a "barren faith" and "vacant yearning" can
bring no profit; and though they may have power
to soar to the heights and dive to the deeps, they
reveal only "phantoms" and dim reflections, and
he sings,—

> "I'll rather take what fruit may be
> Of sorrow under human skies."

CXV. The noble resolve is realised. He sings
of the coming spring. The summer of long ago,
when Hallam sunned his spirit by "seraphic intellect and force," is dead. The winter of his
discontent, when grief, veiled in her sanctuary,
heard only the rain and the falling leaves, is buried.
But now out of dead regrets the spring of life and
hope is born; we see "the greening gleam," and
hear the "happy birds," and feel the coming breath.

> "And in my breast
> Spring wakens too; and my regret
> Becomes an April violet,
> And buds and blossoms like the rest."

CXVI. The song of the spring is continued. It
is "life re-orient out of dust." It strengthens faith
in the resurrection, and he feels the spirit presence
of his friend.

> "Not all regret: the face will shine
> Upon me, while I muse alone."

His spirit has turned now to the future with the hope of sacred reunion,—

> "Less yearning for the friendship fled,
> Than some strong bond *which is to be.*"

CXVII. He finds joy even in the delay, believing that the gain will be richer in the end, "delight a hundredfold."

> "O days and hours, your work is this,
> To hold me from my proper place,
> A little while from his embrace,
> For fuller gain of after bliss."

CXVIII. He still sings of the future, and sees in the evolution of the earth a symbol of the high destiny of the unfolding life of man. If this solid earth were evolved out of "fluent heat" and "cyclic storms," until at last "arose the man," who moved on and ever higher, though like iron-ore "heated hot" and "dipt in baths" and battered into "shape and use," then may not we infer from this evolution "ever nobler ends"? Yes, and in the process man is "working out the beast." The poem rings with the new spirit that fills the soul as it turns from the past to the future. All through we have evidence of the victory of conscious faith over grief and doubt. The grief is chastened by the new joy found in communion with the dead, and in the hope of the reunion. Thus in CXIX he revisits Hallam's old home in Wimpole Street, which he described in VII in language of utter

desolation ; but as he comes back to the scene it
is to speak of the singing of birds, and

"A light-blue lane of early dawn."

His grief is now transfigured with the spirit of
resignation.

"And in my thoughts with scarce a sigh
I take the pressure of thine hand."

CXXI. We have the contrast between the poet's
past and present experience in the symbol of Venus.
As "sad Hesper" she is the evening star wanting
to die with the "buried sun." Thus his grief would
fain have set with the sun of Hallam's life ; but
Venus rises again as Phosphor, the morning star,
and is thus the symbol of the new-born hope that
ushers in the day.

"Thou, like my present and my past,
Thy place is changed ; thou art the same."

CXXIII. The notes of victory swell on as he
pictures the cyclic change in land and sea : where
the tree once grew there rolls the sea, and where
the deep sea lay in stillness there roars the crowded
street. The very hills, like shadows, have changed
their forms.

"But in my spirit will I dwell,
And dream my dream, and hold it true ;
For tho' my lips may breathe adieu,
I cannot think the thing farewell."

He is assured of their reunion.

CXXIV. In this noble tribute to faith we hear the music of final triumph as he finds rest in the consciousness of God.

When assailed by a godless scepticism,

> " And like a man in wrath the heart
> Stood up and answered ' *I have felt,*' " *

and though doubt and fear may come,

> " Then was I as a child that cries,
> But, crying, knows his father near."

CXXVII. Again we hear "all is well" in the thunder of the storm.

> "Well roars the storm to those that hear
> A deeper voice across the storm."

We see then how he has found God in pure heart-love; and in that very feeling, in which his spirit is embraced by the All-loving, he finds again his friend, who comes a spirit presence to mingle with his life.

> " Dear heavenly friend that canst not die,
> Mine, mine, for ever, ever mine ;
> Strange friend, past, present, and to be ;
> Loved deeplier, darklier understood ;

* The thought is contained in Hallam's essay, *Theodicœa Novissima.* " He [God] is for them a being of like passions with themselves, requiring *heart for heart,* and capable of inspiring affection because capable of feeling and returning it,"

Behold, I dream a dream of good,
And mingle all the world with thee. (CXXIX.)

Far off thou art, but ever nigh ;
  I have thee still, and I rejoice ;
  I prosper, circled with thy voice ;
  I shall not lose thee tho' I die." (CXXX.)

The fitful communion is now fixed and the
two spirits live together. In finding God he has
found the life of his friend, and in that sublime
recovery the tears of grief are sunned by radiant
hope, and doubt is dissipated. Thus we have
the way of a soul through grief and doubt on
to final victory. The soul rests on the rock of God
and immortality and love. Faith cleaves its way
through all sophistry, superstition, scepticism, and
materialism ; and when challenged, declares, " I have
felt." The service which " In Memoriam " has
rendered to Christian Faith is great indeed. Its
pure spiritual teaching, through the intuitive faculty
of the poet, clears the mind, and calms the soul,
and breaks like the dawn upon the night.

WE have seen how the poet in varying
phases illustrates the conflicts and victories of
the soul. In " Idylls of the King," we shall
find the same subject taking a wider range and

* " By King Arthur I always meant the soul, by the Round
Table the passions and capacities of man "—TENNYSON *to Mr.
Knowles.*
" The whole is the dream of man coming into practical life

illustrated with perfection of art. It does not fall within the scope of our work to show how through long years the Idylls were constructed not in orderly sequence as they appear, but broken and irregular, and yet it is clear that the poet had in his mind a central truth which drew to itself and harmonized all the parts, so that when finished the Epic rose in " exquisite magnificence," and is probably his greatest work.

It is evident that the poet, for the ethical purpose he had in view, took the greatest liberty with the Arthurian legends, either amending or rejecting, or creating as the ethical necessity arose. Two threads run through the Idylls. The one thread is the romantic and leads into the labyrinth of

and ruined by one sin. It is not the history of one man, or of one generation, but of a whole cycle of generations."—TENNYSON, *A Memoir*, ii., p. 125.

" One noble design warms and unites the whole. In Arthur's coming, his foundation of the Round Table, his struggles and disappointments and departures, we see the conflict continually maintained between *the spirit and the flesh.*"—DEAN ALFORD.

" His Arthurian epic is a great attempt to depict the infusion of a soul into a chaos of stately passions."—R. H. HUTTON, *Literary Essays*, p. 366.

" It was through the pages of Malory that Tennyson made acquaintance with the story of Arthur, and from these he has drawn most of his Idylls. One other source must be mentioned. In 1838, Lady Charlotte Guest published 'The Mabinogion,' a translation of the ancient Welsh legends contained in the 'red book of Hergest,' which is in the library of Jesus College at Oxford. From this book Tennyson has taken the story of Geraint and Enid."—HENRY VAN DYKE.

the old legends. The other thread is the ethical
and leads into the purpose of the poems. This is
the thread we have set ourselves to follow. Ethically
the Idylls fall into two groups and may be thus
classified.

ms of).	*The Coming of Arthur—Gareth and Lynette—Geraint and Enid—Balin and Balan—The Holy Grail* (in part) *—Guinevere* (in part)—*The Passing of Arthur.*
ms of th.	*Merlin and Vivien—Lancelot and Elaine—Pelleas and Ettarre—The Last Tournament* (in part).

Tennyson has left us without doubt as to the
ethical meaning of " The Idylls." It is the war of
Sense with Soul.

In his dedication " To the Queen " he thus makes
clear the serious purport of the Epic.

> ". . . Accept this old imperfect tale,
> New-old, and shadowing Sense at war with Soul,
> Ideal manhood closed in real man,*
> Rather than that gray king, whose name, a ghost,
> Streams like a cloud, man-shaped, from mountain peak,
> And cleaves to cairn and cromlech still. . . ."

In the first group—Poems of Life—we shall find
the principal characters " shadowing Sense at war
with Soul," in which the victory falls to the side

---

* My father thought that perhaps he had not made the real
humanity of the King sufficiently clear in his epilogue; so he
inserted in 1891, as his last correction, " Ideal manhood closed in
real man," etc.—*A Memoir*, ii., p. 129.

of soul. In the case of Guinevere Sense is regnant almost to the end, when Soul awakens and is victorious.

In the second group—Poems of Death—the victory is more or less on the side of Sense, with, of course, the exception of Arthur and Dagonet in " The Last Tournament."

Let us take the first group and watch the war of Soul on its way to the victory of life.

The Coming of Arthur. THE " Coming of Arthur" introduces us to the king, that "Ideal manhood closed in real man," and the purest type in the Idylls of the spiritual man in conflict with opposing forces. He comes to a kingdom which is a wilderness—a moral waste

> " Wherein the beast was ever more and more,
> But man was less and less, till Arthur came."

Sense was regnant over Soul, when the call comes to the King

> " ' Arise, and help us thou !
> For here between the man and beast we die.'"

But when Arthur comes men dispute as to his birth.

> " This is the son of Gorloïs, not the King ;
> This is the son of Anton, not the King."

While Bedivere, in answer to King Leodogran, affirms

"'Sir, there be many rumours on this head :
For there be those who hate him in their hearts,
Call him baseborn, and since his ways are sweet,
And theirs are bestial, hold him less than man :
And there be those who deem him more than man,
And dream he dropt from heaven. . . .'"

Here we have the prevailing views of the origin and nature of the soul. Those who look only with the eyes of sense discern no spirit, and regard the soul as the product of matter—" baseborn." There is a materialism so absorbed in the phenomena of sense that it blinds the vision of the soul, so that it sees only "earthworms," where it might see angels ! There is a grosser form in which the sensuous has become sensual, and would fain drag the spirit into its own moral cesspool.

"... Since his ways are sweet,
And theirs are bestial. . . ."

Others again, who have not sacrificed but cherished the spiritual, contend for the divine origin of the soul,

" And dream he dropt from heaven. . . ."

So that Arthur—the spiritual man—enters upon a realm in which he is opposed from the outset by the animal or sense-bound men. But so kingly is he in the greatness of his spirit and the supremacy of his authority, that soon they yield to his sway. In the great hall they kneel and are knighted, they swear allegiance, accept his will and obey his word.

Then the strength of Arthur seems to pass into them, and they go to fight his battles and to win.

> "'But when he spake and cheer'd his Table Round
> With large, divine, and comfortable words,
> Beyond my tongue to tell thee—I beheld
> From eye to eye thro' all their Order flash
> A momentary likeness of the King.'"

In "likeness" to him lay the secret of their power and of their victories over the heathen. They were loyal to their king. They witnessed the fire of God fall upon him on the field of battle, and their motto was:

> "'The King will follow Christ, and we the King.'"

Thus he fought

> "The heathen hordes, and made a realm and reign'd."

But the scene changes. Arthur, the spiritual man, will marry Guinevere, the carnal woman. Does it not suggest that soul must be joined to flesh to make the flesh pure? May not the higher nature in union with the lower infuse its own vitality so that the lower shall be redeemed, as if by an awakened conscience warring with its passions? Did not "the Word" become "flesh" to redeem the flesh, and was not the union of the twain the secret of redemption? Thus Arthur :—

> "'But were I join'd with her,
> Then might we live together as one life,

> And reigning with one will in everything
> Have power on this dark land to lighten it,
> And power on this dead world to make it live.'"

And when the marriage is celebrated, it is with the suggestive words spoken at the altar:

> "'Reign ye, and live and love, and make the world
> Other, and may thy Queen *be one with thee*,
> And all this Order of thy Table Round
> Fulfil the boundless purpose of their King!'"

But the sequel shows that Arthur wedded to Guinevere—Soul to Sense—may sometimes fail to make flesh one with soul, and that it cannot always be redeemed and vitalized, or only late, " so late," as when Guinevere hides her face in the dust, and feels the breath of the passing King, and sees the shadow of his lifted hands, waved in blessing, ere he goes to be crowned in light.

Slowly Sense begins to win supremacy over Soul in the guilty love of Guinevere for Lancelot; and, as evil is always contagious and taints the very atmosphere, it soon poisons the knights and, working within them, saps their loyalty and scatters their forces and ruins the realm. The King, compelled to arm against his rebel knights, falls at last upon the battle-field; but though he falls he is not vanquished, for he goes to be crowned in the far-off city, and men seem to hear the shout as of welcome to " a king returning from his wars."

The character of Arthur will reveal itself throughout the Idylls. He is the spiritual warrior waging war upon the "heathen of the land." His task is to reconstruct the fabric of society upon a spiritual basis. He would interpenetrate the whole kingdom of Sense with Soul. The powers by which this regeneration is to be wrought are revealed in the beautiful allegories of the "three fair Queens," "the Lady of the Lake," and "Excalibur."

> "Three fair Queens,
> Who stood in silence near his throne, the friends
> Of Arthur, gazing on him, tall, with bright
> Sweet faces, who will help him at his need."

The three Queens may be taken for "three of the noblest women," or "Faith, Hope, and Charity" —those spiritual powers which are as strong angels within the soul as it wars with sense and sin. Ever near the throne of the heart must stand, as sentries on guard, these heavenly powers.

Merlin, subtle and powerful, represents intellect or science divorced from religion.

> "And near him stood the Lady of the Lake,
> Who knows a subtler magic than his own."

The Lady of the Lake is the symbol of religion. She is represented as dwelling

> "'Down in a deep; calm, whatsoever storms
> May shake the world, and when the surface rolls,
> Hath power to walk the waters like our Lord.'"

She gives to Arthur the sword Excalibur

"Whereby to drive the heathen out."

The sword is the symbol either of the spiritual weapon by which the Soul wars with Sense, or the temporal power by which the Church assailed her enemies.

> "'On one side,   .
> Graven in the oldest tongue of all this world,
> "Take me," but turn the blade and ye shall see,
> And written in the speech ye speak yourself,
> "Cast me away!"
>
>   *   *   *   *   *
>
> "Take thou and strike! the time to cast away
> Is yet far off." So this great brand the King
> Took, and by this will beat his foemen down.'"

The reference may be to the temporal power at the time when the Church conquered by carnal weapons, and to the fact that the time had not yet arrived for the exercise of her purely spiritual functions ; but, as Arthur is the centre of the conflict, Excalibur more probably is the symbol of that "sword of the spirit" by which all through life the soul must wage war with sin, and which can only be "cast away" when at last the soul, having "fought the fight," goes out upon the deep with the three fair Queens to the land where is no storm nor hail.

Gareth and Lynette. KING ARTHUR'S court is still unstained and unshadowed. The knights are pure and loyal. There is much fighting in "Gareth and Lynette," but the air is untainted, and light and music play throughout. The romance begins with Gareth, the last of the sons of Lot and Bellicent, who craves to enter Arthur's Hall, but is restrained by his over-anxious mother. He is inspired with a noble ambition, sufficiently clear and lofty to become a fascinating ideal ; he would rise

> "'To the great Sun of Glory, and thence swoop
> Down upon all things base, and dash them dead,
> A knight of Arthur, working out his will,
> To cleanse the world. . . .'"

But such glory is reached, not on swift wings, but only by patient endurance and strenuous effort. The initial difficulty, his mother, is not easily overcome. She would have Gareth remain with her, and promises him "a comfortable bride." She would have him stay to chase the deer and live a life of sensuous delight. Nobly he replies :

> "'Follow the deer? follow the Christ, the King,
> Live pure, speak true, right wrong, follow the King—
> Else, wherefore born?'"

Bellicent alleges that Arthur is not "proven" King. Gareth answers wisely :

> "'Who should be King save him who makes us free?'"

Finding that her appeal to filial feeling and sensuous ease fails to change the purpose of her son, she proposes a condition. He may go to Arthur's Hall, but he must go disguised, and serve for twelve months in the kitchen.

> " Silent awhile was Gareth, then replied,
> ' The thrall in person *may be free in soul.*'"

He accepts the condition.

Gareth represents here, and throughout, the Soul in conflict with the forces that would blind its vision. He strives for the supremacy of the spiritual over the sensuous and selfish. The conflict between Soul and Sense with Gareth begins with the pathetic pleadings of Bellicent. She sees only with Sense, and is selfish. If he had yielded to her he would have followed the deer, not " the Christ, the King." The spiritual would have been lost in the sensuous, and in place of a spiritual warrior we should have had a self-indulgent lord of the manor. Gareth wins the first victory over Sense when he replies to Bellicent:

> "' Follow the deer? follow the Christ, the King.'"

Now he comes disguised to Camelot,* the city

---

* "Camelot, . . . a city of shadowy palaces, is everywhere symbolic of the gradual growths of human beliefs and institutions, and of the spiritual development of man."—TENNYSON, *A Memoir*, ii., p. 127.

built to music, and into Arthur's Hall, where he listens to the plaints of those who seek redress,

> "And all about a healthful people stept
> As in the presence of a gracious king."

In turn he craves his boon to serve twelve months among the kitchen knaves. The boon is granted, and Gareth goes to serve under Kay, the seneschal. Of gentle birth, he finds himself surrounded by the vulgar. He sleeps with "grimy kitchen knaves," while Kay, jealous and exacting, imposes the most menial tasks.

> ". . . And Gareth bow'd himself
> With all obedience to the King, and wrought
> All kind of service with a noble ease
> That graced the lowliest act in doing it."

Thus he gains the second victory over self and circumstance. The conditions were anything but favourable to the high ideal. His ambition was to reach the flashing height, when he finds himself herding in a kitchen with base-born menials! Thus the soul on its way to the highest life may be conditioned by seeming evils that thwart its progress, but which, rightly estimated, become aids to the attainment of the ideal. If Gareth had judged only by Sense he would have chafed and fumed away his life in the servitude of the kitchen; but he judged by the spirit and saw "the soul of good in things evil." He accepted the discipline with patience, and was chastened into beauty. Great lives grow like great trees—in storms.

At the end of a month Bellicent relents, and Gareth, loosed from his vow, hastens to tell the King his ambition, to beg that he may be knighted in secret, and the first quest be granted him.

> " Smiled the great King, and half-unwillingly
> Loving his lusty youthhood yielded to him."

Sir Lancelot is privately informed of the promise, and commanded by the King to follow Gareth.

Now Lynette, a maiden of gentle birth, enters the Hall. She tells how the lands of her sister, Lyonors, are harassed by three lawless knights who had seized three fords of a serpentine river, and how a fourth, the mightiest, had imprisoned Lyonors within her castle, "to break her will and make her wed with him"; and she begs the King that Lancelot may redress the wrong. She further describes the lawless knights. According to their humour they are "courteous or bestial," they have no law but their own wild will, and they

> " . . . Call themselves the Day,
> Morning-Star, and Noon-Sun, and Evening-Star,
> Being strong fools; and never a whit more wise
> The fourth, who always rideth arm'd in black,
> A huge man-beast of boundless savagery.
> He names himself the night, and oftener Death.
>
> * * * * * *
>
> And all these four be fools, but mighty men,
> And therefore am I come for Lancelot."

Suddenly a voice is heard within the Hall—the voice of Gareth, who craves the quest, which the King grants.

"And I can topple over a hundred such,"

" And all hearers were amazed."   But Lynette, flushed with anger, exclaims :

"'Fie on thee, King! I ask'd for thy chief knight,
And thou hast given me but a kitchen-knave.'"

Sir Gareth now enters upon the third stage of conflict.   He gets to horse, and in the "field of tourney," finds Lynette all in a blaze of passion. What right had the King to scorn her ?   If Lancelot could not be spared, he might have sent a trusty knight and not—" O fie upon him—his kitchen-knave ! "

Though Gareth proves his valour by overthrowing Kay, she continues to abuse him as "dish-washer, and broach-turner, loon."   So they ride on, "reviler and reviled."   Entering a deep pine-wood, whence a man rushes, crying, "They have bound my lord to cast him in the mere," Gareth hastens to the rescue, cudgels the knaves, and releases "the stalwart Baron," who recognises in him one of "Arthur's Table."   Lynette admits that he is of the Table, only it is the kitchen table ; she will not sit with him, and tells the Baron the story of her wrongs, and how Arthur, "gone mad," gave the quest to "this frontless kitchen-knave " :

"'Him—here—a villain fitter to stick swine
  Than ride abroad redressing women's wrong.'"

Thus the chivalry of Sir Gareth is rewarded with
the scorn of Lynette. For her he suffers, in obedience to the King, only to be reproached. The
object of his solicitude returns him selfish ingrati-
tude. It is the picture of a noble soul living by
the spirit, following " Christ, the King " through
scorn and derision to the victory of life. The
divinest things are hidden from Sense, but unveiled
to Soul.

He enters now upon the fourth stage of his conflicts.

"Then to the shore of one of those long loops
  Wherethro' the serpent river coil'd they came."

Here he wages battle with the lawless knights in
possession of the bridges and the fords. Sir Morning-Star, living in a gay pavilion by the bridge of
single arch, calls to the "daughters of the dawn,"
three fair girls, to arm him for the fight. On the
bridge Sir Gareth and Sir Morning-Star meet in
fearful shock of battle when

"He drave his enemy backward down the bridge,
  The damsel crying, 'Well stricken, kitchen-knave!'
  Till Gareth's shield was cloven ; but one stroke
  Laid him that clove it grovelling on the ground."

The "serpent river" represents the winding of the
stream of life. The scene of the first conflict at
" the stream full, narrow," is the symbol of youth,

when life is rushing and full within its narrow limits. A single arch takes the bridge at a leap, and suggests the impetuosity of youth to leap by a bound into manhood. Sir Morning-Star and his gaudy pavilion, with the three fair maidens in rosy raiment, symbolise the seductive pleasures which assail the youthful soul.

The soul must wage fierce war with every form of sensual pleasure. To yield is to "reel back into the beast." A pavilion of splendour may hide a skeleton of death. Evil when masked may parade as an angel of light. The spiritual youth, not vigilant as Gareth, may soon waste his substance in the pavilion of "riotous living." The soul must battle with the evils of the sensuous. Temptations must not be parleyed with, but vanquished with sudden and fierce onslaught,

> "Till Gareth's shield was cloven; but one stroke
> Laid him that clove it grovelling on the ground."

Gareth is next assailed by Sir Noonday-Sun.

> "Huge, on a huge red horse, and all in mail
> Burnish'd to blinding, shone the Noonday Sun
> Beyond a raging shallow. . . ."

The stream of life now spreads into a "raging shallow" unbridged. Manhood is thus symbolised. Youth was bridged to manhood by a single arch and taken at a single leap; but in manhood the waters are not so full and rushing. They have broadened and no bridge appears, as in manhood the transitions are not so apparent.

Here he meets the Noonday Sun in mid-stream where " four strokes they struck with swords, and these were mighty "; but in raising his mailed arm to strike the fifth stroke

> " The hoof of his horse slipt in the stream, the stream
> Descended, and the Sun was wash'd away."

He is found " bone-batter'd on the rock," when he yields to Gareth, who sends him to the King.

Thus we have suggested the temptation which most of all assails manhood—the lust of gold. The soul gazing at gold may be quickly dimmed.

> " All sun; and Gareth's eyes had flying blots.'

Fascinated by the gleam of material wealth, it loses the vision of spiritual realities. The curse of life is the love of gold. Men bow in worship of the Noonday Sun and the burnished tinsel blinds them to the glory of virtue. It is better to batter out the love of gold on some rock of adversity than lose the vision of the King.

Now Gareth comes face to face with that lawless knight—Sir Evening-Star. Fierce and long is the deadly struggle. Evening-Star is the symbol of those habits which, once formed, become regnant within the soul, and are like wild beasts on the throne of old age.

> "He seem'd as one
> That all in later, sadder age begins
> To war against ill uses of a life,
> But these from all his life arise, and cry,
> ' Thou hast made us lords, and canst not put
>   us down!'"

Again

> "His arms are old, he trusts the harden'd skin."

While Gareth

> ". . . Hew'd great pieces of his armour off him,
> But lash'd in vain against the harden'd skin."

As rock hardens about the fossil, so evil habits harden about the soul. Evening-Star symbolises the force of habit in old age. Sins repeated become habits, and the habits " hardened skin." Gareth's way is the only way to victory. The soul must assert itself, " straining ev'n his uttermost," and cast them into the deep. There must be no compromise. If the soul is to be victor it must tear from itself encoiling evil, and silence the passionate voices that cry

> ' "Thou hast made us lords, and canst not put us down!'"

They must be put down, or there will be no throne for the soul, only the chains of sense.

Sir Gareth now wages his last war with Night, or Death, an awful monster, who had struck terror into the country round.

"High on a nightblack horse, in nightblack arms,
   With white breast-bone, and barren ribs of Death,
   And crown'd with fleshless laughter—some ten steps—
   In the half-light—thro' the dim dawn—advanced
   The monster, and then paused, and spake no word."

The moment is intense.   Lyonors wrings her hands.
Lancelot shudders as Gareth dashes on the foe with
splendid valour, and with one blow splits the skull
of " Death."

          " . . . And out from this
       Issued the bright face of a blooming boy
       Fresh as a flower new-born. . . ."

The soul, conquering in the crises of life, finds
at last that dreaded death wears the face of a
" blooming boy."   Victorious over sense, it finds
in death eternal youth.   We see only the hideous
mask of death, but it hides the face of a young
angel.

Thus the poem is a parable.   The interpretation
lies in the allegory of the hermit's cave, where
Morning, Noon, Evening and Night, personify the
evils that assail the soul.

   "And running down the soul, a shape that fled
       With broken wings, torn raiment and loose hair,
       For help and shelter to the hermit's cave."

But, as we have seen, in the end the spiritual soul
is victor,

   "So large mirth lived, and Gareth won the quest."

In contrast to Gareth is Lynette, who throughout

judges by the sense. She judges him by the outward and visible. She has no spiritual perception to see the noble and beautiful within him. She sees only the kitchen-knave where she might have seen a kingly knight. Lynette is cheery and charming when not scornful. She is sensitive to nature, ever breaking into song at the sight of birds and flowers. She is entirely sensuous and lives by the outward, and it is only at the last, when the soul sees, that she learns the spiritual worth of Gareth.

> " . . . And she clapt her hands,
> 'Full merry am I to find my goodly knave
> Is knight and noble, . . .'"

Geraint and Enid. IN "Geraint and Enid" we have the first indication of the pure air of the court being tainted, and of its effect upon so brave and pure a knight as Geraint. He had married the lovely Enid, daughter of Yniol, whose fortunes had been broken through the treachery of Edyrn, a discarded suitor and despised nephew. Enid is a great favourite with the Queen, who loves her. The suspicion that haunts Geraint throughout, and shapes itself into a horrible phantom, has its rise in the scandal of the guilty love of Lancelot for Guinevere.

He prevails with the King to grant him leave of absence to defend his own princedom, and to

purge its lawlessness. Once there he becomes so
utterly absorbed in Enid as to neglect all else.

> " He compass'd her with sweet observances
> And worship, never leaving her, and grew
>
> .   .   .   .   .   .
>
> Forgetful of his princedom and its cares.
> And this forgetfulness was hateful to her."

It is the common talk that he is a prince
" whose manhood was all gone." His strength is
being sapped by self-indulgence. The temptation
is to sacrifice the spiritual quality of love for its
sensuous delights. The fact that the temptation
comes through Enid—the ideal loveliness—all
unconscious to herself, made it all the more subtle.
The most seductive temptation may come through
the tenderest object. The passion for the object
loved may sweep aside duties sacred as the love
itself. Absorption in any earthly object weakens
the force of the soul in other directions. Love
indulged to the point of self-indulgence saps manhood, and leaves the man a prey to wildest fancy
and subtlest suspicion. Enid naturally saddens,
and the phantom of fear is again raised in Geraint
" that her nature had a taint."

Thus weakened in his moral fibre, first by suspicion and then by self-indulgence through sensuous
devotion, Geraint is most susceptible to jealousy.
He who lives by the senses is likely to become
a prey to vultures of suspicion that tear out the

heart.   Geraint, with the sorrow of the tainted
court brooding o'er him, begins to doubt the purity
of Enid ; and the doubt seems confirmed as she
bends over him in his semi-sleep and pours out her sad
heart in a soliloquy ending with the innocent words :

> " ' O me, I fear that I am no true wife.' "

Her tears fall in a rain of grief ; he feels the warm
tears and believes that she is

> " ' Weeping for some gay knight in Arthur's hall.' "

He hears the fragments of her words and thinks
she is not faithful to him.

He is now maddened with jealousy, and becomes
reckless in his treatment of Enid, which reveals in
him the soul defeated by sense, and in her the soul
victorious over sense.   Geraint, believing only in
what he can see and hear and feel, becomes the
victim of the most painful self-deception.   The
senses usurp his being and make suspicion and
tyranny regnant.   Let the story reveal the characters,
and note the " Sense at war with Soul."   Confirmed
in his suspicions, Geraint commands Enid—

> " ' And thou, put on thy worst and meanest dress
> And ride with me.' . . ."

His fiery passion only blinds him to the goodness
of Enid.

> " O purblind race of miserable men,
> How many among us at this very hour
> Do forge a life-long trouble for ourselves,
> By taking true for false, or false for true."

They ride into the wilds when Geraint, all un-
knightly, compels Enid to ride on before, and on
her duty as a wife not to speak to him. They go
by the marshes and through the wastes infested
with robbers, Enid pale as a lily, bending in obedience before the storm, Geraint with the dark cloud
of suspicion brooding within him, and the lightning
of jealousy flashing in his eyes! Soon Enid espies
three tall knights, " caitiffs all," concealed within
the shadow of a rock, and the struggle begins
between duty to her husband, and a blind, passive
obedience. She resolves to disobey to save his life.

> "'Far liefer by his dear hand had I die,
> Than that my lord should suffer loss or shame.'"

Geraint is wrathful, but strips "the three dead
wolves of woman born," and commands Enid to
drive on the bandit's horses.

Again, in the shadow of a deep wood she sees
three horsemen wholly armed and "one larger than
her lord," all waiting for their prey. The struggle
between duty and obedience is renewed with the
result—

> "'I needs must disobey him for his good;
> How should I dare obey him to his harm?
> Needs must I speak, and tho' he kill me for it,
> I save a life dearer to me than mine.'"

Again Geraint flings her a wrathful answer, and
Enid, with bated breath and " fits of prayer," awaits
the issue of the deadly conflict! When the victory

7

is on the side of Geraint, and the captured horses are bridle-reined, he utters no word save :

> ". . . 'Drive them on
> Before you,' and she drove them thro' the wood."

They halt now in a meadow where the mowers are mowing, and where they find a boy with victuals which Geraint speedily devours, and Enid, "to close with her lord's pleasure," tastes a little. The delicate touch reveals her character, she is sensitive to his wish when the wish is not to his hurt. The mower-boy flushes with delight on receiving horse and arms for reward, and exclaims that he will tell his Earl, who would welcome Geraint to his palace.

> "'I know, God knows, too much of palaces!'"

is the significant reply.

Geraint and Enid go to a chamber in the little town and there they sit apart, he in sullen melancholy, and she in gentle sadness—voiceless. Then suddenly there breaks upon the scene the Earl Limours, a rejected lover of Enid, who moves Geraint to laughter, and having obtained of him permission to address her, pours into her ear his bibulous sentiments, and suggests that his followers shall capture her sullen prince. Enid, anticipating danger, answers with discretion, and by postponing the plot until the morrow, gains time for action. She disobeys again and breaks the law of silence,

and by the dawn they leave the town and escape
Limours ; but ever that command is laid upon her

> "That ye speak not, but obey."

Swiftly there sweeps down upon Geraint, like a
thunder-cloud, the foiled Limours with his reckless
retainers, when Enid, first to hear the sound, but
bound to silence, turns and lifts her finger in
warning ! The struggle is short and sharp.
Limours is hurled, stunned, or dead, from his horse,
and the rest are put to speedy flight by the vigour
of Geraint ; but he is wounded and bleeding beneath
his armour, and

> ". . . Without a word, from his horse fell."

Enid, hearing the crash, hastens to his side, and
with perfect self-control searches for the wound,
then tears away her veil and

> ". . . Swathed the hurt that drain'd her dear lord's life."

There she waited and wept. At noon the lawless
Earl Doorm " with a hundred lances " appears. To
him Enid appeals, and " since her face is comely,"
he instructs two spearmen to convey Geraint to the
castle. They, cursing all the way, bring him

> "And cast him and the bier in which he lay
> Down on an oaken settle in the hall,"

where he lies in weakness, feigning sleep, and
listening to the voice of Enid like the music of
gentle streams. At last the shameless Earl returns,

and, thinking Geraint dead, strives to bend Enid to his lawless will. He commands her to eat and to drink, to array herself in a splendid silk of foreign loom ! All of which she steadfastly declines.

> " 'Yea, God, I pray you of your gentleness,
> He being as he is, to let me be.' "

The Earl, baffled and enraged, rises, and with flat hand strikes her on the cheek, when Enid " sent forth a sharp and bitter cry." Geraint hears, and with a bound and a sweep of his sword

> " Shore thro' the swarthy neck, and like a ball
> The russet-bearded head roll'd on the floor.
> So died Earl Doorm by him he counted dead."

With the confession of Geraint comes the recon-ciliation, and two souls estranged blend into one, he becoming the " great prince," and she " Enid the good."

Such is the legend ; but what of the ethical teaching, and what place do the characters occupy in the war of Soul with Sense ?

It is evident Geraint is not the ideal. He pos-sesses physical power, is great and strong and brave, but he is suspicious and jealous and tyran-nical towards Enid, because the spiritual is asleep within him. At present with the eyes of Sense he can see only the Enid of sensuous beauty, of whom he is jealous. If he could see with the eyes of Soul he would see her ideal loveliness, and thus

seeing he could never doubt; but as it is he is
suspicious and becomes jealous and tyrannical. If
you say he ought not to have been so, the answer
is that, seeing only by the sense, he could not be
aught else; when the soul awakes he will see
differently, but so long as he is sense-bound he will
see what the sense brings him. Then does Geraint
not love Enid? Yes, indeed; but his love is animal
love; it is the love of the lion for his lioness; the love
of passion and instinct; the love that sees physical
qualities, but, having no spiritual perception, sees no
moral loveliness. There is an animal and instinctive love. There is also a spiritual and perceptive
love. Geraint is a great animal who loves Enid for
her physical beauty, not for her grace of soul. As yet
he is blind to the charms of character that would
have made his cruel doubt impossible. Thus
Geraint stands for the soul stricken through with
Sense. He judges Enid ever by the purblind sense,
he takes "false for true," and forges his own
trouble. While Enid drives the horses through the
waste the angel of pity once stirs within him, but
quickly folds her wings in the sense-bound cage. Still
the angel is there, and in the end will soar beyond
the sense. Now what of Enid? Her own sex
have plunged into the fray and shot envenomed
arrows at her, until Earl Doorm's treatment of her
seems merciful. The whole race of women appears
to have conspired against " Enid the lovely." It

is said that she was weak and silly and ought not to have yielded to the unjust jealousy and mad caprice of her husband, and that there could be no "woman's rights" were we all Enids. We reply, Enid is the ideal of womanhood. Her love is ideal just because she can go on loving and trusting Geraint when he responds only with scorn and suspicion and jealousy. She might have resented his conduct and no one could have blamed her ; she would have been within her woman's rights : but then her love would have fallen short of the ideal—the ideal that can love and wait, believing that the mystery will be cleared and the heart won again by the love and the waiting. Further, the wisdom of her obedience is challenged. She is spoken of as weak and blind in obeying the cruel commands of Geraint. But, observe, she discriminates, she obeys where obedience, painful for her, is no hurt to him, as when she drove the horses on before: but she disobeys when obedience might result in injury to him. Her obedience is thus ideal, because in all it considers the good of the object loved. If she had stood upon her "rights" she would not have won again the heart of Geraint, but because she waived her "rights" and loved him even in the mystery, and obeyed with wise discrimination, she wins the victory in the end. Enid is thus the type of the soul that does not live by sense merely, but by love and trust and obedience when mystery

enfolds it.   So she conquers Geraint, who is now no
longer the sense-bound life, but he sees the spiritual
beauty, the deathless angel, within the soul of
Enid.

Here then we have the central truth which the
poet sings so sublimely, and teaches with ever-wider
range so earnestly—that the highest life is only
reached through that moral energy which strikes
down every lawless passion.   Self-indulgence is
best cured by self-sacrifice.   Ignoble jealousy is
best crushed by the higher love that " thinks no
evil."

> ". . . Nor did he doubt her more,
> But rested in her fealty, till he crown'd
> A happy life with a fair death. . . ."

**Balin
and
Balan.**   IN "Balin and Balan" we trace the tragic
results of cherished evil in Arthur's court.
The air is thickening and the shadows are
deepening.   The taint impregnates the whole atmosphere, and the realm of Arthur is in danger.
Lancelot and Guinevere must be held morally
responsible for the tragedy that follows.   Evil is
gauged by its results.   Its circle may be wide, but
its centre is the same, and the centre must be held
responsible for the circle.

The story begins with Pellam the king, who had
taken sides with Lot and lost his kingdom, which,
however, Arthur had restored on the condition of

his paying tribute. Pellam had become an ascetic, and was so absorbed in " other worldliness " as to forget the duties of earth.

He thinks more about Arimathean Joseph, the saints and the relics, than of his lawful debts. He is the type of asceticism that degraded religion by cherishing its shell and sacrificing its kernel. While he will allow no women to pass his palace gates, his son Garlon is both sensualist and assassin ! He is so dead to the world as to forget he owes tribute. It is a phase of the ascetic life that separates itself from the currents of humanity. It dies into a stagnant pool. The asceticism that makes Pellam a hypocrite also drives his son into secret sensualism and cowardly murder.

The pious Pellam not having paid his tribute, Arthur commands his treasurer to wait upon the defaulter and remind him that " Man's word is God in man." The treasurer hesitates, fearing the two strange knights, Balin and Balan, who sit by the well of Camelot, but, ordered not to molest them, he passes on to the court of Pellam.

King Arthur appears at the well where Balin and Balan are " sitting statuelike." When asked why, they reply, " For the sake of glory," and boast of their victories over Arthur's Knights. The King answers that he too is of Arthur's hall and challenges them to combat ; but he lightly smites them down, and leaves them to their own reflec-

tions. Ere long he sends and commands them to
his hall. Then Balin tells the story of his life,
how he had been a Knight of the King's, but in
nature was " the savage," and had struck in passion
one of Arthur's thralls, with the result that the
King had sent him into exile and his life had been
bitter in its fury ; but now he thought that if the
King could hear of his prowess by the well, he
might make his brother Balan, knight, who was
" ten times worthier." Resolved to tell the whole
truth, he confesses how that very day they had
fallen before an unknown knight. Arthur, impressed by his honesty, restores him to knighthood.

> "'Rise, my true knight. As children learn, be thou
> Wiser for falling ! walk with me, and move
> To music with thine Order and the King.'
>
> Thereafter, when Sir Balin enter'd hall,
> The Lost one Found was greeted as in Heaven."

Balan, the guardian angel of his brother, is also
received into the Order.

The treasurer, returning from the court of Pellam,
reports the mummery of his ascetic life. Pellam,
in his other worldliness, had referred him to his
son Garlon for the tribute, who paid it "railing
at thine and thee." He had also found in the
woods the body of a Knight of Arthur's, " spear-
stricken from behind," and had suspected Garlon :
but a woodman had told him of a demon, once a
man, driven by evil tongues to hate his fellows,

who sallied from a cave, and from behind flashed
his deadly spear.   Superstition thus accounts for
the natural by the supernatural.   The " fiend " was
Garlon disguised.

Arthur at once calls for a Knight

> ". . . 'Who will hunt for me
> This demon of the woods ?' . . ."

Balan claims the quest, and ere he rides away
embraces Balin and warns him against himself.

> " 'Let not thy moods prevail, when I am gone
> Who used to lay them! hold them outer fiends,
> Who leap at thee to tear thee; shake them aside.' "

He commends Balin to the purity and fellowship
of his Order, all unconscious of the serpent coiled
within the " flowery welcome."   To Balan, Arthur's
hall is the ideal life.

> " 'No more of hatred than in Heaven itself,
> No more of jealousy than in Paradise !' "

Sir Balin, left to himself, becomes reflective.   He
is conscious that he is far from having realised the
ideal of Arthur.   The qualities that make the ideal
are courtesy and manhood and knighthood, the last
combining strength and gentleness.

Now observe : Balin is not satisfied with having
the ideal in the abstract, but he must see it in the
actual.   Sir Lancelot, being the favourite of the
King and Queen, is regarded throughout the court
as the ideal knight.   Wherefore Balin " hovered

round Lancelot," but, as the lame-born boy looks to the heights flushed with the sun and sighs because he cannot climb, so Balin as he watches Lancelot sighs in spirit :

> ". . . 'These be gifts,
> Born with the blood, not learnable, divine,
> Beyond *my* reach.' . . ."

Then he imagines that the glory of Lancelot is but the reflected radiance of the Queen—if only he might look upon the Queen and see the realised ideal, he too might win the strength and gentleness of knighthood ; but that being impossible he will crave a boon—a token—upon which he may gaze and thus restrain his violence ; he will ask

> "To bear her own crown-royal upon shield."

The boon is granted.

> ". . . And all the world
> Made music, and he felt his being move
> In music with his Order, and the King."

But as the notes of the nightingale change, so the music in him is broken by fitful gusts of wrath. He strives strenuously to realise the ideal and " seemed at length in peace."

Suddenly the scene is changed and the situation becomes dramatic. Sir Balin is sitting one morning close-bowered within the garden when down a path of roses wanders Guinevere, and from a door emerges Lancelot.

They meet. Eyes flash their message. The
flush upon the face of the Queen tells its story, and
Balin sees and hears and starts from his bower.

> "'Queen? subject? but I see not what I see,
> Damsel and lover? hear not what I hear.'
>
> .   .   .   .   .   .
>
> · · · He sharply caught his lance and shield,
> Nor stay'd to crave permission of the King,
> But, mad for strange adventure, dashed away"

—away into the woods, where his brother Balan
hunts the demon of the cave. The woodman
declares the devil to be genuine.

> ". . . 'Our devil is a truth,
> I saw the flash of him but yestereven,
>
> .   .   .   .   .   .
>
> Look to the cave.' . . ."

But Balin is careless and tempestuous, and does not
see the cave ;

> "Whereout the Demon issued up from Hell."

It is not until a spear flashes by him, and a shape
with pointed lance vanishes into the woods that he
is alarmed, and, blindly pursuing the "fiend," strikes
against a tree and is unhorsed ; then remounts and
rides in haste until he enters Pellam's hall.

> "A home of bats, in every tower an owl."

The crown-royal upon his shield attracts attention.
Garlon is inquisitive, and Balin answers that by

consent of the Queen, " best and purest," he wears
it; whereupon Garlon hisses

> " ' Best, purest ? *thou* from Arthur's hall, and yet
> So simple ! ' "

He assails the honour of the Queen.

By the side of Balin stands a goblet " bossed with
holy Joseph's legend." This goblet Balin grasps
and would hurl at Garlon's head, but the memory
of the crown-royal causes him to relax his hold,
saying, " I will be gentle "; but his words belie him
as he pours out his wrath upon the man who dare
insult the Queen.

In the early morn he walks into the castle yard
and encounters Garlon, who twits him again upon
the " crown-scandalous."

Sir Balin now loses all self-control, splits the
head of Garlon, and only escapes " a score of pointed
lances " by hiding in King Pellam's chapel. Thence
by horse he rides through many miles, when the
weary creature drops at last by a fallen oak.
Thinking he has disgraced himself by violence, he
hangs the shield upon the boughs, withdraws into the
wood and flings himself upon the ground " moaning,
' My violences, my violences ! ' "

Now Vivien, subtle as the serpent, appears upon
the scene. She finds the crown-royal, and comes
upon the prostrate Balin ; she tells a pathetic story
of her simulated wrongs, and claims his protection,
but Balin declares that he is disgraced, and will live

and die a savage of the woods. Vivien conjures up a love scene twixt Lancelot and Guinevere by the great tower of Caerleon, and Balin, struck with horror, breaths in a dismal whisper, "It is truth." He grinds his teeth and yells, tears down the shield, stamps out the crown-royal and, cursing, hurls it into the woods.

Balan hears the wild yell and, believing it to be the "scream of the wood-devil," dashes through the forest all unconsciously on Balin. Both brothers fall to the ground. Balin is crushed beneath his horse and Balan is wounded with a mortal thrust, while Vivien cries, "Fools!" Then she bounds away, with her brood of vipers coiled within her breast to lift their heads—perhaps in Arthur's hall!

The Squire of Vivien had loosed the casques from the faces of the brothers, and they recognize each other. Pathetic is the scene where Balin crawls to his dying brother, and Balan draws down the face he loves and kisses it, with sobs of sorrow.

Then comes the final parting as the shadow falls from out eternity, and Balin utters his farewell.

> "'The night has come. I scarce can see thee now.
> Goodnight! for we shall never bid again
> Goodmorrow.' . . .
>
>   .   .   .   .   .
>
>   Balan answer'd low,
> 'Goodnight, true brother, here! goodmorrow there!'
>
>   .   .   .   .   .
>
>   . . . And slept the sleep
> With Balin, either lock'd in either's arm."

Now how do these two characters illustrate the
" war of Sense with Soul " ? Both brothers are
powerful personalities, but Balin is dominated by
sense and Balan by spirit   Balin by nature is
passionate and volcanic, and his ideas are mixed
in that lava flood within.   He is radically good, but
his goodness is driven by the impulsive and erratic
force that makes him weak when he ought to be
strong.   What he most needs, he most lacks,—the
clear, calm vision of spiritual realities apart from
persons.   He had been " the savage," but the good
within revolts and asserts itself, and he longs for the
purer life of Arthur's hall.   When restored by
favour of the King he has a clear conception of
the ideal of knighthood—courtesy, manhood, strength,
gentleness—but he must see it in bodily form.   An
ideal has no power over Balin unless it take flesh
and live before him, a veritable incarnation.   Unless
he can see he will not believe.   He must have
" signs " for his faith and his ideal must have an
objective reality.   So he turns to Lancelot and
" hovers round " the ideal knight, only to find there is
a higher ideal—the source of his inspiration—the
Queen.   If only he may gaze upon the Queen, she
may flash her nobility of soul into him, but failing
that he will beg to wear the crown-royal upon his
shield, that, looking upon it, he may win self-control.
Thus Balin lives by the sense.   His ideal is good,
but he must see it in the flesh.   His motive is good—

self-control ; but the control can only come through Sense, he must have the crown-royal to look upon.

Now mark how Sense wars with Soul. When Balin is a witness of the scene in the garden, Sense seems to say to him, There is your ideal ! What do you think of it now ?

Then did the senses deceive him ? No, they saw what was. The senses saw only the outward —true as far as the senses could see. The persons were false, but that did not prove the ideal to be false ; it only proved that Balin was living by Sense, and not by Soul.

If he had looked through Soul at the ideal he would have been saved, but he looks through Sense at the persons, and is lost. Thus we learn that no human life has ever perfectly realised an absolute ideal. Faith must not be fixed on persons, but on principles. Men on earth reflect only faint rays of the sun in heaven. The Sun is infinitely greater than the rays, and purer. To live by the sense, to believe only what we see, is to see little of heaven in man but much of earth, until earth seems greater than heaven, and, with Balin, the soul plunges again into the wilds, and lives the life of a savage. The character that depends on the sensuous for its ideal is in danger of losing it. The sensuous is as likely to degrade the spiritual as the spiritual is likely to redeem the sensuous.

Balan is the antithesis of his brother, and is the

type of the spiritual man. He does not confound principles with persons, ideals with individuals, but is careful to discriminate. He soars beyond the sense, sees the spiritual and the eternal, and though Lancelot and Guinevere may fail to incarnate goodness, and though Vivien may hiss like a serpent in Eden, and though the realm of Arthur may be shattered, yet Balan knows that goodness lives ; and when death begins to chill the fire of life, and Balin falls back into materialism, with pathetic despair crying :

> "'Goodnight! for we shall never bid again
> Goodmorrow,'"

then Balan, living by the spirit, "seeing Him who is invisible," replies with radiant hope, as if the dawn were already breaking :

> "'Goodnight, true brother, here! Goodmorrow there!'"

and lifts him by the power of his own spiritual victory into the coming light, and once again Soul triumphs over Sense by "the evidence of things not seen."

.

IN "The Holy Grail"* the war of Sense with Soul is clearly portrayed. The soul is pictured throughout in conflict with the

* "The Holy Grail" is one of the most imaginative of my poems. I have expressed there my strong feeling as to the Reality of the Unseen.—TENNYSON, *A Memoir*, ii., p. 90.

8

dangers arising out of the life of mystic musing and uncontrolled ecstasy and sensuous allurement. The Holy Grail represents the Cup used in the Last Supper.

> ". . . And if a man
> Could touch or see it, he was heal'd at once,
> By faith, of all his ills. . . ."

Sir Percivale, who had "passed into the silent life of prayer," sitting by the cloisters under the yew-tree, tells the story to the monk Ambrosius. His sister, a pure and gentle nun, first heard the legend of the Grail from the lips of an old man, who hoped it might have come when Arthur cleansed the court, "but sin broke out." She, longing for the vision, gave herself to prayer and fasting. One day she sent for Percivale and told him how the Holy Grail had come to her. A silver beam flashed in upon her cell "and down the long beam stole the Holy Grail."

> "'And tell thy brother knights to fast and pray,
> That so perchance the vision may be seen
> By thee and those, and all the world be heal'd.'"

And he went and, told the story to all men, and himself fasted and prayed. Galahad was the first to come under the spell of the holy legend and the deathless passion of the saintly maiden. "Then came a year of miracle," and Sir Percivale tells how one summer night

> "'That Galahad would sit down in Merlin's chair,'"

when suddenly there came a storm—thunder and lightning—and in a radiant beam the Holy Grail appeared "covered with a luminous cloud." Then the Knights of Arthur longed to go in search of the sacred cup. They entered into solemn vows without the knowledge of their King. He returned to find tumult in the hall, and when he heard the cause his face darkened as if he saw the shattering of his realm. He told them they had sacrificed the chance of doing noble deeds in following "wandering fires," but their vows were sacred and they must go. So the Knights were scattered. They went their way, some through wilds and wastes, others through conflicts and self-torture, striving to win the vision of the Grail. The war of Soul in varying experiences is pictured in the conflicts of Percivale, Galahad, Bors and Lancelot. The conflicts differ with the differences of character. Each has his battle to wage on the way to the victory of life.

Sir Percivale at the outset of the search had to battle with his own self-consciousness. When he recalled his prowess in the lists, the strong arm that had defeated the great and brave, he felt that Heaven smiled upon him as on a favoured son, and that he would surely find the Holy Grail. Then came the memory of the words of Arthur and of his own deeds, as if crying "This Quest is not for thee," and he found himself "in a land of sand

and thorns." The soul that would make itself great by its conceits is made little by its conscience. It was the temptation to trust in the outward. The outward may conform to all the rules of decorum and the earthly standards of greatness, but what if the inward be stained with sin and veined with self? Then the supremacy of Sense falls into dust before the eyes of the spirit, and the soul finds itself, in the words of Percivale,

> "'Alone, and in a land of sand and thorns,
> And I was thirsty even unto death.'"

Then he rode on with that ever-burning thirst, and came to a brook that made music to his ears, on whose banks goodly apples grew, tempting to the taste, where lawns of tender verdure invited him to rest, and he drank of the brook and tasted of the apples and would have rested on the lawns, when lo! all fell into dust, and the great thirst remained " in a land of sand and thorns."

The symbol reveals the charms of the sensuous, and how they fail to slake the thirst of the inner life. The vision of sensuous beauty, when abused, can only result in spiritual indolence. The streams of worldly indulgence only leave the living soul with the fever of its thirst. Divine realities are won, not in sitting by the stream eating the fruits of sensuous delights, but by strenuous conflict with the evil.

Still on he rode, and came to a fair house with a kindly woman spinning at the door. She welcomed him to rest, but at his touch they "fell into dust and nothing."

The delights of domestic life—the loves of home —are thus symbolised as tempting the soul from its high and noble quest. May it not rest here in the joys of human love, with the prattle of little children, "those truants from heaven"? No. Though natural love may be pure and sweet as the winds blowing down from the hills, no soul that thirsts for the sacred vision can be satisfied. It cannot find its best and highest in human loves, be they never so gentle and good. Well if they lead it on to the divine, but ill indeed if they cause it to rest in things human. At the last these must fade, and when death takes all, there will be naught to slake the burning thirst.

"And on I rode, and *greater was my thirst.*"

Then came a golden light, and as it flashed across the world he thought, "The sun is rising," but it was one crowned and robed with gold, whose splendour dazed his sight, and who seemed to be "Lord of all the world."

It is the symbol of wealth, and of the temptation it presents to the soul in its search after life. To yield to the lust of gold, to exhaust the energies of being in the absorbing desire to be rich, is to find at last cravings of heart and voices out of the deep that wealth cannot satisfy. Gold may give pleasure to the senses, but it gives no satisfaction to the soul that feels the pulse of immortality and cries, "Give me God." The gold fell into dust.

> "And I was left alone,
> And wearying, in a land of sand and thorns."

He next arrived at a great hill, where a city rose with spires piercing the heavens, and a crowd at the gateway cried, "Welcome, Percivale!" But when he reached the heights it was to find the ruins of a city with the silence of death. The crowd had vanished, save one old man, who "fell into dust" as Percivale strove to ask

> "'Whence and what art thou?'"

The fleeting glory of human ambition is thus portrayed. Fame, like the pinnacles of the city, may soar into the heavens to-day, and fall into the dust of oblivion to-morrow. Though the soul may scale the heights and win the glory it is still conscious of the ever-living thirst. The wind of death passes over the city of human greatness, when it falls into ruins, and the living walk on the graves of the dead! Thus, Percivale could not find in fame enough to satisfy the thirst of the soul.

> "And I was left alone."

Then he found himself within a lowly vale where was a chapel and a holy hermit to whom he spoke

of his strange adventures, of the allurements of the
way, and of his failure to find the Holy Grail. The
hermit warned him that the secret of his failure
was his lack of true humility.

> " ' Thou hast not lost thyself to save thyself
> As Galahad.' . . ."

Percivale, continuing the conversation with Ambrosius, further relates the appearance of Galahad,
and tells how he was made " one with him, to
believe as he believed "—how he had followed him
up the hill of death where storms raged, and had
seen him pass amid a blaze of fire and a roar of
thunder, like the " shoutings of the sons of God "—
pass like a silver star into the spiritual city, and
then it was there flashed upon him the vision of the
Grail and he was satisfied, and returned to Arthur's
hall.

Ambrosius would know whether he had come
only upon " phantoms " in his Quest, and learns of
a carnal temptation. It was the Princess of the
castle, who, with artful wiles, had striven to win him
from the holy Quest to a life of sensuous delights.
She was beautiful and rich, and the love of his
youth.

The conflict waged between love and duty : self
and self-renunciation glows fiercely in the lines—

> " ' O me, my brother! but one night my vow
> Burnt me within, so that I rose and fled,
> But wail'd and wept, and hated mine own self,

And ev'n the Holy Quest, and all but her;
Then after I was join'd with Galahad
Cared not for her, nor anything upon earth.'"

The war of Sense with Soul is thus portrayed in
the character of Percivale and in the symbolism of
his experience. He is simply a creation standing
for the living soul seeking purity and truth and
God. His experiences depict the varied conflicts
of Soul with Sense. All through Percivale is
attacked on the sensuous side of his nature, where
he is most susceptible. He is weak, and he is
conscious of his weakness. He is not strong enough
to stand alone, and is only girded by the might
of Galahad, and redeemed from evil by the power
of his spirituality, yet even after he has won the
sacred vision he cannot trust himself, but goes into
" the silent life." So strong are the allurements of
Sense. He is by nature carnal, but is made spiritual
by grace. Finding no satisfaction in the temporal
he wins at last, through Galahad, the vision of the
eternal. Thus the victory is won over Sense. The
thirst of the soul cannot be slaked until it drinks of
the life of God. The storm must rage within the
deeps of being until the peace of heaven falls.

"Then fell the floods of Heaven, drowning the deep."

Sir Galahad is the most beautiful of the
characters and the most difficult to delineate. He
is too ethereal and spiritual for analysis. He is not

of earth, but of heaven. Little is related of his conflicts with self and sense. His spiritual career begins as he looks upon the glowing face and listens to the warning words of the holy maiden.

> "She sent the deathless passion in her eyes
> Thro' him, and made him hers, and laid her mind
> On him, and he believed in her belief."

His nature was sensitive to the spiritual. He moved in white armour among the knights, symbol of purity, and when knighted

> "'God make thee good as thou art beautiful,'"

said Arthur. The soil of his nature was well fitted for the seed of grace that grew into a flower of heavenly beauty. But was there no worm to wither the flower? There is something in the spiritual making of Galahad which suggests that the flower had a worm at its root, and the worm had to be killed, or it would surely kill the flower.

The clue is supplied in the symbolic chair of Merlin

> "'For there,' he said,
> 'No man could sit but he should lose himself:'
> And once by misadvertence Merlin sat
> In his own chair, and so was lost; but he,
> Galahad, when he heard of Merlin's doom,
> Cried, '*If I lose myself, I save myself!*'"

The chair, with its mystic scrolls, is the symbol of knowledge. Knowledge involves responsibility.

To know the difference between good and evil and
to choose, as Merlin did, the evil—to sacrifice the
spiritual for the sensuous—is to be lost in the chair
of knowledge. But to make the sacrifice of self,
and all pleasant but fatal things of sense, and
become the willing slave of truth and goodness, is
to save one's life. Here was the worm of self at
the root of the flower. Self would have him sit in
Merlin's chair and choose the evil. It is the old
conflict waged between flesh and spirit ; the tragedy
played on the curtained stage of every human soul.
But Sir Galahad said,

> "'If I lose myself, I save myself!'"

He will make the sacrifice of self that he may win
the vision of the spirit, and find the higher self
born in the death of the lower. It is the great
truth of self-renunciation which he sees to be
essential to the victory of the soul. The throne
of life is only reached over " the stepping-stones of
our dead selves." And he made the sacrifice, at
what cost the idyll does not tell, for what reward
the sequel shows. Ambrosius, the not too spiritual
monk, had enough perception to detect the secret
of the saintly Galahad when he rebuked the sensuous
Percivale, saying

> "'Thou hast not lost thyself to save thyself
> As Galahad.' . . ."

The King also recognised his spiritual supremacy

over his brother Knights when, in reply to his
declaration, "I saw the Holy Grail,"

> "'Ah Galahad, Galahad,' said the King, 'for such
> As thou art is the vision, not for these.'"

In the conflict between self and self-renunciation,
the higher nature is triumphant in Galahad. He
shapes into the spiritual warrior. The new forces
that awake within him are transmuted into mighty
energies that strike down the evil and redress the
wrong. The life that thrills his being does not
waste itself in pietistic brooding, but leaps, like a
sword from its scabbard, to purge the land. The
process of his spiritual evolution marks the progress
of the living soul from the lower to the higher.
First comes the victory over Self and Sense ; then,
with the strength born of victory, he becomes the
iconoclast of evil.

> ". . . 'And in the strength of this I rode,
> Shattering all evil customs everywhere.'"

Having won the battle within, he is armed for the
battle without. Galahad is the type of the spiritual
warrior drilled into efficiency by the discipline of
his own soul. He loses himself in God and in the
service of man, and goes at last through the storm
and lightning of death to live with God.

> "'And hence I go ; and one will crown me king
> Far in the spiritual city.' . . ."

Thus Soul, through sacrifice of self, is victor over Sense.

Sir Bors also wins the vision of the Holy Grail. There is naught in him of the mystic warrior or the religious enthusiast.

> "'If God would send the vision, well: if not,
> The Quest and he were in the hands of Heaven.'"

And that calm faith is unshaken though severely tested. Among the crags in a lonely part of the realm he finds a heathen people with their ancient cult. They fail to make a convert of him by persuasion, and would bring him to his senses by coercion. They bind him and bury him in a cell of "great piled stones." There, with faith tested in prospect of death, through the gap of a fallen stone, he wins the vision of the Holy Grail.

> ". . . 'Beyond all hopes of mine
> Who scarce had pray'd, or ask'd it for myself.'"

The cause of success or failure is to be sought in the character. Sir Bors is the type of a perfectly honest man, transparent in rectitude. He is not in the least emotional, and is incapable of great religious fervour, but he has honest simplicity and pure-heartedness, and unshaken conviction, which enable him to win the victory of Soul without much effort. That he is beautifully altruistic glows in the words ;

"' He well had been content
Not to have seen, so Lancelot might have seen,
The Holy Cup of healing.' . . ."

This was not indifference to but tender pity
for the anguish of Lancelot, so that the very cell
in which he was buried may be regarded as a
symbol of the buried self. And may we not
think of the Maiden of Faith who set him free,
as a type of the deathless angel that opens to the
spirit the barred gates of Sense? When the soul
stirs within the grave of its dead self it wins the
sacred Quest, it sees the angel of the resurrection.

Sir Lancelot, in his complex character and
tragic experiences, sounds deeper depths in the
conflict of Sense with Soul. What a character
he is! We pity him while we blame him. We
love him while we spurn him. He stirs within
us such mingled feelings, possibly because his life
is so human and real. He charms us when the
greatness of heaven seems to be about him. He
was built for heaven, but marred by earth. He
might have been a strong angel, but his wings
were broken, and soiled by one subtle sin.
Heaven and earth, angel and devil, contend for
the mastery. Thus, throughout, Lancelot seems
a dual-man. He photographs his inmost self in
the confession :

"' . . . But in me lived a sin
So strange, of such a kind, that all of pure,

Noble, and knightly in me twined and clung
Round that one sin, until the wholesome flower
And poisonous grew together. . . .'"

His guilty love of Guinevere was the poisonous
weed that would suck the life of the flower of
goodness. "Who shall deliver me from the body
of this death?" was the agonising cry of Lancelot.
The spiritual and the carnal on the silent secret
field of every human life wrestle for supremacy.
The victories of soul are not chronicled on earth,
but they are written in heaven. Its tragedies are
not seen by men, but lie open to the eyes of the
All-seeing. Lancelot reveals the contest between
Sense and Soul at its fiercest, and in the Gethsemane
of his agony we catch a glimpse of the blood-red
way that leads for some up to the heights of victory.
To the King he relates his experiences, and as he
states them we are conscious of their spiritual
significance. In the effort to tear the "twain
asunder" in his heart, the weed of evil and the
flower of good, he tells how he was driven into
waste places, where he was "beaten down by
little men"!

Sir Lancelot, once so strong, is now so weak.
His sin had sapped the moral energies of his life.
He had cherished it so long that it was like a
parasite sucking his strength, so that he succumbs
to little sins. It is a vital lesson which the soul
struggling with Sense and self must learn—that to

cherish sin, even in desire, is to cherish a vampire that drains the life and leaves the soul a prey to every creeping thing of evil. There can be no compromise. Either sin must be slain or the man.

Then he tells how he came to a "naked shore" where nought but "coarse grasses" grew.

It is the wilderness of the soul that once knew God and goodness, but lost the sacred vision. The soul, like the naked shore, is bereft of the beautiful ; no flowers of heavenly grace grow within, only the coarser growths. It is burnt and hardened by the fire of evil and swept by the storm brewed in the deeps of death. Lancelot is caught in the roar of its tumult. A great blast is heard, louder than the voices of the deep, shaking the clouds into confusion and the sands into sound. What are they but the symbols of his own unrest—the reflex of of the storm that surges and sobs within his own vexed being ?

Then he saw a boat in the wild surf and said :

> "'"I will embark and I will lose myself,
> And in the great sea wash away my sin." '"*

What does it mean ? Why, he will fight the storm, or it will beat out his life : he will take "arms against a sea of trouble" and in the great sea of spiritual conflict will wash away his sin.

> "'Seven days I drove along the dreary deep.'"

---

* "Will all great Neptune's ocean wash this blood clean from my hand ?"—*Macbeth*.

They are the seven days of Soul in struggle with Sense. His guilty love is like the passion of the sea. The soul would be pure, but Sense storms about it, and yet there is hope.

> " 'And with me drove the moon and all the stars;
> And the wind fell. . . .' "

And these are symbols of the heavenly lights that come out like angel-pilots to guide the soul into the diviner way of peace.

Then he came to the enchanted towers of Carbonek, " a castle like a rock upon a rock." The symbolism is now most significant. He found the steps that met the breakers guarded by two lions, and when he drew his sword to smite he heard a voice:

> " ' " Doubt not, go forward; if thou doubt, the beasts
> Will tear thee piecemeal." ' "

Thus the Soul in conflict with Sense, in its struggle to be pure, must learn the lesson of Faith. To doubt is to be lost ; doubt is the paralysis of action. The soul that lingers to question the possibility of its purity practically renews the invitation to its darling sin, and becomes a lost soul on the very steps of victory. Faith that not all is lost, that God is in heaven, and that the moon and stars still gleam across the dark sky—faith in the possibility of regeneration—is half the battle, and Lancelot believed, and passed on and up into a " sounding hall." In the hall was no picture or shield upon the wall, no bench or table upon the floor.

It is the hall of prayer and meditation. Why the emptiness of the hall ? Surely to teach that the heavenly sounds can only be heard in the being empty of self and Sense and all things that distract. Into that deep silence of being with naught but God comes the heavenly voice of hope.

Thus with Lancelot

> " ' But always in the quiet house I heard,
> Clear as a lark, high o'er me as a lark,
> A sweet voice singing in the topmost tower
> To the eastward. . . ." '

It is the voice of Divine hope that sings its " Excelsior " in every soul fighting its doubts and sins, struggling to be pure and free. It must not live in the lower, it must ascend to the higher.

> " ' . . . Up I climb'd a thousand steps
> With pain : as in a dream I seem'd to climb
> For ever. . . .' "

They are the steps of persistence.

Not in a flash may the mingled results of the poisonous weed and the wholesome flower be separated. Not in a day will the lower vacate the throne for the higher. The victories of Soul are won through long years of discipline and conflict.

> " Move upward, working out the beast
> And let the ape and tiger die," *

is ever the call of that sweet voice out of the East ;

* *In Memoriam.*

9

but the soul cannot soar to that high life and Divine—it must go by way of the thousand steps of persistent effort: yet ever in the "sounding hall" of prayer may be heard the heavenly voice of hope.

Sir Lancelot toiled on and upward until at a door he heard

> "'"Glory and joy and honour to our Lord
>   And to the Holy Vessel of the Grail."'"

He forced the door and entered, was blinded with the glare as of a great furnace, and swooned in the awful light that smote him.

> "'O, yet methought I saw the Holy Grail,
>   All pall'd in crimson samite, and around
>   Great angels, awful shapes, and wings and eyes.
>
> .   .   .   .   .   .
>
>   . . . But what I saw was veil'd
>   And cover'd; and this Quest was not for me.'"

The unveiled vision is not permitted Lancelot, that he may learn the lesson of reverence. Reverence will wait with deep humility praying, "Lord, Lord, open unto us," but Lancelot "essay'd the door." Thus, in the ascending series of faith and prayer and persistence, we find that reverence in the presence of the Awful Purity is essential to the unveiled vision ; but Lancelot is permitted to see the veiled glory. He sees enough to make him pure, and in the end he dies a "holy man."

What, now, is the King's estimate of the conduct and the character of his Knights?

> " ' " Blessed are Bors, Lancelot and Percivale,
> For these have seen according to their sight."

The Holy Grail was to them a symbol of purity, and their spirits were cleansed by fiery trial or spiritual warfare.   But the many knights—like Gawain—who sought the Holy Grail, not for its spiritual significance, but because of superficial sentiment cr sensuous excitement, followed "wandering fires."   In them Sense triumphed over Soul. The spiritual Knights saw "according to their sight"; looking for purity they found purity.   The sensuous knights—the greater number—won no vision of the spiritual, for they had no eye for it. They would have lived more noble lives, and done more noble deeds, if they had been content to do the work nearest to them.   The King had uttered a prophecy which in the end was verified.

> " ' Your places being vacant at my side,
> This chance of noble deeds will come and go
> Unchallenged, while ye follow wandering fires
> Lost in the quagmire!   Many of you, yea most,
> Return no more. . . .' "

Thus the Round Table of the King was broken, and the Knights, upon whose souls he had momentarily flashed his likeness, who had fought his foes and won his battles, were scattered.   The idyll surely teaches that highest life is found and holiest vision won at the "Table Round" of duty, and in strenuous effort to fulfil the plain prosaic duties of life, however loveless. To some few, like the "holy maiden," it may be given to find the highest and the best in spiritual mysticism, but, for most of us, the safest way lies in making the best of our life where it is, and, like the King himself, in never "wandering from the allotted field," and in fighting our evil where we are bravely and patiently. So we shall find a light not of earth, and a vision that shall not pass.

> "'"Who may not wander from the allotted field
> Before his work be done ; but, being done,
> Let visions of the night or of the day
> Come, as they will ; and many a time they come,
> Until this earth he walks on seems not earth,
> This light that strikes his eyeball is not light,
> This air that smites his forehead is not air
> But vision—yea, his very hand and foot—
> *In moments when he feels he cannot die,
> And knows himself no vision to himself,
> Nor the High God a vision, nor that One
> Who rose again. . . ."'"

Guinevere.   THROUGH all these years the victory had been on the side of Sense. When Guinevere first rode with Lancelot among the flowers the evil was wrought. She learned to love this courtly Knight, with his warmth of colour. As years passed love deepened ; they met in secret and pledged their vows. Suspicion haunted the court,

* "These three lines in Arthur's speech are the (spiritually) central lines of the Idylls."—TENNYSON, *A Memoir*, ii., p. 90.

and conscience grappled with their heart-strings. Soul clashed in furious battle with Sense. The agony of Lancelot was stamped upon his face.

> "The great and guilty love he bare the Queen,
> In battle with the love he bare his lord,
> Had marr'd his face and mark'd it ere his time."

And so, with Guinevere, Sense did not become regnant without a struggle. She is stronger on the sensuous than on the moral side, her mental powers dominate the spiritual, but she has just enough conscience to make her feel. The remorse of Guinevere, in the earlier scenes, never deepens beyond regret.

> ". . . 'I for you
> This many a year have done despite and wrong
> To one whom ever, in my heart of hearts,
> I did acknowledge nobler.' . . . ."

The regret is not deep, though it suggests a spark of conscience which may flame again. As years pass her reason is more alive to the danger. The guilty love being cooler and more calculating, she becomes suspicious of Modred.

> "She half-foresaw that he, the subtle beast,
> Would track her guilt until he found, and hers
> Would be for evermore a name of scorn."

The sense of shame and regret awakens, but even the regret is almost selfish. There is no thought of the great wrong done to Arthur, or of the loss to herself in not having "loved the best and highest."

As yet she thinks only of her fair name, defamed, should Modred learn the secret.

But shame for a lost name is a moral quality which may be strengthened. The fact is, Guinevere had not yet realised the badness of her sin. She had toyed with it so long that its features had changed, and ceased to be repulsive. She does not as yet see her sin, only herself lost to fame and name; but conscience is stirring, and a pulse of nobler life begins to beat. We feel how much stronger it has grown in the lines,

> "Henceforward too, the Powers that tend the soul,
>   To help it from the death that cannot die,
>   And save it even in extremes, began
>   To vex and plague her. . . ."

Even in her dreams conscience makes her coward. She dreams that a shadow falls from out the sun; it broadens and blackens until land and cities are swathed and burned in the fiery darkness.

It is the shadow of her evil which she sees through the eyes of awakened conscience, falling dark and deadly over the fair realm of the King.

This slow awakening of the moral nature in Guinevere is an instructive study. Conscience has now so far reasserted itself that she seriously proposes to Lancelot their final separation!

> "'O Lancelot, get thee hence to thine own land,
>   For if thou tarry we shall meet again,

And if we meet again, some evil chance
Will make the smouldering scandal break and blaze
Before the people, and our lord the King.'"

Lancelot promised, but failed to perform, and must be held responsible, for "still they met and met." Whatever specious arguments he used he failed to soothe her deep unrest or hush the holy voice that cried through the soiled sanctuary of her being.

". . . Again she said,
'O Lancelot, if thou love me get thee hence.'"

The night for the long farewell is fixed; "passion pale they met," when suddenly the voice of Modred shouts—

"'Traitor, come out, ye are trapt at last."

The guilty secret is out. The cherished evil of two hearts will work its own tragedy; "the end is come."

Sir Lancelot would have the Queen fly across the sea, where he would defend her with his life. She reminds him of the farewell, and calls him "friend," to indicate how final is the separation. At last they come to the parting of the ways. She decides to renounce him. Sense had clashed with Soul for the guilty love, but in the end Soul is victor.

"For I will draw me into sanctuary."

It reveals moral possibilities in Guinevere that she should gain her greatest moral victory at such a crisis. She breaks with Lancelot at the moment she most needs him. Love and expedience and Lancelot plead for elopement, but conscience pleads for right, and conscience wins. It must not be forgotten that Guinevere met the crisis of her life, strangled her guilty love, and banished her lover when in dire necessity.

Thus Soul wins supremacy over Sense, and her higher nature slowly emerges to the point of a new vision. Sir Lancelot leaves for his castle, while the Queen travels all night to Almesbury across the "glimmering waste," where her sense of utter loneliness is voiced by nature in the moaning of the spirits of the weald and in the rush of the cold wind, and in the croak of the raven in the dawn, when she thinks the raven "spies a field of death," the slain of the land! Thus conscience is working out remorse.

In the nunnery, all unknown, she finds refuge. Here the little novice chatters of the scandal of the court and sings her sweet song :

"Late, late, so late! and dark the night and chill!"

The talk of the innocent child is as fire in the heart of Guinevere, and the voices of the song go wailing through her desolate soul.

"No, no, too late! Ye cannot enter now."

Then the agony of the heart stricken with remorse beats its fevered pulse of pain in the line

"Will the child kill me with her foolish prate?"

Her every word, as she tells the legend of Arthur, burns like fire, when, with conscious guilt, the Queen flashes out upon the child,

"· · · 'Thou their tool, set on to plague
And play upon and harry me, petty spy
And traitress' . . ."

The moral sense thus works in flame of passion falling back into the smouldering ashes of reflection, out of which is wreathed at last the form of repentance.

"'But help me, heaven, for surely I repent.
For what is true repentance but in thought—
Not ev'n in inmost thought to think again
The sins that made the past so pleasant to us."

And yet, even as she prays, she forgets her own definition of repentance, and her thoughts wander back to Lancelot, through the flowers and over the sunny glades of those forbidden days, when the King seemed cold and colourless and not like Lancelot.

". . . While she brooded thus
And grew half-guilty in her thoughts again,
There rode an armed warrior to the doors."

It is the King! Down the long gallery she

hears the sound of his step, coming nearer. She falls from her seat, and with her arms and hair makes her face a darkness to the king. She cannot look up to his pure, marred manhood, as he stands beside her and tells the story of his vanished hopes.

His tones tremble with mingled wrath and love as he speaks of his once great ideal—how he would have driven the heathen out and reconstructed the realm by drawing to himself the flower of men.

> "'I made them lay their hands in mine and swear
> To reverence the King, as if he were
> Their conscience, and their conscience as their King,
> To break the heathen and uphold the Christ.'"

But what had happened ?

> "'And all this throve before I wedded thee,
> Believing, "lo mine helpmate, one to feel
> My purpose and rejoicing in my joy."'"

She had fallen ! Through scandal and contagion of evil his realm had been shattered.

> "'Till the loathsome opposite
> Of all my heart had destined did obtain,
> And all thro' thee.'"

Then the King paused, and she crept nearer and " laid her hands about his feet." It was the better self, striving to articulate the speech of conscience, saying, " I have sinned : forgive ! " The King feels the meaning of the touch, and his tones change.

> " 'Lo ! I forgive thee, as Eternal God
> Forgives : do thou for thine own soul the rest.' "

Leaving her the assurance " I love thee still," he speaks of possible purity and hope of reunion " in that world where all are pure."

> " ' . . . Leave me that,
> I charge thee, my last hope. . . .' "

Over her prostrate form he waves his hands in blessing, and then goes out into the night.

She fain would see his face, " which then was as an angel's," as he commands the nuns to cherish and to guard her. Then he rides to the great battle in the west.

Guinevere, now left alone, passes into her night of agony, and we have all the phases of the working of conscience, self-loathing, remorse, penitence, despair and hope. In all her being storms rage, and waters moan, and lightnings flash, until the angel of peace comes across the troubled deep. In the midst of all, her sin looms out of the night, tormenting, and she talks of suicide.

> " ' What help in that ? I cannot kill my sin,
> If soul be soul ; nor can I kill my shame.' "

No, she cannot. Then is there no hope ? Did not the King speak of hope ? Did not he forgive ?

> " ' . . . And left me hope
> That in mine own heart I can live down sin.' "

Thus the gleam of possible purity shoots through the night of despair.   Her repentance is complete, and out of it will grow that diviner vision of a · soul no longer chained to Sense.   She sees, through her growing purity, what she had not seen before, the real glory of Arthur.

> "'Who wast, as is the conscience of a saint
> Among his warring senses, to thy knights.'"

Her vision grows to the height of his pure sublimity, and the radiance of it flashes down upon her, like living fire to consume her evil.

> "'. . . Now I see thee what thou art,
> Thou art the highest and most human too,
> Not Lancelot, nor another.   Is there none
> Will tell the King I love him tho' so late?'"

She had looked upon him ever with the eyes of Sense, and seeing no "warmth and colour" she had turned to Lancelot.   Now she sees him through Soul, and "that pure severity of perfect light," his spiritual supremacy, charms her into love and adoration.   The result is that, knowing now the real Arthur, her pain is great, in that she had not known him before.

> "'Ah, my God,
> What might I not have made of Thy fair world,
> Had I but loved Thy highest creature here?'"

But she is saved by the thought of his love.   Long ago by the stately altar he had vowed "I love thee

to the death," and when she lay in the dust, under
the shadow of her shame, and Arthur stood within
the shadow of his death, he was still unchanged,
and out of a broken heart declared

"'Let no man dream but that I love thee still!'"

It is the memory of his love that saves her, and
we hear the resolve of a nobler life breathing in
the line,

"'I must not scorn myself: he loves me still.'"

Thus in Guinevere the carnal nature is redeemed at last by love. For her good deeds and
pure life she was chosen Abbess, when she lived
for three years and then passed "to where beyond
these voices there is peace;" and Soul, though late,
triumphed over Sense.

The poem is a parable. Arthur is the spiritual
man, subduing and moulding his Knights of the
lawless passions into chastity and obedience, until
he becomes as the conscience of a saint among
them.

Guinevere bodies the sensual or carnal nature to
which Arthur, the spiritual soul, is wedded. The
antagonism between Arthur and Guinevere is the
conflict waged in every human life between flesh
and spirit. The problem for the spirit is how to
save and purify the body. Arthur's love redeems
both body and soul. A pure spiritual fire in the

house of the body will burn up its evil, so that it becomes the shrine of the saintly life.

When the senses, like the Knights, submit to conscience, then the. soul flashes down its splendour, life is redeemed in its depths as well as in its heights, and the union is complete.

> " ' Hereafter in that world where all are pure
> We two may meet before high God, and thou
> Wilt spring to me, and claim me thine, and know
> I am thine husband. . . .' "

The Passing of Arthur. IN " The Passing of Arthur " the soul wages its last war with death. When the Knights are dead and Guinevere a dream and Arthur a memory old Sir Bedivere tells the story of the last great battle.

As he walked among the sleeping warriors, nearing the tent of the King, he heard the pathetic lament of Arthur, who had seen God in the stars and the flowers—

> " ' But in His ways with men I find Him not.
> I waged His wars, and now I pass and die.' "

His own work seemed a failure.

> " ' . . . All my realm
> Reels back into the beast, and is no more.
> My God, thou hast forgotten me in my death.' "

The soul in conflict with death is tremulous with doubt ; but only for a passing moment.

> " ' Nay—God my Christ—I pass but shall not die." '

There is a life which death cannot kill, an immortality of deeds that flows on, like a pure stream, to sweeten other lives. There is for such a deathlessness in death. The doubt of Arthur is slain by the consciousness of immortality. His work may be a seeming failure, and the ways of God a mystery; but he is assured " I shall not die." His pure soul, by noble deeds, had wrought itself into humanity.

Then Sir Bedivere relates how the King had slept and dreamed of the ghost of Gawain wailing on the wandering wind

> ". . . 'Hollow, hollow all delight!
> Hail, King! to-morrow thou shalt pass away.
> Farewell! there is an isle of rest for thee.'"

In the old superstition it was usual for an apparition to predict a battle with its results. The ghost of Gawain suggests, moreover, that what a man is here, he will be hereafter.

Gawain had lived a frivolous, empty human life, with corresponding results in the other world. He had sown to the wind and he reaps the whirlwind; death does not change character, it merely projects it within the curtain; we start in eternity where we leave off in time.

> "Light was Gawain in life and light in death,"

and light after death!

The dream troubled the King, but Bedivere was

not superstitious ; he did not believe in apparitions and omens ; he was calm and practical, with calculating common-sense.   He relates how he urged the King to shake off the nervous dread and fling himself with courage into the battle ; he had heard the tramp of Modred and the rebel knights, then, let the King

> " ' Arise, go forth and conquer as of old.' "

We feel the gloom in the heart of Arthur, and the closing of the night about him in his pathetic reply :

> " ' Yet let us hence and find or feel a way
> Thro' this blind haze, which ever since I saw
> One lying in the dust at Almesbury,
> Hath folded in the passes of the world.' "

Then the King rose and flung himself into the last weird battle.   In that "deathwhite mist" we hear the clashing of steel, the wail of voices, and the moan of dying men.   The death-storm sweeps into silence both friend and foe.   The realism of the description suggests the spiritual significance.

The sun is burning low, and is a symbol of the flickering fire of life.

A "deathwhite mist" sleeps o'er land and sea ; in which we have the image of death veiling the vision of the dying.

The cold creates a "formless fear"; suggesting the fear of the soul tremulous on the threshold of the unknown.

Some had "visions out of golden youth"; and they are the pure loves and delights of long ago gleaming through the mists of death.

"Some beheld the faces of old ghosts"; and these are the evil deeds done in life rising in the dread hour like mocking spectres.

Wailing voices filled the air with "shrieks after the Christ," and they suggest the passing souls who feel their need of Him in death.

Cursing voices rent and stained the night; and we hear the despair of those who know not God, and take their wild leap into darkness.

"Cryings for the light"; in which souls awakened to a sense of their need seek the kindly light.

Now through the storm of battle upon all alike there fell the last deep sleep, and we are reminded of one who died, and who conquered in dying.

> "Last, as by some one deathbed after wail
> Of suffering, silence follows. . . ."

Thus the mist of death fell on the gory scene; and when the mist had cleared Bedivere tells how the King, looking across the field, saw—

> ". . . Only the wan wave
> Brake in among dead faces. . . .
> .   .   .   .   .   .
> And rolling far along the gloomy shores
> The voice of days of old and days to be."

It was the voice of time, not the voice of battle, ringing in his ears.

10

> " ' Hearest thou this great voice that shakes the world,
>   And wastes the narrow realm whereon we move ? "

Time, like ocean hungry for the land, eats away the ever-narrowing ground of life and sweeps us into the great deep.

The voice had called for the King, and, for a moment, he was overwhelmed, and doubted his own spiritual ascendency.

> " ' Confusion, till I know not what I am,
>   Nor whence I am, nor whether I be King.' "

It is the final war with death, when the soul begins to question its origin and dignity and destiny. Doubt seizes upon it. What if it be only matter, to be blown on the wandering winds ? What if it change and lose itself in other forms ? For a moment Arthur doubted, staggered, and cried—

> " ' Behold, I seem but King among the dead.' "

Bedivere was not troubled with such doubts. He believed in the kingly supremacy, and relates how he urged the King to one more deed of valour to establish faith. He pointed out Sir Modred, that incarnation of evil. The King fell upon him and slew him, but was well-nigh slain himself. The soul best kills its doubts by rising and slaying the evil. It comes back to its throne through moral victories. Arthur fell, but he fell victorious, no longer doubting that he was King.

Then came the final scene. Sir Bedivere tells
how he was told to take Excalibur and fling it
into the deep ; but he had made excuse, and only
after the third command, with threat, had he flung
it across the wave, when an arm clothed in white
samite rose, caught the sword, brandished it three
times, and drew it into the deep.

Excalibur, as we have seen, was the symbol of
the spiritual weapon by which the victories of the
King were won ; but now that his work was done
it was time to "cast away" the sword. In the
eternal deep to which he goes there is eternal
peace.

The King, mortally wounded, was borne by Bedivere to the margin of the wave, when across the
deep loomed a dusky barge with three crowned
queens and other stately forms ; and Arthur mur-
mured, " Place me in the barge." As it moved
away, Bedivere tells of his own lament—

> " ' For now I see the true old times are dead.' "

But the passing King replied in those immortal
words :

> " ' The old order changeth, yielding place to new,
>   And God fulfils Himself in many ways,
>   Lest one good custom should corrupt the world."

The loyal Knight had watched the barge sail out,
a speck upon the misty waters, and "vanish into
light." What does it mean ? The barge is death,

but it is death passing into life.   The three Queens suggest " Faith, Hope and Charity."   Charity is the symbol of the infinite love where the weary victor rests after his last war with death, and where he sleeps into the tender dawn, with the welcome voices of the city chanting as if

" Around a king returning from his wars."

Thus Arthur is a parable of the human soul warring in life with Sense and all its evils, yielding at last to death, but only to win its greatest victory through death.

Now what shall we say of Arthur as an ideal ? It is evident that he cannot be regarded as perfect. It would be easy to point out the flaws of his character.   We must hold him partly responsible for the sin of Guinevere.   His duties to his realm did not release him from his duties to his Queen. To allow her to ride in the early spring with Lancelot, while he was absorbed in state affairs, was to create an opportunity fraught with danger.   All through we miss in Arthur that tender humanness that makes the ideal man and husband.   He is ever on the far-off heights, very pure, but far too frozen. Even divinity is not perfect without humanity. When the Queen grovels in her shame at his feet, he betrays no sense of imperfection.   He utters no word of self-reproach, though his conduct had not been blameless, and, to say the least, we should have

POEMS OF DEATH, OR VICTORY
OF SENSE.

---

*Merlin and Vivien. Lancelot and Elaine. Pelleas and
Ettarre. The Last Tournament (in part). The Vision of
Sin. The Lotos Eaters. The Sea Fairies. The Islet.*

**Merlin
and
Vivien.** VIVIEN is attached to the court of Mark, the
Cornish King. She hates Arthur and his
Knights, with their high ideals ; she is a cynic
and laughs to scorn the Table Round, and her
cynicism grows to active malevolence. She is an
incarnate reptile, this smooth-tongued Vivien. She
will leave the court of Mark and enter Arthur's Hall,
where she will watch for scandal and circulate her
poison. Thus she comes to Camelot and, casting
herself weeping at the feet of the Queen, appeals
against the perfidy of Mark. The Queen listens to
her plaint, bids her bide awhile, and rides away
with Lancelot, while Vivien, through the portal arch,
watches with evil-glowing eyes every sign of innocent
intimacy and mutters :

> " ' . . . They ride away—to hawk
> For waterfowl. Royaller game is mine,' "

The character and conduct of Vivien are power-fully focussed in the lines

> "But Vivien half-forgotten of the Queen
> Among her damsels broidering sat, heard, watch'd
> And whisper'd: thro' the peaceful court she crept
> And whisper'd: then as Arthur in the highest
> Leaven'd the world, so Vivien in the lowest,
>
> .   .   .   .   .   .
> Leaven'd his hall. . . ."

In the hall and near the King is one Merlin, who is bard, astrologer, architect and wizard. He possesses a "charm" which Vivien covets and sets herself to win. Merlin, under the power of her subtle spell, falls into melancholy.

> ". . . He found
> A doom that ever poised itself to fall,
> An ever-moaning battle in the mist,
> World-war of dying flesh against the life,
> Death in all life and lying in all love."

In the heart of the doubt was a foreboding of doom, in that war of Sense with Soul, when the worm of flesh would eat into the spirit of life. He would escape her baneful influence, but she follows him into the boat, and they are driven across to Breton sands, where they pass on into the wild woods. Merlin is morose and taciturn, as if the chilling shadow of some tragic doom lay athwart his spirit. Vivien is playful and loving, intent on winning the secret of the mystic charm.

"The which if any wrought on anyone
With woven paces and with waving arms,
The man so wrought on ever seem'd to lie
Closed in the four walls of a hollow tower,

.   .   .   .   .

And lost to life and use and name and fame."

How tenderly she pleads and caresses until that
"dark forethought rolled about his brain"!   Then
her mood changes into humorous sallies and sober
argument and flippant satire, but Merlin answers
with discretion.   Yet there are signs of weakness;
she wins upon his confidence and stirs the pulse of
age.   He "half believes her true," but when she
plays the *rôle* of scandal and breathes suspicion
from the lowest to the highest of those in Arthur's
hall, Merlin is vexed, and mutters, "Tell her the
charm," and falls into a soliloquy.

"'What did the wanton say?
"Not mount as high"; we scarce can sink as low:
For men at most differ as Heaven and earth,
But women, worst and best, as Heaven and Hell.'"

Vivien, angered at the muttered words, leaps erect
as a frozen viper; her lips are white and bloodless.
She breathes in puffs of wrath; her cheeks are
blanched; her hand steals down to grasp her dagger!
Then suddenly her mood changes and she is
reproachful and sentimental.

She had hoped her life might have been a path
of flowers with him, but now she can only weep

her life away.   A storm is gathering and brooding.
Merlin begins to relent, and calls her to shelter from
the storm.   She replies with simulated passion, and
the storm grows nearer.   She challenges the lightning to strike her if she lie.   The storm breaks,
the lightning flashes, an oak is riven, and Vivien,
crying, "Save me!" creeps closer, with terms of
endearment.   The storm rages, the winds wail,
the rotten things snap.   Merlin tells the charm
and sleeps.

> "Then crying, 'I have made his glory mine,'
> And shrieking out, 'O fool!' the harlot leapt
> Adown the forest, and the thicket closed
> Behind her, and the forest echo'd, 'Fool!'"

The idyll portrays the complete victory of Sense
over Soul.   Vivien is a repulsive character, but she
is necessary.   She incarnates the evil that broke the
realm and scattered the Knights, and personifies its
most seductive and revolting influence.   In none of
the Idylls is the heinousness of sin drawn with
such deep dark colours as in Vivien.   A woman is
chosen because man at his worst is "as earth," but
woman is "as hell."   Evil has no conscience, neither
has Vivien.   She is beautiful flesh without soul.   She
possesses intellect and imagination, but the soul
lies coffined in her lovely body.

Merlin stands for intellect divorced from religion ;
he has knowledge, but not self-control ; he is strong
intellectually, but weak morally.   His centre of

gravity lies in reason rather than in conscience, and, being more easily shifted, he quickly falls, and dies to life and use and name and fame. The fallen soul, conquered by Sense, is thus dead to purity. The greatness of being lies in ruins, through which wanders a mocking laughter as of fiends crying, " Fool ! "

lot   A TOURNAMENT is arranged. The central
       diamond and the last of Arthur's is the
).   prize. Lancelot feigns sickness to remain
with Guinevere, but she orders him to the joust. He doubts her love, but is reassured :

> " For who loves me must have a touch of earth ;
> The low sun makes the colour: I am yours,
> Not Arthur's. . . ."

On his way to the Tournament, he calls at the castle of Astolat where dwells the lily maid Elaine, who falls at once in love with him, though he is twice her years, " and loved him with that love which was her doom." * As he tells the stories of the wars or falls to traits of pleasantry, love weaves his meshes round her tender heart. She cannot sleep, and, in the early dawn, steals down the tower stairs, when she hears the voice of Lancelot as he strokes his steed. She draws near, " rapt on his face as if it were a god's " ; she

---

* " The Lily Maid " seems to me the fairest, purest, sweetest love-poem in the English language."—PROFESSOR JOWETT.

would have him wear her favour at the joust,
and, as he leaves with her his shield, she " lives in
fantasy."

Lancelot goes to the Tournament disguised, and,
being borne down by numbers, receives a well-nigh
fatal wound, and vanishes into a wood whence a
hermit bears him to a cave.   Meanwhile the King
tells his fear to the Queen, but hopes " that
Lancelot is no more a lonely heart," for he wore
a sleeve of scarlet, doubtless the gift of a gentle
maiden.   The effect upon the Queen is electric ; she

> " Past to her chamber, and there flung herself
>   Down on the great King's couch, and writhed upon it,
>
>   .   .   .   .   .   .
>
>   And shriek'd out, ' Traitor ! ' . . . ."

For weeks the life of Lancelot hangs on a thread,
when the King, handing Gawain the diamond of
the joust, bids him seek the missing Knight and
deliver him the prize.

Sir Gawain comes to Astolat and lightly falls
in love with Elaine.   In vain he pleads his suit,
but, divining her secret love for Lancelot, drops
poison into her pure mind, and gives her the
diamond, believing that she knows his hiding-place.
Then carolling a song he rides away to the King,
and is severely reprimanded for disobedience.   He
merely stares and circulates the story of Lancelot
and Elaine, with the result that jealousy consumes
the heart of the Queen.

Meanwhile Elaine, with her father's consent and her brother's help, goes in search of the lost and wounded Knight, and, finding him in the hermit's cave, gives him the diamond. He kisses her, saying, " Rest you must have " ; but as he gazes on the gentle maiden he sees her secret blaze upon her simple face and he is sore perplexed.

Then follows a pathetic story of the tender love that flits between Camelot and the cave, hovering like a dove o'er the sorely-stricken Knight, alluring him from the grave; and, with the sweet charm of its tenderness, nursing him into life and strength.

Sir Lancelot calls her friend and sister, but love he cannot give, as his heart is not his own.

> " The shackles of an old love straiten'd him,
> His honour rooted in dishonour stood,
> And faith unfaithful kept him falsely true."

Elaine knows how hopeless it is, and wanders across the fields into the city with that plaintive cry, " Must I die ? " Through the long, lone night she mutters, " Him or death." Sir Lancelot, on recovery, presses on Elaine some friendly gift, when her self-control is swept away by a surging torrent of feeling.

> " Then suddenly and passionately she spoke :
> 'I have gone mad. I love you : let me die.' "

And Lancelot replies :

> " . . . ' Had I chosen to wed,
> I had been wedded earlier, sweet Elaine.' '

Her pathetic answer rings the knell of passing hope : "My good days are done." Lancelot leaves the castle.

> " So in her tower alone the maiden sat :
> His very shield was gone ; only the case,
> Her own poor work, her empty labour, left."

What a picture of desolation and heart-breaking despair !

The Lily Elaine droops beneath the storm. In her chamber she sings the song of love and death. It is the wail of a dying heart. The brothers hear the last notes of the passing cry, " Let me die ! " and hasten to her, only to receive her dying wish that, after death, upon the bed on which she died, she might be placed within the barge decked like the Queen's, and that the old dumb servitor might row the barge to Arthur's palace. She dictates a letter to Lavaine, which she herself will deliver.

The promises are made, the letter laid in her hand, and Elaine sleeps her last sleep.

The barge is palled in samite, and the body carried to the river ; in her right hand she holds a lily, and with her left she clasps the letter.

> " ' For Lancelot and the Queen and all the world.' "

The brothers kiss her. The dumb man takes the oars and rows with the flood to the palace of the King.

". . . And that clear-featured face
Was lovely, for she did not seem as dead,
But fast asleep, and lay as tho' she smiled."

In an oriel window of the palace may be witnessed another scene.

The stately Queen gives audience to Sir Lancelot,
who kneels at her feet, proffering her the jewels
he had won in many a joust.   The Queen receives
them coldly and her words are hot with jealousy—

" '. . . Not for me !
For her ! for your new fancy. . . .'"

Then suddenly she flings the diamonds through
the open casement into the stream below.

Lancelot in disdain of love and life leans upon
the window-ledge when,

". . . Slowly past the barge
Whereon the lily maid of Astolat
Lay smiling, like a star in blackest night."

The barge arrives at the palace doors.   The
servants wonder and ask, " What is it ? "   The King
comes out, and the body, at his command, is borne
by Percivale and Galahad into the hall.   Gawain
and Lancelot and the Queen look on in pity.   The
King spies the letter, telling all the secret of her
love, with that pathetic farewell, " My true love
hath been my death."

Then follows the defence of Sir Lancelot, with
tender regret for the lovely dead, and the rebuke
of the jealous Queen and the burial of Elaine.

The scene in the oriel window is thus contrasted :

> " . . . The Queen
> Who mark'd Sir Lancelot where he moved apart,
> Drew near, and sigh'd in passing, 'Lancelot,
> Forgive me ; mine was jealousy in love.'
> He answer'd with his eyes upon the ground,
> ' That is love's curse ; pass on, my Queen, forgiven.' "

Thus the war of Sense with Soul is seen in the struggles of Lancelot and Elaine and Guinevere. An estimate of each character may help us to understand the conflict waged and the victory won by Sense.

Sir Lancelot as the hero of the idyll stands between Elaine and Guinevere. He is the object of a dual-love, the love of Elaine, pure and tender and clinging, and the love of Guinevere, guilty and jealous and suspicious. The question for Lancelot is, Shall he break with the Queen and free himself from a guilty bond by accepting the love of Elaine, or shall he continue bound ?

That is the problem out of which emerges the war of Sense with Soul. Soul would say, Free yourself from a false and fatal position, and grow pure again in the face of a pure love. But Sense would say, Cling to the one who has suffered for you and whom you love, though the love be guilty. We have an insight into the struggle of Lancelot when Lavaine calls him " great," and when, feeling his guilt, he shows his inner life in the sad reply :—

> " 'In me there dwells
> No greatness, save it be some far-off touch
> Of greatness to know well I am not great :
> There is the man.' "

Again, when the white face of her who might have made

> " This, and that other world
> Another world for the sick man,"

appeared in the palace, his pain is great.   Her pure love might have been his to break his bonds, but she is dead through love of him, dead because he deemed his honour bound him to the Queen.

> "His honour rooted in dishonour stood."

And when he sits by the river, watching the returning barge that bore the body of Elaine, and dreams of love and jealousy and knighthood, we hear the cry of a great soul chained to Sense, half hugging the chains, but with conscience enough to know that they are chains.   Shall he break the bonds that bind him to the Queen ?   Shall he sacrifice her love and rise again to purity and chivalry ?   If she willed it, has he the power ?   It is the conflict of Sense with Soul, and we hear the clash of it in the warring lines :—

> " ' . . . I needs must break
> These bonds that so defame me : not without
> She wills it : would I, if she will'd it ? Nay,
> Who knows ? but if I would not, then may God

I I

> I pray Him, send a sudden Angel down
> To seize me by the hair and bear me far,
> And fling me deep in that forgotten mere
> Among the tumbled fragments of the hills.'"

Lancelot knows that his will is weak, and yet his conscience is still alive.

> "So groan'd Sir Lancelot in remorseful pain."

His pain was great, for he was great save for that one sin. The nobler the nature the more sensitive it is to evil, and the keener is its suffering. Thus Lancelot suffers first because of Elaine, for her pure love wasted and life blighted, then because of Guinevere, for the guilty love that chained and defamed him, lastly because of Arthur, the stainless King, who loved and trusted him when he was guilty of treachery. Ever side by side with the crystal purity of the King moved this dark sin of his, and the vision of the contrast was his torment :—

> "The great and guilty love he bare the Queen,
> In battle with the love he bare his lord,
> Had marr'd his face and mark'd it ere his time.
> Another sinning on such heights with one,
> The flower of all the west and all the world,
> Had been the sleeker for it: but in time .
> His mood was often like a fiend, and rose
> And drove him into wastes and solitudes
> For agony, who was yet a living soul."

The conflict is fierce and the victory lies with Sense. Lancelot, throughout, clings to the guilty love that degrades.

Now, what shall be said of Elaine ?   It is clear she is weak in reason and judgment, but she is strong in feeling.

She is the ideal of pure emotion ; the deepest thing in her is love ; she cannot balance it, for she has not the power ; she cannot control it, for it is the stronger force. Elaine is the embodiment of pure and lofty feeling flinging itself against the barred gates of Sense. Her strong, impetuous love, like a torrent met · by rocks, dashes back upon herself in a frenzy of passion. Like the torrent, too, she cannot soften the rock upon which her love beats wildly. Her love can only fall back into the surge of her own heart, there to gather strength and spend itself until life is wasted with the backward rush of foiled feeling.

Thus the ethical truth emerges that the soul may waste its best force on the impossible. It can only feed itself upon an object rich in noble feeling and responsive. To find and to love what is possible and best and highest, is to become like the object loved. And yet Elaine, weak in intellect and will, is beautiful because of her wonderful capacity for love. " She loved much," though foolishly, and we can forgive her defects, seeing that the charm of womanhood consists in the power to love. Elaine, throughout, is brought into sharp contrast with Guinevere. It has been well said, " The maid of Astolat is the lily of womanhood ;

the Queen is the rose, full-blown and heavy with fragrance." In the love of Elaine we have simplicity and freshness and purity and faith. In the love of Guinevere we find the mingling of suspicion and jealousy and duplicity and doubt. The full-blown rose of her love nourishes the worm of jealousy.

When she hears of the "favour" worn by Lancelot, she writhes upon the couch,

> "And clench'd her fingers till they bit the palm."

And when the fickle Gawain spreads a story of Lancelot's love for Elaine, she in anger

> "Crush'd the wild passion out against the floor."

How fiercely her jealousy flames again in the oriel window :

> "'Tell her she shines me down.'"

But the contrast between Elaine and Guinevere is finely imaged in the flinging of the diamonds into the stream.

> ". . . And down they flash'd, and smote the stream.
> Then from the smitten surface flash'd, as it were,
> Diamonds to meet them, and they past away."

Thus Lancelot stands between these two loves, and must choose. When he decides for the guilty love Soul is chained to Sense. The passing diamonds are symbolic of purity passing from Arthur's realm.

18   PELLEAS, a simple youth, but pure and brave,
        comes to Arthur's court and is knighted.
:e.   One day he rides across the Forest of Dean
to seek Caerleon and the King, when he lights
upon a company of gay damsels and knights who
had lost their way.   The lady of the party appeals
to Sir Pelleas to direct them :

> ". . . But while he gazed
> The beauty of her flesh abash'd the boy,
> As tho' it were the beauty of her soul."

This is the Lady Ettarre, an important personage
and an accomplished flirt.   Pelleas is so impres-
sionable that Ettarre seizes her opportunity, and,
seeing him strong in frame with heart all ablaze,
she will have him fight for her and win the circlet,
" that I may love thee."

Pelleas in ecstasy, deceived by the false pressure
of her hand, not seeing the mocking glance she
flashed around until a smile wriggled over every
face, promised, " nor slept that night."

In the Tournament of Youth he wins the golden
circlet, which the Lady Ettarre accepts, and wearing
for " the last time is gracious to him."   On their
return he is treated with cold and cynical snubbing.
She " cannot bide Sir Baby."

The damsels are to keep him back and feed him
on pap-meat.   Arriving at the castle gates he is
shut out and left to wander in a field, where he
consoles himself with an analysis of woman's mind,

" These be the ways of ladies," he says, and thinks she is testing his fidelity, and he will persevere ; so all day long by the castle wall he sits upon his steed.   The lady in anger bids her minions drive him hence, when Pelleas receives their charge and they are overthrown ; and still he keeps his watch.

They charge again, when he submits to be bound, and is carried to Ettarre, with the result that he is "smitten" more deeply, and believes in her and in her word.   He thinks she is putting him to the proof, and she will yield in the end.   Alas! how she mocks his knightly vows and thrusts him out of doors, railing—

> " '. . . For save he be
> Fool to the midmost marrow of his bones,
> He will return no more.' . . ."

But at the end of the week he is still there, crouching like a faithful dog!

Ettarre now would have him slain, or bound, and brought once more before her.   The caitiffs, three to one, charge upon him, when Sir Gawain flashes on the scene with proffered help to Pelleas, which, however, he declines, and overthrows the minions. They leap again, bind him, and bring him to Ettarre. The lady wreaks her wrath upon the caitiffs, and commands them to thrust him bound from the palace gates.   At last upon the love-lorn youth the fact dawns that he has been cruelly fooled ; and yet his love burns on !

> ". . . 'Farewell;
> And tho' ye kill my hope, not yet my love.'"

A glimpse of the better nature in Ettarre, like a star-gleam across a dark sky, is revealed in her reflection :

> "'I deem'd him fool? yea, so? or that in him
> A something—was it nobler than myself?—
> Seem'd my reproach? He is not of my kind.'"

Meanwhile the bound lover is being released by Gawain, who, wayward as the wind, yet doubtless sincere, offers to be proxy. He will do the wooing and bring the lady to her senses ; he will play upon her feelings by assuring her that he had slain Pelleas, and, when he wins her confidence, he will chant the praise of Pelleas "from prime to vespers." Sir Gawain enters the castle, but he lingers within, as Pelleas without sings the song of his "rose."

Weary of waiting, Pelleas passes through the open gates across the court into a garden with three pavilions,

> "And in the third, the circlet of the jousts
> Bound on her brow, were Gawain and Ettarre."

His pure young heart burns with indignation as he creeps away in moral loathing to the castle bridge, when his shame flames into wrath. He will go back and slay them there. With drawn sword he stands over the guilty sleepers, but the vow of brotherhood restrains him. He passes out, but returns to lay the gleaming sword across their naked throats.   Then he rides moaning, like a madman, from the castle, calling up the doom of hell upon its walls and women, wailing over the pure love he had wasted on that loathsome creature of sensuous beauty, and exclaiming:

> " ' I loathe her, as I loved her; to my shame,' "

wildly dashes into night.

The guilty sleepers wake with the cold of the sword upon their throats.   Ettarre, in wrath, with awakened conscience, charges Gawain with falsity.

> " . . . And he that tells the tale
> Says that her ever-veering fancy turn'd
> To Pelleas, as the one true knight on earth,
> And only lover; and thro' her love her life
> Wasted and pined, desiring him in vain."

Sir Pelleas rides madly on through the starry darkness to the tower " where Percivale was cowled," and there beside the walls he sleeps and dreams of Gawain setting fire to Arthur's hall, when hands are laid upon him and he starts crying

> " 'False ! and I held thee pure as Guinevere.' "

He is thinking of the lady Ettarre, but Percivale hears the words and asks if he is dreaming or has he heard of Lancelot ?   Pelleas, like a wounded man, cries—

> " 'Is the Queen false ?'   And Percivale was mute."

Then Pelleas mounts his steed and, riding over

a cripple, dashes on like a fiend until in sight of
the tall towers of Arthur's hall.

> " ' Black nest of rats,' he groan'd, 'ye build too high.' "

Suddenly Sir Lancelot appears and Pelleas bears
down upon him, declines to give his name, and
comes as a poisonous wind to

> " ' . . . Blast
> And blaze the crime of Lancelot and the Queen.' "

He madly dashes, without sword, upon the great
Knight, when, his weary steed staggering at the
shock, Pelleas falls, crying, " Thou art false as hell."

Sir Lancelot, with his heel upon him, in fierce
but passing anger, speaks.

> " ' Rise, weakling ; I am Lancelot ; say thy say.' "

They pass together into the hall of Arthur.   The
Queen learns they have fought, but knows not why.
She bids him speak if he have plaint to make.

> " But Pelleas lifted up an eye so fierce
> She quail'd ; and he, hissing ' I have no sword,'
> Sprang from the door into the dark. . . . "

Then rose between the Queen and Lancelot the
phantom of retribution.   They saw in the face of
each the shadow of the coming doom, that Nemesis
which is the penalty of sin.

> " Then a long silence came upon the hall,
> . And Modred thought, ' The time is hard at hand.' "

It is a painful picture, but, like the picture of

Merlin and Vivien, it is necessary in order to portray the progress of evil in the court. It had demolished the citadel of knowledge in Merlin; old age with its wisdom had fallen; but the picture must be completed by the wreck of a young, pure life in Pelleas. He deserved a better fate, and Mr. Hutton thinks he ought to have had it; but that could only be at the cost of the finished portrait of the tragedy of evil, which is no respecter of persons.

In Pelleas the victory falls back to Sense, and delineates the young, pure life rudely awakened to the falsities concealed within the sensuous. Pelleas stands for the ingenuous soul allured by the senses, not seeing how sensuous beauty may conceal moral ugliness, or a worm be curled within a rose, or evil pass as an angel of light.

The danger is lest the shock of the discovery may cause such revulsion of feeling that faith in humanity shall be lost and the young life fling itself into the night of infidelity.

There is, further, the danger of confusing the sensuous with the spiritual. Pelleas confounds physical beauty with beauty of soul, and when he finds that he has been allured and deceived by the physical, he loses faith in the spiritual. He does not see that the face of gentle culture may hide the meanest of souls. The pure soul gives a subtle beauty of its own to Sense, but Sense may have beauty without Soul, which may allure to death.

The bloom of many a life has been blighted by
the loveliness of Sense.   The soul is only beautiful
when goodness dwells within.   It can make lovely
the loveless face with its own spiritual glory.
Beware of physical beauty without moral goodness,
is the lesson of " Pelleas and Ettarre."

The Last THE war of Sense with Soul is shaping to its
Tourna- tragic end.   The evil, wrought by the guilty
ment. love of Lancelot and Guinevere and by the
scattering of the Knights through following " wandering fires " of superstition, now rushes on to its final
conflict in " The Last Tournament."

The characters are powerfully drawn.   In Arthur
and Dagonet the victory is on the side of Soul,
but in Tristram and Isolt it falls to Sense.

Let us watch the unfolding of the spiritual and
the sensuous, and note the glory that circles the
one and the shame that darkens the other.   We
have seen how Arthur, the King, stands for the
spiritual principle, authoritative and supreme within
its own realm, striving to bring all its conflicting
forces into obedience.

For a time the spiritual was regnant, but we
noted the gathering shadows and dying light within
the court.   We saw the deepening of the moral
gloom as that spell of superstition, working secretly
among the Knights, drew them into the wastes.
Now the night grows darker, and we begin to hear

the muttering of the storm that wrecks the goodly
realm of the King.

We hear its echoes in the insolent message of
the Red Knight brought by the maimed churl who
escapes to Arthur's Hall.

> " ' " Tell thou the King and all his liars, that I
> Have founded my Round Table in the North,
>
>   .   .   .   .   .   .
>
>   . . . and say his hour is come,
> The heathen are upon him, his long lance
> Broken, and his Excalibur a straw." ' "

The King is not only well informed of the rebel
forces without who band themselves to violate the
order of his realm, but he is also conscious of a
lower tone within his Knights.

> " ' Or have I dream'd the bearing of our knights
> Tells of a manhood ever less and lower ? ' "

He had laboured to construct a kingdom of
spiritual men, but the carnal forces had not been
slain, only maimed, and the recreant rebels lift their
heads again.   Sense would wrestle with Soul for
supremacy.

" The Last Tournament " is the symbol of the ·
battle growing ever fiercer between the higher and
lower nature.

The old question asked in " The Coming of
Arthur " we hear once again :

> " Asking whence
> Had Arthur right to bind them to himself ?
> Dropt down from heaven ? wash'd up from out the deep ?

They fail'd to trace him thro' the flesh and blood
Of our old kings ; whence then ? A doubtful lord
To bind them by inviolable laws."

It is Sense at war with Soul, questioning its
origin and right to reign. It is the gross materialism
that would choke the soul out of the universe.
Because it cannot · trace its genesis through flesh
and blood it will deny its supremacy. It will
spurn the categorical imperative

"Thou shalt and shalt obey and do my bidding
And fight my wars."

It would pull down the higher nature. The
philosophy that would resolve all of man into matter
chokes the soul. So Arthur prepares to wage war
with the fleshly forces.

The description of the fierce onslaught images
the fervour and force with which spiritual battles
ought to be waged.

"Swording right and left
Men, women, on their sodden faces, hurl'd
The tables over and the wines, and slew
Till all the rafters rang with woman-yells,
And all the pavement stream'd with massacre.
                .   .   .   .
So all the ways were safe from shore to shore,
But in the heart of Arthur pain was lord."

Once again Soul is regnant over Sense. Arthur
is still King, and the spiritual is supreme ; conscience is alive and Sense has been defeated. But

why pain ?   Because it is the law of life that we
pass from the lower to the higher through struggle.
Life only comes to its crowning through Gethsemane.
It must wrestle with Sense in the red rain of its
agony if the angel is to be seen.   Arthur had not
yet won the final victory, and so " pain was lord."

We do not vault into thrones, we wade to them
through blood.

Sir Tristram had won the jewels in the joust
and proclaimed, without the name, Isolt as Queen
of Beauty.   What more of evidence is needed that
the glory of the Round Table had departed !   What
an elevation and a crowning of the sin of Guinevere
and Lancelot, when, by implication, an adulteress
is proclaimed, by the co-respondent, Queen of
Beauty in the Tournament of Arthur !   No wonder
that Guinevere sits and sighs in her high tower as
Arthur passes.   No wonder the great Sir Lancelot
languidly watches the jousts,

> " . . . Sighing weariedly, as one
> Who sits and gazes on a faded fire,
> When all the goodlier guests are past away."

Was there not a root of the ruin in his own
heart ?

The Tournament is over, and Tristram whiles
away the time with Dagonet.

Dagonet is court-jester, and little of stature, but
great of soul.   No Knight of Arthur was ever more
chivalrous.   His quick penetration into the causes

working the ruin of the realm ; his keen sabre
thrusts into the fleshly jeering of Tristram ; his
clinging to the feet of Arthur, as he climbs "the
stairway to the hall," sobbing his secret grief, " I
shall never make thee smile again," all reveal the
greatness of the soul in so small a body, and the
power of the spiritual to clothe even deformity
with the robe of beauty.   It is interesting to follow
Dagonet in his mingled moods of satire, and note
how in him Soul riddles Sense in the fleshly target
of Tristram.

Dagonet refuses to dance to the music of Tristram,
and when asked why,

> " Made answer, ' I had liefer twenty years
>   Skip to the broken music of my brains
>   Than any broken music thou canst make.' "

Tristram answers :

> " ' Good now, what music have I broken, fool ? ' "

Dagonet replies :

> " ' Thou makest broken music with thy bride,
>   Her daintier namesake down in Brittany—
>   And so thou breakest Arthur's music too.' "

The delicious play upon the words, the keen
retort, and the subtle perception of the discordant
notes within the realm that break the music of the
King, are most suggestive.   Dagonet clearly sees
the evil, and makes war upon it.   The gross mate-

rialism of Sense reeks in the answering song of
Tristram :

> "'" New life, new love, to suit the newer day:
> New loves are sweet as those that went before:
> Free love—free field—we love but while we may."'"

The war of Sense with Soul could not be more
clearly portrayed. Purity wallows in the ethics of
the sty. Dagonet sums it up in one significant
word—" mud ! "

One of the little maidens who sat by the fountain
had offered him a draught from her golden cup.

> "'. . . And thereupon· I drank,
> Spat—pish—the cup was gold, the draught was mud.'"

Tristram answers :

> "'Was it muddier than thy gibes ?
>
> . . . For here be they
> Who knew thee swine enow before I came,
> Smuttier than blasted grain. . . .'"

Dagonet replies :

> "'Swine? I have wallow'd, I have wash'd—the world
> Is flesh and shadow—I have had my day.
> The dirty nurse, Experience, in her kind
> Hath foul'd me—an I wallow'd, then I wash'd—
> I have had my day and my philosophies—
> And thank the Lord I am King Arthur's fool.'"

It is the triumphant answer of Soul to Sense.
A life taught by experience, having tested materialism,
is redeemed from wallowing by the vision of the

pure splendour lying on the heights of Arthur ;
and yet Dagonet sees, in replying to Tristram,
how unlikely it is that even the King will succeed
in lifting all men from the troughs of evil to the
thrones of good.

> "'Conceits himself as God that he can make
> Figs out of thistles, silks from bristles, milk
> From burning spurge, honey from hornet-combs,
> And men from beasts. . . .'"

In Tristram and Isolt the victory is all on the
side of Sense, and we watch it wrestle on its evil
way, through love and songs, to its swiftly tragic
end.   Isolt, the Queen of Mark, had cherished
the guilty love of Tristram.   She hears his footstep
in the hall and flies to meet him at the door.

The intensity of her feeling burns in the lines :

> "'My God, the measure of my hate for Mark
> Is as the measure of my love for thee.'"

It is well to contrast the high character of
Dagonet with the character of Tristram and Isolt.
Compare the spiritual heights that gleam through
the serious jesting of Dagonet with the sensual
deeps that lie within the words and songs of the
guilty lovers.

Isolt, as she thinks of the deserted bride of
Tristram, is jealous, and declares—

> "'O were I not my Mark's, by whom all men
> Are noble, I should hate thee more than love.'"

12

Then her mood changes into passionate yearning for assurance of his ever deeper love. She will be satisfied if he will but flatter and lie to her!

> "'Swear to me thou wilt love me ev'n when old,
> Gray-hair'd, and past desire, and in despair.'"

There we have the character of Isolt, shallow, sentimental and voluptuous, so maudlin that she will be content to suck honeyed words filled with flies of falsity. How Soul must have lost itself in Sense when satisfied with sweet sounds of love empty of reality!

The reply of Tristram rings with a mocking void:

> "'Wine, wine, and I will love thee to the death,
> And out beyond into the dream to come.'"

In a laughing mood he sings the song of the two stars.

> "Ay, ay, O ay, the winds that bend the brier!
> A star in heaven, a star within the mere."

The song is a self-conscious and vivid contrast of himself to Arthur.

Arthur's star is the star of spirituality, calm and clear and abiding, shining far away in the heavens. Tristram's star is the star of Sense shining near within the mere, ever shimmering with unrest, swept by gusts of passion "as if a phantom thing," doomed to pass.

The song is prophetic of his destiny, fulfilled in tragedy.

> " Behind him rose a shadow and a shriek—
> ' Mark's way,' said Mark, and clove him thro' the brain."

Tristram and Isolt are thus epicureans of the lowest type. They make unlawful pleasure the end of existence. There glimmers o'er all their sensuous life and talk a spiritual ideal which they persistently sacrifice to lower ends. The result in character with Isolt is a selfish voluptuary, who seeks to win Tristram from his lawful bride with heartless indifference, and with Tristram a callous sensualist, who is dead even to woman's tears and pleading, who is cynical, with a coldness that shivers in his words, as he speaks to one bereaved, or to Isolt as she pleads for love in old age, or of his wife forsaken and lonely. Thus in Tristram and Isolt Sense is regnant and Soul is trampled in the slime of unholy passion, while the tragedy that sweeps the star of Tristram into oblivion is the symbol of moral retribution standing like an avenging angel within the folds of Sense, awaiting the hour of doom ; " the mind of the flesh is death."

The Vision of Sin. IN " The Vision of Sin " we have another illustration of the working of spiritual death in a human soul. It is often complex, always invisible, and only known by its dire results. No one has ever seen a soul die, but when it dies there are mostly signs of death. "The Vision of Sin" portrays the outward aspect of a dying soul. The cause is sensuality and the subject a young man.

> "A youth came riding toward a palace-gate.
> He rode a horse with wings. . . ."

The horse with wings is, doubtless, borrowed from Plato's "Phædrus" and is suggestive of high spiritual possibility. The youth has the power to soar, but his pinions are weighted with cloying sensualism. First he is allured by "a child of sin." Then we are introduced to an altogether sensuous scene with its "low voluptuous music" which, as it trembles and dies away, touches the soul into sighs and whispers. Again it "storm'd in orbs of song," shaking them all into a frenzy of sensuality.

> "Then they started from their places,
> Moved with violence, changed in hue,
> Caught each other with wild grimaces."

The whole picture portrays the effect of voluptuous music on the quivering nerves of Sense. Wings cannot soar in that reeking atmosphere of sensuous song. Then the scene is changed.

The soul is still conscious of its capacity and possibility. The great ideals have not all faded ; upon the mountain lies the light of noble things.

> "God made Himself an awful rose of dawn."

It is far withdrawn, but powerful enough to penetrate the dense atmosphere and stir the soul in its slumber. That "rose of dawn" is the call to spiritual vigilance and the prophecy of the day of nobler life. But sensuality numbs moral sensibility, with the result that the dawn is

> "Unheeded: and detaching, fold by fold,
>   From those still heights. . . ."

And as the neglected light slowly fades, the nemesis comes creeping down.

> "A heavy vapour, hueless, formless, cold,
>   Came floating on for many a month and year,
>   Unheeded. . . ."

The moral atmosphere grows denser and finally wraps the soul in deadly folds, when the young life of soaring genius is shrivelled into an old age of sodden cynicism. The man is dying while living. The withered heath and ruined inn are symbols of wasted, empty being, where no flowers grow and the winds wail a requiem.

His talk at the inn with the ostler and barmaid and waiter reveals the man.—Sensuality generates subtle evils. Cold-blooded cynicism, contempt of virtue, and blatant infidelity constitute the staple of his speech.

> "'We are men of ruin'd blood;
>   Therefore comes it we are wise.
>   Fish are we that love the mud,
>   Rising to no fancy, flies.'"

His cynicism is the dye which gives a colour of vice even to virtue. He assails the Church and religion and liberty. All men are hypocrites, life is a delusion, death is king, and the skull of the dead is a hideous mockery of the divine.

> "'Lo! God's likeness—the ground-plan—
> Neither modell'd, glazed, nor framed.'"

In the last picture we have the death of the old sensualist. He is dying, when there rises again that "mystic mountain range," and the sound of voices is heard.

> "Then some one spake: 'Behold! it was a crime
> Of sense avenged by sense that wore with time.'"

The voice pleads that his sins were due to sensuous passion, that the higher nature took no active part, that sufficient penalty was exacted of the body and that thus Sense was avenged.

> "Another said, 'The crime of sense became
> The crime of malice and is equal blame.'"

Precisely! It was impossible for the man to sin only through Sense. He could not divorce intellect and conscience and feeling. All sin is by consent of the higher nature. His sensuous sin begat malice, but the will was involved in the malice. The soul is a unity and is not divisible. All its moral actions are determined by its executive, the will. Thus the man was to blame.

Yet another voice on the slope pleads.

"... 'He had not wholly quench'd his power;
A little grain of conscience made him sour.'"

It is urged that he was cynical and contemptuous, not because of malignancy, but because of his own sense of failure, and that, though he had wasted his life and abused his gifts, he had still something left. And the question is asked, "Is there any hope?" The answer comes, but it is vague and uncertain. Man may not determine the destiny of such an one. God alone knows the hidden things of the soul and whether nobler life can be fashioned out of the wrecks of ruin. But the fact that the dawn wholly withdrawn flushes once again the mystic mountain may carry a suggestion of hope.

"And on the glimmering limit far withdrawn
God made Himself an awful rose of dawn."

Thus "The Vision of Sin" vividly portrays the career of the sensualist and the slain greatness of a human soul.

The Lotos-Eaters. IN "The Lotos-Eaters" we do not find vulgar passion at work with its vein of cynicism or crime of malice, but merely the *abandon* of the whole man to the sensuousness of nature. The senses are captivated, with the result that love and duty and great ideals and noble effort are sacrificed for the greatest number of pleasing sensations. "The Lotos-Eaters," with its minute detail and exquisite colour, is a perfect picture of the moral effect wrought by sensuous absorption. If we think with one critic only of its artistic merits, as "picture and music and nothing more," or if we regard it exclusively on its physical side as "the apotheosis of sensuous enjoyment" we shall miss its deepest meaning.

The mariners come to the lotos land and eat of the lotos fruit. They bask in the summer light and breathe the perfumed air. They watch the "crisping ripples on the beach" until their senses steal away their souls. They forget the claims of country and home, love and duty. Sense absorption weakens human feeling, and in hedonism they sacrifice altruism. They would take an oath—

"In the hollow Lotos-land to live and lie reclined
  On the hills like gods together, careless of mankind."

So the higher nature dies in self-indulgent ease. When used as a means the sensuous may aid the spiritual, but when regarded as the end it becomes a parasite of the soul to suck its life.

Mr. Bayne would like to have seen "the atmosphere of Epicurean repose over the heads of the lotos-eaters shaken by the thunder of some higher truth, by the tumult of passionate acting men, by the roar of battle."

Artistically, doubtless, that would have been a gain, but ethically it would have been a loss ; we should have lost the moral force of the slow nemesis that creeps with death upon the soul abandoned to sensuousness.

> "And all at once they sang, ' Our island home
> Is far beyond the wave ; we will no longer roam.' "

The Sea-Fairies. AGAIN in " The Sea-Fairies," the temptation to live for the senses rather than the soul rings like a charming bell in the siren call of the fairies to the weary mariners.

> "Who can light on as happy a shore
> All the world o'er, all the world o'er ?
> Whither away ? listen and stay : mariner,
> Mariner, fly no more."

The Islet. AND again in " The Islet," when the wife of the singer would charm him from a life of action to indolent ease we hear the song of death.

> " 'Whither, O whither, love, shall we go ? ' "

And when he asks in the crashing music, if it shall be

> " 'To a sweet little Eden on earth that I know,' "

She at once replies :

> " 'Thither, O thither, love, let us go.' "

But he knows that in the Eden of sensuous in-
toxication there is spiritual death, and bravely
answers,

> " ' No, love, no.
> For the bud ever breaks into bloom on the tree,
> And a storm never wakes on the lonely sea,
> And a worm is there in the lonely wood.' "
>   *   *   *   *   *

THE EMOTIONAL POEMS

THE SANCTITY OF LOVE.

TENNYSON is not only the finest of English poets in the exquisite finish of his art, but he is one of the purest. He has not written a line which may not be read in the presence of the most chaste and sensitive. He never leaves a stain upon the whiteness of the tender flower of our home. The breath that breathes through his Idylls is ever fresh and pure. When he sings of the sanctities of love we are in that Eden of long ago, where pure · hearts and calm imaged the perfect face of love.

Our poet touches the most delicate subjects with a hand so steady and with eyes so clear, that the finished picture impresses us, not with the sensuous, but with the spiritual. Within the veil of Sense he shows the sanctities of the soul. We pass quickly through the porch of the human into the temple of the divine, and within he reveals the altar, where burns the sacred fire. Only a pure great soul, finely sensitive to the nobility of love, love in the home, breathing its pure air, soothed by its "voice of gentle stillness," or inspired by its vision of lofty sanctity, could ever have written these "Idylls of the Hearth." With the poet the home is the unit of the nation. Its true greatness lies not in her army and navy, but in the sacredness of home. What the home is the nation will be ; hence the domestic idylls in which the nobility of love is more persistently taught than in any other English poetry. The ideal of its sweetness and strength gleams through these idylls, and should love be degraded by passion or pride or hypocrisy, should the holy place of the soul be desecrated, the anger of Tennyson bursts like a lava flood upon the shameless seducer.

Love and Death.   IN "Love and Death" we have the key-note of the song which the poet sings sublimely through the first five poems of this group. Love and Death are represented as meeting in the walks of Paradise, when Death claims to be proprietor. Love concedes the supremacy of death on earth, but flings back the retort that Death is only the shadow of life. As the tree standing in the light of the sun casts its shadow,

"So in the ligi
Life eminent grief had deepened the river-bed
The shadow prow had cut a window in "the
But I shall reign to which they looked beyond.

Thus with clear vision the comfort he had
deepest instinct of the human
immortal.   wrought

The   THE note struck in "Love and Death set and
Miller's   heard in "The Miller's Daughter."   that
Daughter.   It is in the pure loves of home that the
sanctity of the ideal is most nearly realised.   And
here we have an exquisite picture of domestic love
flowing serenely through tender scenery and fragrant
flowers and sweet songs. We listen with delight
to the old man's prattle as he tells over again to
Alice, his wife, their love-story—how, when angling
in the pool, he was haunted with a love-song and
saw a reflection in the "level flood," the beauteous
form of Alice leaning from the casement ; and when
he raised his eyes and looked in hers—

> "Such eyes ! I swear to you, my love,
> That these have never lost their light."

In the new love his being awoke and nature
seemed to awake as well in responsive sympathy.

> "I loved the brimming wave that swam
> Thro' quiet meadows round the mill."

The story runs on through those golden days of

190 THE TEACHING OF TENNYSON.

quickly through the porch of ily natural are the
temple of the divine, and wi'
altar, where burns the sisly, half-shy,
great soul, finely sen id would not, little one!
love in the home, aded tenderly,
and I were all alone"!
its "voice of
vision of ie won the consent of his mother, who
these " le excuse—for the heart of a mother keeps
hom is watch over the love of a son ; but at last
I'

"'Go fetch your Alice here,' she said :
Her eyelid quiver'd as she spake.'"

Then he asks Alice to sing the "foolish song"
he gave her in those blissful days, and the two
lyrics, interrupting the flow of the story, are
exquisitely musical and tender.

"It is the miller's daughter
And she is grown so dear, so dear."
.   .   .   .   .
"Love that hath us in the net,
Can he pass, and we forget ?"

What a vision of sanctity in the heart of home
is revealed in the lines—

"Look thro' mine eyes with thine. True wife
Round my true heart thine arms entwine"!

How tenderly he touches their sacred sorrow!

"Although the loss had brought us pain,
That loss but made us love the more,

With farther lookings on. . . ."

The dredge of grief had deepened the river-bed of their love.   Sorrow had cut a window in " the narrow house " through which they looked beyond. Pathetically he speaks of the comfort he had found in her.

> " But that God bless thee, dear—who wrought
> Two spirits to one equal mind."

Then together they go out into the sunset and die with the sun into the life of the day that never dies.   It is a perfect picture of the sanctity of love in the home, making pure all the fires on the altar of the heart.

The Gardener's Daughter.   THE same ideal, clothed with equal tenderness, and singing as sweet a song, gleams through " The Gardener's Daughter."   For clear penetration into the heart of love with its subtle working, for the finished picture of the English garden, the whole of this charming idyll is unique. It fills us with wonder at the great skill of the artist, and the clear penetration of the poet-seer into the secret chamber of the heart.   The conception of love is pure and noble, and all the pictures glow with its sanctity.   The garden, with its sylvan beauty, seems to make visible that other garden of the soul where the flowers of love are pure and sweet as those of Eden.   The story is simple.   Two young men living together in the city are brothers in art and friendship, when the one, Eustace, is drawn by some law that holds in love, the attraction of opposites, to Juliet.   She is a kind of *multum in parvo*, and outwardly most fascinating, such an one to be

> "The summer pilot of an empty heart
>   Unto the shores of nothing ! . . ."

Of the pure grace and inward loveliness that adorn the spirit and make it the Shekinah naught is told.   As a work of art, a child of sensuous beauty, Juliet is captivating.   Thus thinks adoring Eustace, who paints her picture and chaffs his friend on its finished beauty, saying, "When will you paint like this ? "   He answers that it is all the work of love.   "A more ideal artist he than all."   At this Juliet, laughing, bids him

> ". . . 'Go and see
> The Gardener's daughter : trust me, after that,
> You scarce can fail to match his masterpiece.'
> And up we rose, and on the spur we went."

Then follows the description of the garden in which Rose lives.   It is well to linger and to note with what power of imagination the garden is pictured.   We may sit, "muffled in dark leaves" and hear the minster clock, and look out over fields of dewy freshness,

> ". . . Wash'd by a slow broad stream,
> That, stirr'd with languid pulses of the oar,

> Waves all its lazy lilies, and creeps on,·
> Barge-laden, to three arches of a bridge
> Crown'd with the minster-towers."

We may see the large lime-trees making a summer-house for "murmurous wings." This sylvan beauty of our English scenery in many a rural district is faithfully portrayed. The poet dwelt in seclusion, communing with the soul of nature, watching all her mystic moods and wondrous ways, and tells us ever what he sees. Here Rose lived, "hoarded in herself," her little world the garden, her greater, the sweet self in which she dreamed ; but even flowers in hedgerows are not quite hidden, and bees are allured by their fragrance and beauty. Thus Rose becomes a centre of attraction, and even the vulgar drones buzz about her.

> ". . . The common mouth,
> So gross to express delight, in praise of her
> Grew oratory. Such a lord is Love,
> And Beauty such a mistress of the world."

Ere he sees her the young artist falls in love ! Her imagined beauty flashes on his vision, and her tender grace flushes his life like the dawn. He reads the unerring instinct and passionate yearning within and says

> "'My heart was like a prophet to my heart,
> And told me I should love.'"

Then follows a delightful description of the

desires and hopes created by love, setting fire to the heart, and making imagination glow and giving colour to all things.

> " . . . A crowd of hopes,
> That sought to sow themselves like winged seeds,
> Born out of everything I heard and saw,
> Flutter'd about my senses and my soul."

The passage is an illustration of our poet's power in penetrating and describing subtlest feeling. He is master of the finest woven threads in the delicate web drawn across the chamber of the heart, but his power lies not only in subjective analysis of emotion, but in sympathetic interpretation of nature and in the skill with which he blends the moods of nature with the moods of the soul. He is more than a scientific observer of nature, noting with calm and practised eye her lights and shades; as when he describes

> "The curled white of the coming wave
> Glassed in the slippery sand before it breaks,"

and

> "The golden autumn woodland reels
> Athwart the smoke of burning weeds."

Or when he paints a tempest with vivid realism :

> "The forest cracked, the waters curled,
> The cattle huddled on the lea
> And wildly dashed on tower and tree
> The sunbeam strikes along the world."

And when he touches the colours of the Alps with fine delicacy :

> "How faintly-flushed, how phantom-fair
> Was Monte Rosa, hanging there
> A thousand shadowy pencilled valleys·
> And snowy dells in a golden air."

Tennyson is thus a student and lover of nature, who registers what he sees with scientific accuracy. When he tells us that a skylark comes down sideways on the wing, or when he writes

> "More black than ashbuds in the front of March,"

we may be sure that he is right. But when we have said that the poet is a scientific observer of nature we have not said all, nor is it just to say with one critic that "nature to him is neither love nor thought, she is law." Nature to him is law, for law is order, and he sees order everywhere. He owns and reflects the scientific spirit, but he sees much more than law, symbol of the force that drives through all the currents of life. Force is pitiless ; but to the poet nature is much more than force. He sees also a mystic life with moods having their counterpart in human emotion, so that the one seems a reflex of the other. He sometimes interprets nature as if she were an infinite mother in tender sympathy with the joys and sorrows of her children, and so not all law but love as well. Nature may not be to him what she was to Words-

worth ; but it is evident that he feels the power
of a Person behind and within nature, evolving
beauty and order, and ever in sympathy with the
best and purest.   He does not merely " describe "
nature with scientific accuracy, but he interprets her
mystic moods, and, with something of the skill of
Shakespeare, shows that she is married to man not
merely to serve him, but to sympathise with him
in all pure delights and chastise him in all wrong-
doing.   Take an illustration of this poetic sympathy
of nature with the joyous passion of love when the
young artist makes his first call upon Rose—

> " All the land in flowery squares,
> Beneath a broad and equal-blowing wind,
> Smelt of the coming summer, as one large cloud
> Drew downward: but all else of heaven was pure
> Up to the Sun, and May from verge to verge,
> And May with me from head to heel. . . ."

And so nature is interpreted not merely as law,
but as love,* for all her voices blend with the
passion of the lover's heart, who replies to Eustace—

> " . . . 'Were there nothing else
> For which to praise the heavens but only love,
> That only love were cause enough for praise.' "

In the garden the two friends come suddenly
upon Rose, and beautiful is the portrait of the
modest maiden among her flowers.

---

* " I report as a man may on God's work—*All's love yet all's
law*."—ROBERT BROWNING.

" But the full day dwelt on her brows, and sunn'd
Her violet eyes, and all her Hebe bloom.
                . . . Half light half shade,
She stood, a sight to make an old man young.
So rapt, we near'd the house; but she, a Rose
In roses, mingled with her fragrant toil."

The fascinated lover begs a flower of the un-
suspecting maiden, who hesitates and is slightly
nervous; she drops the branch, and "braids her
looser hair," and shapes her lips as if to answer,

" Nor yet refused the rose, but granted it,
And moved away, and left me, statue-like,
In act to render thanks."

He keeps watch all day long "till every daisy
slept" with the hope of seeing her, but his beautiful rose had gone to hide her crimson blush in
the seclusion of her home. The friends return
to the city, when the love-lorn man is assailed by
the good-natured banter of Eustace. Night comes,
but he cannot sleep for the vision of her beauty
and the call of the voice of love. How charmingly
natural is his declaration !

"Henceforward squall nor storm
Could keep me from that Eden where she dwelt."

Then comes the old story, yet ever fresh and
beautiful as the morning. He attends the wedding
of Eustace, and as example is better than precept
in life, he will follow the example of his friend.

So we have the delightful story of his wooing, and
how at last

> "The silver fragments of a broken voice,
>   Made me most happy, faltering, 'I am thine.'"

Then of aspirations realised and hopes fulfilled
he may not speak.   There are sacred things in the
heart veiled by the wings of the cherubim.

> ". . . Here, then, my words have end."

But he longs to tell the story of the sacred past, and
gives an exquisite outline in the words beginning—

> "Yet might I tell of meetings, of farewells,"

until at last

> "Night slid down one long stream of sighing wind,
>   And in her bosom bore the baby, Sleep."

And he is left alone and yet not alone, for she
is a spirit-presence, a memory and an influence to
keep his heart pure and young in old age, and at
last to stand with him in the sunset.

> "The darling of my manhood, and, alas!
>   Now the most blessed memory of mine age."

Thus the poet sings sublimely of the sanctity of
love, making life richer and fuller, love giving
the glow of tender colour to prosaic things, love
inspiring the soul to true nobility, and, when the
eventide draws on, filling it with light and music,

THE power of a pure great love is further illustrated in " Dora."

The scene of the story lies in the rural home of farmer Allan, who has a son named William and a niece called Dora. The old man having set his heart on the marriage of William and Dora, one day calls his son and tells him how he and Dora's father " had once hard words and parted," and when he died he took Dora to his home, and his one wish had ever been that William might marry Dora. William cuts the conversation short by declaring

> " ' I cannot marry Dora ; by my life,
> I will not marry Dora.' "

Allan in a violent passion threatens to disinherit William unless he complies with his wish.

> " ' . . . Take a month to think,
> And let me have an answer to my wish ;
> Or, by the Lord that made me, you shall pack,
> And never more darken my doors again.' "

Two strong wills thus clash, with added heat. William, feeling that he is being coerced into love, turns madly from his father's house, becomes a farm labourer and marries Mary Morrison, a labourer's daughter. Allan now pours the vial of his wrath on the patient Dora, forbidding her to speak to William or Mary on pain of expulsion.

> " ' . . . My will is law.'
> And Dora promised, being meek . . . .' "

Misfortune falls on William, who passes his father's gate half starving, but is scorned by the unforgiving man.

Dora, however, proves to be the guardian angel who, out of " what little she could save," provides for the pressing needs of William and Mary and their boy, until fever cuts short the life of William. Then Dora goes to Mary, and we have a woman's plot to soften the heart of Allan. Believing in the subduing power of love, Dora suggests that she should take the boy into the harvest field and set him among the wheat that

> " 'He may see the boy,
> And bless him for the sake of him that's gone.

The first day the plot fails, but on the second day Dora returns to the field with her little cupid, places him on a mound and wreaths him with harvest flowers,

> " To make him pleasing in her uncle's eye.

Allan appears on the scene with the question, " Whose child is that ? " When he learns the truth he is angry, and Dora makes the pathetic appeal—

> " 'Do with me as you will, but take the child,
> And bless him for the sake of him that's gone.' "

Allan cannot tolerate opposition, and yet relents ; he will take the boy, but Dora must not see him again. He disappears with the struggling urchin ;

Dora, returning to Mary, finds her grateful for the prospect opening before her boy; but when she learns of the hardness of Allan, she repents, saying :

> "'For he will teach him hardness, and to slight
> His mother. . . .'"

They resolve to go to Allan's house and to claim the boy, and through the partly open door they witness a lovely scene—

> "The boy set up betwixt his grandsire's knees,
> Who thrust him in the hollows of his arm,
> And clapt him on his hands and on the cheeks,
> Like one that loved him. . . ."

The women enter. Mary tells Allan the pathetic story of his son William and the last broken utterance of his sorrow. She begs of him her son and, further, pleads for Dora.

The sequel is described in words of tragic pathos, simple and natural.

> "'I have kill'd him—but I loved him—my dear son.
> May God forgive me!—I have been to blame.
> Kiss me, my children.'"

Thus Allan softens into contrition and his children come home.

> "So those four abode
> Within one house together."

The characters need no comment; they stand self-revealed, and the moral lies upon the surface. The story might have been called " Redeemed by

Love " in illustration of the truth " A little child shall lead them." Allan enthrones law with inflexible tyranny as if it were moulded in iron to break the offender. He enthrones it in heart and home, forgetting that law itself must be administered under the sway of a higher power—love. He forgets that charity must go beyond justice and lay her angel hand upon the sword and teach that rigid rule of will and tyranny of selfish desire are not to crush tender emotion.

Allan rolled the engine of an iron will across the field of his heart and hardened it into rock, and his nature could only be redeemed, its waste places restored and the seeds of heaven sown by a little child. Thus love, that "greatest thing," reasserts its sway, and the young angel comes back into the heart of an old man.

If in " Dora " we have natural emotion wrought into an idyll of exquisite tenderness, then what shall be said of " The May Queen " ?

The May Queen. IN " The May Queen " the first thing we feel is its strange emotional power over us. And emotion is stirred so deeply because the delineation of feeling is natural and simple and pathetic. Tennyson is sometimes a little too ornate to be natural, but in " The May Queen " the lines of light and shade are finely drawn. He has flashed his spirit into the character; he feels with Alice in her varying moods, and gives clear expression to them. There is a scale of emotion rising from the lower notes of self, ascending to the higher in nature and reaching the climax in the divine.

That ascending music which she hears in her dream marks the progress of her own spirit from the lower to the higher. In the opening stanzas we have a child filled with frolic and mirth, absorbed by the sweet expectation "I'm to be Queen o' the May." The thought dominates her and makes her authoritative and selfish. She addresses her mother imperatively

"You must wake and call me early, call me early, mother dear."

And her self-consciousness is clearly unveiled in the lines

"But none so fair as little Alice in all the land they say."

Further, her wayward, selfish humour leads her to be cruel to the love-lorn Robin. There is really no excuse for playing the ghost on him, and her words have a cold ring about them,

"They call me cruel-hearted, but I care not what they say,

They say he's dying all for love, but that can never be: They say his heart is breaking, mother—what is that to me?"

The Alice, in those first stanzas, in the rushing spring of life, with the expectation of being crowned

queen of the shepherd lads and lasses, is obviously
a vain and selfish girl.   She is already a tyrannical
little queen ; all her subjects must be her slaves.
We feel instinctively that she lacks the beautiful
soul—tender sensibility to the joys and sorrows of
others.   She has not yet found the selfless, altruistic
life.   She has not yet become a Christ-child.   She
is bright and charming in her talk and ways, but
she does not know the infinite grace of sacrifice.

Now, in the stanzas of " New-Year's Eve " we
trace the subtle change wrought in the character
of Alice.   She is fast wasting away in consumption,
and suffering is having its desired effect.   In its
furnace the dross of self is being destroyed, and
the gold of character is being sublimated.   Her
spirit is becoming fine and sensitive and gentle.
The first indication of the change is apparent in
the first line, where the imperative becomes an
interrogative, in addressing her mother.

> "You must wake and call me early."

is now chastened by suffering into

> " If you're waking, call me early."

It is a delicate touch, so fine that we almost pass
it, and yet it marks the transition of the spirit from
the lower to the higher.   As the spring is prophetic
of the summer, so these changes in the disposition
tell of a new vitality bearing the promise of richer

life and fuller. The second indication of awakening
out of self lies in the effect wrought by nature upon
her. As if the self-soul, not finding any peace
within, had gone out of its broken doors to look
for it in the soul of nature. Her sweet talk is all
about the sun and the blossom on the blackthorn,
and the flowers and the hazel copse and the rook
in the old elm-tree and the plover piping by "the
fallow lea," and the swallow coming with the
"summer o'er the wave." The choir of nature
sings to her again. Lovely scenes move like
pictures in the brain before the eyes of the dying
girl, filling her with pathetic yearning for the
coming spring and summer. It is the physical
craving of a consumptive patient, but deeper still
it is the hunger of a heart seeking peace in the
sensuous and outward. She has seen the white
robe of God and would fain "touch and hold."
What pathos sobs in the simple lines—

"There's not a flower on all the hills: the frost is on the
    pane :
  I only wish to live till the snowdrops come again :
  I wish the snow would melt and the sun come out on
    high :
  I long to see a flower so before the day I die"!

It is the self-child wandering through sunlight
and woods and flowers, charmed by the nature-spirit,
caressed into tenderness and won from waywardness,
so that thus she speaks :

"I have been wild and wayward, but you'll forgive me now;
You'll kiss me, my own mother, and forgive me ere I go."

Thus far under the influence of suffering the movement of the spirit has been from self into nature, but the climax is reached in the "Conclusion."

She lives through the winter to hear again the bleating of the lambs and to see the blowing of the flowers, but, strange to say, the sensuous beauty and the stirring voices of nature no longer satisfy her.

"It seem'd so hard at first, mother, to leave the blessed sun,
And now it seems as hard to stay, and yet His will be done!"

It is evident that she has realised some higher life and won some sweeter vision. A new movement has taken place in the spirit.

The charm of nature is not lost, but she is under the spell of a diviner charm. She finds the vision of God in Christ, who is the pure image in time of what the Father is in eternity. In His sublime sacrifice she finds the life which is the life of God. She sees the sin of self in the pure splendour of the self-less Christ who died, and she is made pure.

"He taught me all the mercy, for he show'd me all the sin.
Now, tho' my lamp was lighted late, there's One will let me in."

Then comes the dream of the calling voices and

of the sweet music swelling up the valley, passing,
as if on rhythmic wings, to heaven, when her spirit
interprets the sounds of nature as expressing the
movement and mood of her own heart.

> "... I know
> The blessed music went that way my soul will have to go.
> And for myself, indeed, I care not if I go to-day.
> But, Effie, you must comfort *her* when I am past away.
>
> And say to Robin a kind word, and tell him not to fret."

Here we have the climax, the ascending music
of her own spirit out of self into nature, then on
into the divine.   Her last thoughts are for her
mother and Robin ; she has become a Christ-child.
The essence of the Christian consciousness is that
it can project itself into other lives and bear their
sickness and heal their wounds.

Thus she passes, feeling that her new life here in
Christ is the ever old and yet ever young life, a life
which death cannot touch.   It is the vitality of
God.

> "To lie within the light of God, as I lie upon your breast—
> And the wicked cease from troubling, and the weary are
> at rest."

It may not have been in the mind of the poet
to trace in this pathetic idyll the passing of a
human soul out of self and the sensuous into the
spiritual and the divine, but it is there.

One of the marks of a great master is that there
is always more in his work than he himself is

14

conscious of, and it is left for his disciples to follow
the gleam of his genius or fit the broken chord into
the rhythmic whole.

The music of the sanctity of love still sings on
in "Lady Clare," "The Lord of Burleigh," and
in "The Beggar Maid,"—a beautiful trio in which
one great truth is illustrated. The poet links love
with worth. He recognises its supremacy over all
material wealth, and earthly titles, and pride of
birth, and centres it in natural instincts, and
spiritual affinities and the merits of character.

He enters a noble protest against the tyranny
of a caste that will not allow love to wander
beyond the boundaries of ancestry, and against
the sordid avarice that would bind the soul with a
chain of gold to some clod of earth.

In the "Lady Clare" this protest is first made.

Lady Clare. THE Lady Clare is engaged to Lord Ronald,
her cousin ; she is, apparently, a rich heiress,
but she dwells on the thought that he loves her
not for her wealth, but for her worth.

> " ' He does not love me for my birth,
>   Nor for my lands so broad and fair ;
> He loves me for my own true worth,
>   And that is well,' said Lady Clare."

She soon has an opportunity of learning whether

Lord Ronald loves her for her gold, or for her goodness.

The old nurse comes upon the scene and breaks to her the disquieting news :

> "'Lord Ronald is heir of all your lands,
> And you are *not* the Lady Clare.'"

The Earl's daughter had died, and the nurse had substituted her own child. Lady Clare being the daughter of the nurse, Lord Ronald is the legal heir to the property. The situation is embarrassing for all concerned, and there is scope for intrigue and deception. The secret is known only to Lady Clare and her mother-nurse. The supplanter finds it easy to become the temptress and suggests that the secret be kept for life, and the property retained at the marriage. But Lady Clare is incapable of duplicity and, nobly indignant, retorts :

> "'If I'm a beggar born,' she said,
> 'I will speak out, for I dare not lie.'
>
> .   .   .   .   .   .
>
> 'Nay now, my child,' said Alice the nurse,
> 'But keep the secret all ye can.'
> She said, 'Not so: but I will know
> If there be any faith in man.'"

The nurse has lost all faith in man, and believes that Lord Ronald will simply claim his right— enthrone property over love. The Lady Clare will put him to the test, and designs a little plot in which she will appear in the dress of a peasant girl to Lord Ronald—a russet gown with a rose in her hair ; and she will tell him the story of the nurse.

She starts for the castle when Lord Ronald meets her.

> " ' Why come you drest like a village maid,
>   That are the flower of the earth ? ' "

The crisis has arrived ; man is to be weighed in the balance !

> " She look'd into Lord Ronald's eyes
>   And told him all her nurse's tale."

And the result ! To the honour of manhood and the sanctity of love we read that he turned and kissed her with the tender assurance :

> " ' We two will wed to-morrow morn,
>   And you shall still be Lady Clare.' "

Thus Lord Ronald proved himself superior to pride of birth by wedding the child of poverty. We wonder how many, under similar circumstances, would have acted with the honour of Lord Ronald !

The Lord of Burleigh. THE sanctity of love—its superiority to birth and fame and power—is further illustrated in " The Lord of Burleigh." The Lord of Burleigh appears in the character of an artist, and woos and wins a village maiden. They are married without her knowledge of his real title and estate.

His motive in the concealment does not appear

to have been selfish. He would awaken within
her joyous surprise on learning his social position.
The motive is good, but the result is sad. They
pass from her father's roof, she thinking only of
the cottage home among the flowers and the
happiness of her artist husband, and he of the
great surprise in store for her. He leads her by
the handsome houses of the wealthy nobles, through
the ancient parks with oak and chestnut and by
the well-ordered gardens ; but all their glory fades
in the light of her ideal.

> "Evermore she seems to gaze.
> On that cottage growing nearer."

They arrive at a stately mansion, when the gates
swing open and domestics flutter about the doors,
as the landscape painter, to the surprise of the
village maiden, passes with her on "from hall to hall."

> "Proudly turns he round and kindly,
> 'All of this is mine and thine.'
> Here he lives in state and bounty,
> Lord of Burleigh, fair and free."

But the effect upon her is not what he had
fondly hoped. Upon a nature so sensitive the
impression is quickly flashed that she is not
equal to the exalted station—there had been no
preparation and the transition is too swift ; but she
strives to fit herself for the place, and succeeds,
by inherent grace and careful culture in growing
to the gentle life.

> "And her gentle mind was such
> That she grew a noble lady,
> And the people loved her much."

But the weight of honour hangs heavily on her
sensitive spirit, and she longs that the Lord of
Burleigh

> "Were once more that landscape-painter.
>
> .   .   .   .   .   .
>
> So she droop'd and droop'd before him,
> Fading slowly from his side."

The end is pathetic; and yet we may admire
the Lord of Burleigh for placing love above wealth,
and marrying for worth.   And we see how a
village maiden, under gentle culture, may become
a noble lady.   The secret of the chastened culture
lay in the sacred love by which the inferior
assimilates the qualities of the superior.   He was
a gentle consort and she, by a true philosophy,
became like the object loved.   But the experiment
is fraught with difficulty!

**The
Beggar
Maid.**   IN "The Beggar Maid" the protest against
mere class marriages is further voiced.   The
King Cophetua becomes enamoured of a
beggar maid, who is "more beautiful than day."

> "As shines the moon in clouded skies,
> She in her poor attire was seen;
> One praised her ancles, one her eyes,
> One her dark hair and lovesome mien.

So sweet a face, such angel grace,
   In all that land had never been:
Cophetua sware a royal oath:
   'This beggar maid shall be my queen!'"

In this trio the supreme thought is the pure sanctity of love, and that it shall be allowed freedom in the choice of its object—that no considerations of birth, or name, or fame, shall ever be permitted to crush any noble passion when directed towards a noble object, and that marriage only ensures domestic peace in the realisation of dearest hopes, when it is the result of spiritual affinities, soul answering to soul, whether in king and beggar maid, or lord and village peasant. Where the affinities do not exist marriage too often ends in painful tragedy.

We have further illustrations of the sanctity of a pure love, with wider variations, in "The Talking Oak," "The Brook," "Sea Dreams," "Maud," and in "Enoch Arden."

The Talking Oak. IN "The Talking Oak"* we find a tender sympathy on the part of inanimate nature with the joys and sorrows of mankind. We are borne along on its theme, as if on wings, through

---

* "Its author told me that this poem was an experiment, meant to test the degree in which it is within the power of poetry to *harmonise* external nature," etc.—AUBREY DE VERE, *A Memoir*, i. p. 510.

a fairyland. The oak overlooks Sumner-place, where the fair Olivia lives. Her sentimental lover, not sure whether

> "The love, that makes me thrice a man,
> Could hope itself return'd,"

comes to the "talking oak" to hear the stories of the lovers of long ago folded within its shadowy arms, and of all that Olivia does and feels for him, and to listen to the garrulous babbler as he contrasts Olivia's charms with those of the many who had sought his kindly shade.

> "Yet, since I first could cast a shade,
> Did never creature pass
> So slightly, musically made,
> So light upon the grass."

This most friendly oak reveals the secret of Olivia's love, and pours into the rapt soul of the lover all the story of her coming to kiss the spot where his name was cut into the tree, until the "heart of oak" was deeply moved.

> "Hard wood I am, and wrinkled rind,
> But yet my sap was stirr'd."

In the end the lover pronounces a *pax tecum* over this aged and parental tree, capable of such young and tender emotion. The idyll is playful and sunny ; its loves, as they come and go in those centuries of change, are chaste and good, and through the leaves of the lover's tree a pure wind wanders and sunbeams play as if no serpent had ever coiled itself in Eden. The sanctity of love gleams through all. The idea of "The Talking Oak" affords an illustration of what has been well called Tennyson's "sensuous-sympathetic" use of nature. The oak is an incarnation of the lover. What he thinks and feels and would say are transferred to the oak. It is a kind of transmigration of a soul into a tree, in which the tree speaks. This use of nature we shall find peculiar to the poet; he often projects his characters into nature in such a way as to blend them in one current of sympathy—almost identity. His characters do not stand outside nature, merely, and talk to her, but he makes them go inside, so that nature speaks for them, and she becomes a kind of second self, as in the lines—

> "For oft I talk'd with him apart,
> And told him of my choice,
> Until he plagiarised a heart,
> And answer'd with a voice."

"The Talking Oak" is naturally linked to "The Brook."

The Brook. ITS charm does not lie in the simple love-story of sweet Katie and James Willows, with their lover's quarrel, along with the incessant chatter

of Philip, the old farmer, who insists on breaking
in upon the tender scene of reconciliation.

> "But evermore her father came across
>   With some long-winded tale and broke him short,"

until a friend beguiles the farmer across the farm
that Katie and James may not be interrupted, and
has inflicted upon him, by the garrulous old man,
the pedigree and the peculiarities, the beauties and
the blemishes, of every animal upon the farm.
When they return they

> "Found the sun of sweet content
>   Re-risen in Katie's eyes, and all things well."

Nor does the end of the story charm, but sadden.
The old farmer dies—

> "Poor Philip, of all his lavish waste of words
>   Remains the lean P. W. on his tomb."

Katie goes abroad, and years after, Lawrence
Aylmer, now an old man, seated on a stile, is
startled by a lovely maiden. He recalls the vision
of a vanished face, and finds that she is the
daughter of the Katie who wandered

> "About these meadows, twenty years ago."

She tells him how they had returned and bought
the farm, and bids him welcome.

> "My brother James is in the harvest-field:
>   But she—you will be welcome—O, come in!"

The charm of "The Brook" lies in the lyric threading the story: in its musical modulation, and in mingling moods of soul with moods of nature. "The Brook," like "The Talking Oak," "plagiarises a heart" and with a tongue of tender eloquence tells the story of its travels through sylvan beauty and brambly wildernesses. We forget the chastened love-story in the fascinating lyric-flow. It is one of those illustrations, in which Tennyson abounds, of his marvellous use of nature. He seems to penetrate by his peculiar sympathy into her mystic life and reveal her secrets, showing us beauty where we never saw it before, leading us into the "sound of many voices" where stillness reigned. "After all that philosophers have said, the essentially correct definition of poetry in the concrete is the beautiful in sight wedded to the beautiful in sound."

The song of the "The Brook"—

> "I slip, I slide, I gloom, I glance,
>   Among my skimming swallows;
> I make the netted sunbeam dance
>   Against my sandy shallows."

is a perfect illustration of the definition.

IN "Sea-Dreams" we have a story of a
18.   gently born and bred city clerk who had married an unknown artist's daughter. They live on slender means in the city with their only child Margaret. He had been led by an unctuous rogue,

trading on religion, to invest his capital in Peruvian
mines.   Margaret fading for lack of air, they take
her to the sea.   The first Sunday they stray into a
chapel and hear a " heated pulpiteer " who,

> "Not preaching simple Christ to simple men,"

deals with the dogmatism of a narrow school
delighting in a hard theology.

The preacher predicts the speedy and tragic end
of the world.   The gentle-hearted woman shudders,
and her husband conjures up the mocking spectre
of his ruin.   They had entered the sanctuary with
troubled hearts, seeking the vision of God and the
Infinite Love, when they are regaled with the
picture of the scarlet woman !

Out of the confines of the chapel, with its narrow
views of God, they come and walk under the wide
heaven, and by the vast sea.   They drink the
larger air and wander on the cliffs and watch the
white-winged vessels sail into the west until curtained
with the folds of night, or into the east, where they
are " touched with roseate hues."   Then homeward
they return, she haunted by the text :

> "' Let not the sun go down upon your wrath,'
>   Said, 'Love, forgive him : ' but he did not speak."

Then follows a magnificent description of the
rising tide and the roaring sea in the lines :

> "Dead claps of thunder from within the cliffs
>   Heard thro' the living roar. . . ."

They all awake, the man crying, "A wreck, a wreck!"

The sea suggests his own ruined fortunes; he recalls the words of his wife and falls into a soliloquy, descanting on the word forgive and reflecting on the conduct of the unctuous hypocrite —how he had been warned, as if by something divine, not to trust him, had fought with his own lack of charity, had partaken of the hospitality of the man, had listened to his silvery talk, and had invested with him all his savings, and now

> "'Ruin'd! Ruin'd! the sea roars
> Ruin: a fearful night!'"

His wife thinks he dreamed, and asks, 'Had you ill dreams?" Yes, and he tells his dream; and we have an illustration of how imagination in sleep weaves into the fabric of a dream the sounds and sights of nature. Nature becomes a reflex of the storm within the man, or of the peace for which he craved. His dream—the tossing on the deep, the shelter of the cavern, the lovely star upon the night, and the landward exit of the cave filled with light, the strong woman with the pickaxe, and the deep bearing him on, the woman upon the brink who had worked within the mines scaling the mountain and he following, the vision from the summit of the fleet of glass, as if jewelled, sailing down before a dark cloud and in the distance a reef of gold, the fleet bearing down upon the reef and himself frantic to save it, but all in vain—portrays the power of imagination in sleep to construct a dream out of the familiar objects of life which shall reflect the moods of the soul. The ocean, now in wild unrest sobbing through the night, and now in gentle sleep under the summer light, is a picture of life. The woman in her strength, with pickaxe in her hand, stands for noble labour. The fleet of glass wrecked on a shining reef of gold, is the symbol of delusive dreams and broken hopes and vanished ideals. We never fully realise on earth our cherished hopes : we struggle up to some far-off gleaming peak, only to find the height flashing beyond us ; or if we reach the Pisgah of our aspiration, it is only to look upon the promised land and die in the wilderness with unrealised hopes and unfinished life. But God lives and eternity is long, and His completeness will flow around our little life and realise our noblest aspiration. We must shift the centre of gravity from the material to the spiritual if we would adjust the focus. To be spiritual is to be in God, and to be in God is to win the vision of life sailing across the troubled deep to the land of untroubled peace.

Still the wife thinks it is only a dream, and she says :

"'A trifle makes a dream, a trifle breaks,''

He replies that it is no trifle and goes on to speak of his interview with the fraudulent hypocrite, that worst type, with sleek smooth face and biblical quotations and grip of the hand with poison secreted in the heart! The slimy envenomed reptile, with its glittering eyes, that charms to its death the innocent bird, is not more repulsive than the man who uses the spell of religion by which to ensnare the trustful.

Here is a vivid picture of the loathsome reptile.

> "'. . . I should find he meant me well;
> And then began to bloat himself, and ooze
> All over with the fat affectionate smile
> That makes the widow lean. "My dearest friend,
> Have faith, have faith! We live by faith," said he;
> "And all things work together for the good
> Of those"—it makes me sick to quote him—last
> Gript my hand hard, and with God-bless-you, went.'"

Or when his wife urges that he may be wrong.

> "Perhaps he meant, or partly meant, you well,'"

we have the hypocrite chiselled in the cutting reply of the injured man,

> "'Who, never naming God except for gain,
> So never took that useful name in vain,
> Made Him his catspaw and the Cross his tool,
> And Christ the bait to trap his dupe and fool;
> Nor deeds of gift, but gifts of grace he forged,
> And snake-like slimed his victim ere he gorged.
> .   .   .   .   .   .
> How like you this old satire?'
>   'Nay, she said,
> 'I loathe it. . . .'"

But she too had a dream that went to music. She dreamed of a belt of luminous vapour in which music lay concealed and swelled at last into a thunderous fulness, that drew into its mystic light the grey cathedrals, broke the statues of king and saint and founder, caught up the cavilling discords of contending mortals into the ascending music, so that their wild wailings were never out of tune with its sweet note, until at last the great wave, " mixt with awful light," swept

> " The men of flesh and blood, and men of stone,
>   To the waste deeps together."

Yes, replies the man, but in that music harmonising our wild cries hate cannot blend.

> "One shriek of hate would jar all the hymns of heaven."

His conscience, even in his wrathful mood and fiery indignation, is sensitive.   Hate belongs to hell.

> " True Devils with no ear, they howl in tune
>   With nothing but the Devil ! "

Love belongs to heaven, and the wild passions of men may not blend with its holy music.   Hate cannot harmonise with heaven.

The injured man, seeing thus the fitness of things, is conscious of wrong in cherishing the spirit of hatred, and his wife is quick to teach him the lesson of forgiveness.   She tells him now of the sudden

chasm where the sea dashes into foam, leaving behind the yellow gleaming sand.

Beyond there is a wharf about which cluster the red roofs of the fishermen, and yonder a mouldering church speaks of ancient days. We see the long street leading up to a tall-towered mill, and behind it and higher a grey down, where a hollow holds a hazelwood. In this sequestered village lived, a hundred years ago, three families whose children play upon the beach. There is pretty Annie Lea and Philip Ray, the miller's son, and Enoch Arden, whose father lost his life in a winter's shipwreck.

These three, like sunbeams alternating with shadows, spend their childhood in mimic games upon the beach or in a narrow cave within the cliff. They play in childish glee at keeping house, and when the boys quarrel, Annie settles the dispute by saying "she will be little wife to both ! " Thus in sweet innocence the rosy dawn of childhood glides into the growing day of manhood, when the hearts of the two men focus their love on Annie. Enoch, of stronger, rougher nature, tells his love. Philip, gentle and reserved, nurses his love in silence. Annie loves Enoch, but she is kind to Philip.

Enoch, resolute and resistless, with his heart all aflame sets himself to realise a noble purpose ; he will hoard all his savings, and buy a boat and

build a home for Annie. He prospers, and wins
a name for bravery and caution. One year he
served on a merchantman and in the rush of the
seas thrice rescued some drowning life. At the
age of twenty-one he had saved enough to purchase
the boat and make a little home for Annie. The
time had come to claim her. It was a golden
autumn evening when the village youth went
nutting to the hollow in the down, and self-denying
Philip, who had remained behind to tend his ailing
father, climbs the hill and witnesses a lover's scene.
Close by, hand-in-hand, Enoch and Annie are
whispering, and we read the deep passion of Enoch
in the vivid lines—

> "His large grey eyes, and weather-beaten face
> All-kindled by a still and sacred fire,
> That burn'd as on an altar. . . ."

Poor Philip, seeing in all the vision of his doom,
broken and bleeding,

> ". . . Like a wounded life
> Crept down into the hollows of the wood,"

there to pass through his Gethsemane and carry
ever after a hunger in his heart.

On a day we hear in the old church the ringing
of the bells and Enoch and Annie are wed.

Seven years pass of happiness and prosperity,
and little children make merry laughter in their
peaceful home, when a shadow falls! Enoch meets

with an accident, a broken limb, and loses his
trade. He is tormented by doubt as to what may
befall Annie and the children when his old master
offers him the place of boatswain in a vessel bound
for China. Before leaving he will make provision
for his family ; he will sell the boat to stock a
store with all that fisher-folk require. He will then
trade in the far-off land and voyage to and fro
and grow rich and buy a bigger craft and educate
his children and live in peace among them. It
is the loving dream of a noble spirit. Annie, with
her sickly babe, greets him, and on the morrow
he makes known his plan when she, with womanly
instinct foreboding ill, pleads with tears and caresses
that he may remain. The scene is one of rich and
tender feeling. All the deepest things surge out
of the heart of the woman and flow like subduing
waves across the spirit of the man, only to leave
him firm as a rock, not because of the proverbial
obstinacy of his sex, but for the sake of Annie and
the children. The pain of Enoch is no less keen
than hers. He could endure because he loved.

> " He not for his own self caring but her,
> Her and her children, let her plead in vain ;
> So grieving held his will, and bore it thro'."

Then the boat is sold and the goods are pur-
chased and he fits the little sitting-room as a store
while in the clang of the hammer Annie seems
to hear the sound of her own death-knell. The

last morning dawns, and with it farewell, and, though he cannot share in Annie's fears,

> "Yet Enoch as a brave God-fearing man
> Bow'd himself down, and in that mystery
> Where God-in-man is one with man-in-God,
> Pray'd for a blessing on his wife and babes
> Whatever came to him. . . ."

He rocks the cradle of the sickly child, as he talks in sailor fashion of providence and trust, but Annie declares

> ". . . Well know I
> That I shall look upon your face no more."

He laughs at her fears, tells her to get a seaman's glass and spy him out as the vessel passes ; he bids her cast her care on God, he puts his strong arms round her, and kisses the wondering children and the now sleeping babe.

> "But Annie from her baby's forehead clipt
> A tiny curl, and gave it; this he kept
> Thro' all his future. . . ."

Then Enoch sails away, and Annie bravely strives, but thrives not in her trade, and the sickly child fades and goes to seek its health in heaven.

Now Philip comes upon the scene.

He has a true, great heart, and, seeing that Annie weeps over the root of her faded flower, thinks he ought to be a friend in need. The motive is good, but the situation is perilous, He

goes to the lonely woman who is nursing her grief,
not caring to look on any human face, but thinking
only of the angel child. With fine delicacy he
intrudes himself within the sanctuary of sorrow and
speaks of what Enoch would have most desired, the
education of his children.

> " ' Now let me put the boy and girl to school :
> This is the favour that I came to ask.' "

Annie, having no doubt that her husband lives
and will refund the money, with swimming eyes
of gratitude fixed on his kindly face, accepts his
pure and generous offer. Philip sends the boy and
girl to school, though he seldom passes her threshold
for fear of gossip ; but he does not fail to forward
kindly gifts by the children. They are deeply
attached to him, and call him " father Philip," for
he is real, but Enoch seems a dream.

Ten years pass without tidings of the long-lost
man, when one evening Annie's children, bent
on nutting with her, hasten to the mill for Philip,
who consents to join them. She, weary of climbing
the hill, needs must rest as the children scamper
to the hazelwood. Philip remains with her, recalling
the scene of years ago and how like a stricken
deer he had crept into the hollows. Then he
speaks, " Tired, Annie ? " but her face is buried
in her hands.

> "At which, as with a kind of anger in him,
> ' The ship was lost,' he said, ' the ship was lost !

> No more of that! why should you kill yourself
> And make them orphans quite?' And Annie said
> 'I thought not of it: but—I know not why—
> Their voices make me feel so solitary.'"

So solitary! They are words of hope for Philip, and the sequel shows they are the sigh of a soul weary of its loneliness. The heart of Philip reads the meaning of the sigh and speaks its hidden thought—Enoch could not be living, she was poor, and he would prove a father to her children ;

> "'And we have known each other all our lives,
> And I have loved you longer than you know.'"

In that last line is condensed the pathos of his life. Annie asks if one loves twice? Philip is willing to be loved a little after Enoch. She pleads a year's delay, to which he consents, but she must feel that she is free. The year passes and he comes to claim her promise, but she puts him off a month and then six months. The neighbours gossip: Philip is trifling and Annie is coquetting; they know not their own minds! Her son and daughter press the marriage.

One night Annie is distracted and cannot sleep, and prays for a sign—"My Enoch, is he gone?" Then, with the usage of the Puritans, she seizes a Bible and, throwing it open, reads, "Under the palm tree," and, closing the book, she falls asleep—

> "When lo! her Enoch sitting on a height,
> Under a palm-tree, over him the Sun;

'He is gone,' she thought, 'he is happy, he is singing
Hosanna in the highest . . . .' "

She is convinced that Enoch is dead, and sends
for Philip.

" So these were wed and merrily rang the bells."

But she is haunted with fears until the new
child comes, when Philip takes the place of Enoch.

Again the scene changes, and we trace the
pathetic story of the long-lost Enoch.

His ship *Good Fortune* after fair and foul at
last drops anchor in an oriental haven. On her
return voyage she is driven by storms and wrecked
upon the breakers. Enoch and two comrades
are saved upon a raft,

". . . Stranding on an isle at morn
Rich but the loneliest in a lonely sea."

Nature had made every provision for the wrecked
mariners, and they built a hut " in a seaward-gazing
mountain gorge " and dwell in eternal summer. The
comrades die, and Enoch is left alone in that seagirt
isle of tropic splendour. The genius of the poet
revels here in descriptive imagination, and the
lonely isle is made to live before us with its glow
of colour in the magnificent lines—

" The mountain wooded to the peak . . .
.   .   .   .   .   .
The scarlet shafts of sunrise—but no sail."

The very profusion of the life of nature intensifies

the terrible loneliness. Enoch hears the many voices, the shriek of the ocean fowl, the thunder of the sea and the whisper of trees ; he sees the flash of insect and of bird, the beauty of flowers that " coil around the stately stem " ; he watches the shafts of sunrise as they pierce the precipices and the golden day shimmer over the water ; but he never sees a human face, and among all the voices he never hears one kindly voice. What a picture of loneliness is framed in the two lines—

> " Sat often in the seaward, gazing gorge,
> A shipwreck'd sailor, waiting for a sail " !

They suggest a finished copy of the Homeric original.

> "He sat weeping sore
> Hard by the breakings of the barren wave,
> Where he did oft afflict his soul before,
> And through the floods unfruitful evermore
> Yearned a set gaze with many a tear and groan,
> Heart-broken captive on a hated shore."

Imagination is active and peoples the hut of Enoch with the phantoms of those whom he loved ; he lives in the past and hangs pictures in the chamber of memory, of Annie and the babes and the old love scenes.

> " Once likewise, in the ringing of his ears,
> Tho' faintly, merrily—far and far away—
> He heard the pealing of his parish bells,"

and shudders !

> ". . . Had not his poor heart
> Spoken with That, which being everywhere
> Lets none, who speak with Him, seem all alone,
> Surely the man had died ot solitude."

The danger is more philosophically but less poetically expressed by Wordsworth.

> "The innocent sufterer often sees
> Too clearly, feels too vividly, and longs
> To realise the vision with intense
> And ever-constant yearning—there—there lies
> The excess by which the balance is destroyed."

At last release comes for Enoch from his beautiful but hateful prison. Another vessel hove in sight, and Enoch suddenly emerges from his mountain-gorge, wild and muttering, signing to the crew in search of water. He is taken aboard, where he finds speech again and tender human kindness, and in time they land him in the harbour whence he sailed.

Then Enoch makes his way to his old home where Annie once lived, only to find a bill of sale! His heart sinks, and he goes down to the wharf and seeks the tavern, now kept by Miriam Lane, and here for many days he rests. Garrulous Miriam, all unknowing, tells him the story of his house, and the grey head drops and the lips mutter, " Cast away and lost ! "

Now comes the yearning to see his Annie again, and know whether she is happy. In the dull November evening he climbs the hill, with its girdle

16

of sacred memories, and is allured by the light of Philip's house,

> ". . . As the beacon-blaze allures
> The bird of passage, till he madly strikes
> Against it, and beats out his weary life."

Only the bird has this advantage that while it is one of a flock Enoch is solitary. He passes through the gate into the little garden and there under a yew-tree near the window looks upon a scene of domestic peace; he sees Philip stout and rosy and his *own* daughter, fair-haired and tall, playing with a babe, and in the midst the face of Annie, smiling. What a passion of feeling rose and swept and wailed through the breast of Enoch! We feel the shock and hear the fatal rush of it in the tragic lines which describe how he

> "Stagger'd and shook, holding the branch, and fear'd
> To send abroad a shrill and terrible cry,
> Which in one moment, like the blast of doom,
> Would shatter all the happiness of the hearth."

He creeps from under the yew-tree out upon the waste, and, falling, digs his fingers into the wet earth and prays that he may not break in upon her peace. Then he comes back to the tavern, repeating the words, lest memory fail him, "Not to tell her, never to let her know."

He knew from Miriam that Annie lived in dread of his return.

> " . . . And he thought
> 'After the Lord has call'd me, she shall know.'"

Bravely he works for a living, and bears his secret sorrow until he sickens and sees the coming of death. He calls for Miriam, and makes her take an oath not to reveal his secret until he is dead. Then comes the whole sad story of the noble man, and the secret messages to Annie and the boy and girl, with blessing upon Philip ; and his children may come and see him when he is dead.

> " ' . . . But she must not come,
> For my dead face would vex her after-life."

The curl of his babe, which Annie had given him the day of their parting, he hands to Miriam for the mother. On the third night he dies—

> " Crying with a loud voice 'A sail! a sail!
> I am saved ;' and so fell back and spoke no more."

Such the pathetic story told by the poet who is master of the subtle chords of human feeling, and can at will sweep his hand across the chords. But the story, though simple, gives rise to many questions and creates various impressions. The interest circles round the character and conduct of Enoch.

Are we to take him as the type of actual character or is he ideal? With regard to Philip and Annie there is no difficulty. Philip is perfectly natural, a gentle, loving soul who, while he does not force himself upon the notice of Annie and is sensitive to her position, is still human enough to send her flowers and fruits and to keep himself in tender touch with the children. He is strictly honourable, but like a wise man has an eye for possibilities. Annie, also, is entirely natural, with the emotional side of her character dominating intellect and judgment, making her weak where she ought to have been strong ; she is shallow and sentimental, with a dash of Puritan superstition ; she believes in dreams and signs, and so, not having heard of her husband for ten years, she accepts another and builds a new home on the ashes of the old. Thus Philip and Annie are types of actual, ordinary character. But coming to the character and conduct of Enoch, we are at once upon a higher plane. The natural and legitimate thing for him to have done would have been to have claimed his own. So strong is the popular conviction that an illustration was afforded in the reply of one to the query, "What is your estimate of Enoch ? " His answer was more practical than poetic : "I should like to kick him ! " Upon further inquiry as to the ground of this violent attack the reply was : "Because Enoch was not natural, he did not claim and vindicate his own rights ; he ought to have made himself known to his family ! " Precisely, on the supposition that the portraiture of Enoch is actual, not ideal. But it is evident that the poet did not intend Enoch as an actual type.

Viewed as an ideal character the parts fall into
something like harmony ; conceived as natural we
have dire confusion. Supposing he had claimed
his legal and moral rights, what would have been
the result ? Why, the wrecking of the home !
Annie, with divided affection, would have been
placed in a position most appalling. The children
of Enoch must have shared in the dread calamity.
Philip's life would have been blasted as if with
lightning. All this and more would have happened
if Enoch had only been natural, and had claimed
his rights. No one could have blamed him, and
the many would have applauded him ; but rather
than wreck the peace of that domestic circle, rather
than break the happiness of Annie and blight the
life of Philip and darken the days of the children,
he sacrificed his rights and himself for the greater
good. Such a character is clearly ideal, though
the ideal may be defective in its portraiture. What
then is the ethical value of the poem ? Surely, that
the best and highest life is only attained by self-
renunciation. It has been well said, If one were
always claiming one's rights the world would be
a hell. Yes, we are not here for self-conservation
and the demand of all our privileges. We belong
to the social order, and if claiming our rights means
for others pain and loss, we are to surrender them
in obedience to that higher law of love, which goes
beyond justice, seeking the larger good. We may

demand them if we choose, and the world-voices will cry, You are right and none can blame you; and yet we shall have missed the highest, that law of the life of God, " It is more blessed to give than to receive." Better to sacrifice our rights and ourselves in blessing men, than to hold our life and claim our rights in self-conservation. But will not the surrender kill the joy of life? No, it will deepen and cleanse our joy. In voluntary acceptance of the cross of duty that looms before us we shall find the gladness of the Son of Man, who for the joy set before Him "endured the cross." In the bitterness of our sacrifice we shall find, with Enoch, the mingling of the sweet spring of an eternal joy, and know that the secret of Jesus is self-renunciation.

> "He was not all unhappy. His resolve
> Upbore him, and firm faith, and evermore
> Prayer from a living source within the will,
> And beating up thro' all the bitter world,
> Like fountains of sweet water in the sea
> Kept him a living soul. . . ."

THE DEGRADATION OF LOVE.

Aylmer's Field. Lady Clara Vere de Vere. Edwin Morris. The Northern Farmer. The Sisters. Guinevere. The Wreck. Mariana. Mariana in the South. Oriana. Edward Gray.

THE purity that gleams like snow through the group of poems on the sanctity of love, prepares us for the moral indignation that flashes like a sword through the poems on the degradation of love. The purer a poet the more sensitive he will be to impurity, and the higher his ideal of the sacredness of love the fiercer will be his wrath when the ideal is desecrated. We shall now find that when the shrine of love is violated Tennyson is the avenging angel with drawn sword. "Aylmer's Field" and "Lady Clara" voice the protest against pride of birth, "Edwin Morris" voices the protest against pride of wealth, and the "Northern Farmer" is a protest against love of property.

ər's   IN "Aylmer's Field" we are introduced to two homes. Sir Aylmer Aylmer is lord of the manor and a county magnate. His wife is a faded beauty of the baths, and a mere machine moved by his imperious will. They have one child,

Edith, who is beautiful and finely strung. Sir Aylmer loves her

> "As heiress and not heir regretfully.
> But 'he that marries her marries her name.'"

The other home is the rectory where Averill, the rector, lives, shared by Leolin his brother, a young barrister. The two homes are closely bound by many years of intimacy.

Edith and Leolin are frequently together, but the possibility of love never disturbs the conceit of Sir Aylmer. The mere suggestion that once there had been an Aylmer-Averill marriage is quickly brushed aside by the baronet. Meanwhile Edith and Leolin meet, when a passion

> "Lay hidden, as the music of the moon
> Sleeps in the plain eggs of the nightingale."

With that hidden music in their hearts, not knowing that they loved, they wander through the parks and visit the cottagers and hear a good mother whisper, " God bless 'em, marriages are made in Heaven." Then Edith awakes to the knowledge of the hidden music. An Indian kinsman comes to the hall and lavishes upon Edith his Oriental gifts ; among the gifts is a richly jewelled dagger, which Edith shows Leolin, who petulantly remarks that the dagger is not " a gracious gift to give a lady." Quick to detect the lurking jealousy and to allay it, Edith proffers him the weapon, which

now he values as her gift. Sir Aylmer passes,
hears and sees and is suspicious !

The next day a neighbour calls with neighbourly
hints of the danger of a love-match. The baronet
merely stiffens and observes, " The girl and boy,
sir, know their differences " ; but his eyes are opened
to possibilities.

The same night a scene occurs and Edith is
brought up to judgment. The thunder of her
father's rage breaks upon her and she bends before
the rushing storm. Leolin enters by a counter
door, and, as she passes out, he is caught in the
hurricane. Sir Aylmer glares at him, panting for
breath, ejaculating envenomed adjectives ; he charges
Leolin with playing on Edith's feelings, and
demands of him a letter denying any serious
purpose. Leolin replies :

> " ' . . . I
> So foul a traitor to myself and her,
> Never oh never.' "

Then the storm bursts. Sir Aylmer, red with
fiery passion, forbids Leolin the house under threat
of being lashed like a dog ; he swears and kicks
the footstool, stammering out " Scoundrel ! " between
gleaming teeth. He follows the retreating culprit
to the door, and, standing there in the light of
a pale moon, he storms out his rage, with uplifted
hands and a face twisted by the madness of his
passion !

Leolin dashes on to the rectory and " foams away his heart at Averill's ear," vents his indignation on " this filthy marriage-hindering mammon," and is cynical at the conceit that rests on an ancient name.

> " Fall back upon a name! rest, rot in that!
> Not *keep* it noble, make it nobler? fools,
> With such a vantage-ground for nobleness."

He, Leolin, will go and win a noble name and fortune, and shame those " mouldy Aylmers in their graves."

The scene is changed.

Yonder, under the familiar pines, with the winds sighing and the rain falling, the lovers meet and pledge eternal fidelity. In tender sympathy with their passion the dirge of nature mingles

> "As they kiss'd each other
> "In darkness, and above them roar'd the pine."

Leolin goes to his chambers and reads hard, and the benchers talk of him as the coming man. In the hall of Sir Aylmer there are banquets and balls, with the eldest-born of wealth and rank drawn to the feet of Edith ; but she rejects them all. Her foiled parents limit her freedom at last " to her own home-circle of the poor " ; and yet colour is in her cheek and light within her eyes !

There is an old oak broken to the base and crumbling into decay. It has a charm for Edith.

Watching eyes see her flit between the hall and
the oak. So the baronet will go and rake the
touch-wood dust—when he finds a sealed packet,
breaks it, and reads with writhing a letter from
Edith to Leolin. As he reads a crippled lad
appears, bearing a letter from Leolin to Edith which
the baronet demands. He enters into collusion
with the lad, and all the letters pass into his hands.
He reads the letters, only to rage and rend and
burn them. Leolin, receiving no reply, comes down
to the hall to watch, but Edith is closely guarded.
Once only the savage mood of Sir Aylmer softens,
and he kisses her ; but as quickly the mood changes,
and she is greeted with cold sneers, so that she

> "With twenty months of silence, slowly lost
> Nor greatly cared to lose, her hold on life."

The result being that fever seizes upon her
weakened frame,

> "And flung her down upon a couch of fire,
> Where careless of the household faces near,
> And crying upon the name of Leolin,
> She, and with her the race of Aylmer, past."

That night, and at that moment, a startling scene
occurs in the room of Leolin. A shriek, " Yes, love,
yes, Edith, yes," and there is Leolin, with a weird
look, palpitating with emotion, his body flung
forward, arms outstretched, not knowing why he
cried. The next day, the Indian kinsman rushes
into the room, only to find a dead man and a red

dagger and a black-bordered letter! The rector comes to look upon the face of his brother and grows old in looking. Lady Aylmer would have the rector speak of Edith to the people. Then follows the scene in the church. The text is, "Behold your house is left unto you desolate." The sermon is terrible; the thunders of retribution roll, and the lightnings flash. Some weep, others frown, but Sir Aylmer sits "anger-charmed from sorrow, soldier-like." The voice of the preacher changes, the storm dies away, as if into sweet music, as he speaks of the gentle Edith, and the iron mouth of the baronet twitches. Then the tones swell again into anger at the ancestral pride that wrought the death of two pure lives pledged to noble love and, like "a rushing tempest of the wrath of God," the preacher sweeps down upon the guilty parents, shaking their life to its very root. The stricken lady creeps towards her husband as if for shelter, shrieks and swoons, and is carried out. Sir Aylmer follows; his courage forsakes him in the aisle; he reels and grasps the pew, but with final effort he gains his carriage.

In a month the lady dies, and Sir Aylmer, with the word "desolate" burned into his brain and ever trembling on his lips, dies an imbecile!

"Then the great Hall was wholly broken down."

The poem is a powerful delineation of the judgment that falls on the shameless desecration of love. The situations are daring and dramatic, and the characters clearly cut. Sir Aylmer is a type of the ignoble aristocracy that roots itself, not in its own honour, but in its ancient name. He is cold and cynical and cruel, a self-centred county god, whose egoism is magnificent, whose pride of birth deadens sensibility to love, and whose self-esteem transforms him into a tyrant. Lady Aylmer is the sickly shadow of her husband's sun.

The two, unconsciously, compass the death of the sweetest of maidens and the noblest of youths, and simply through pride! There is naught against the character of Leolin, but in the opinion of the baronet character, without birth, is of little worth. Because Edith is loyal to her lover she is done to death and he is driven to suicide; but judgment is exacted. Imagine the situation! In the pew are the parents of the dead girl, and in the pulpit is the brother of the suicide, letting loose that tempest of moral wrath upon the parents whose false pride is responsible for a dual tragedy. The retribution that follows is the poet's protest against the folly that enthrones birth and wealth above love and worth.

The character of Sir Aylmer, when contrasted with that of Sir Ronald or Lord Burleigh, is repulsive, and " Ichabod " is written in flame over the selfish and proud life that would sacrifice pure divinity of love for ignoble pride of ancestry.

Lady Clara Vere de Vere. LADY CLARA is as heartless as Sir Aylmer, but with more refined cruelty in her method. A country youth voices the protest against her cynical flirtations. She had practised her alluring arts upon him and he had discovered the base motive that would make him the toy of her weary hours. Aware of her ignoble pride of ancestry, masked by her winsome smile, he replies:

> "'At me you smiled, but unbeguiled
> I saw the snare, and I retired.'"

He knows the worth of a pure and simple love far above name and wealth and coats-of-arms. But his protest becomes serious when he charges the Lady Clara with moral murder. She had wrought her spell upon young Lawrence, first coquetting with him and then scorning him, with the result that he was found dead!

> "But there was that across his throat
> Which you had hardly cared to see."

In law the lady would be innocent, and the verdict "temporary insanity," but in morals she is a murderess, and the protest is just.

> "The guilt of blood is at your door:
> You changed a wholesome heart to gall."

The young country moralist, with a satire upon the claims of ancestry, not rooted in nobility of goodness, utters the pure sentiment that—

> "Kind hearts are more than coronets,
> And simple faith than Norman blood."

He concludes by urging the Lady Clara to use her time and wealth in the relief of suffering, and to redeem her life by service.

In all this the poet draws a painful picture of one feature of our social life. He utters a passionate protest against the degradation of love and the refined selfishness and sensuous luxury of those who have no pity for the lives wrecked by sin and suffering. It is the voice of a seer who sees that the West End must find a way into the East, not with patronising doles, but with the pity of the Christ.

dwin
[orris.   THE failure to recognise the sanctity of love, whether in the heart of a country yeoman or village maiden, is not confined to the aristocracy, but is shared, apparently, by the middle class, with its commercial spirit. Purse is too often flaunted in the face of purity. Wealth sits upon his throne and makes love his footstool. Goodness and culture come in the garb of poverty with their offering of love, only to be swept away by the ruthless hand of a wealthy cotton spinner. This protest against pride of wealth is voiced in " Edwin Morris."

Three friends, Edwin Morris, poet, Edward Bell, curate, and an artist, relate their love experiences. The young artist had suffered cruelly in his devotion to Letty Hill, who lived by the lake. They met only once, and that by stealth, when in the early morn he rowed across the lake and crept up into the garden where she was gathering flowers. When least desired a relative appeared and vanished, and when the lovers were in fond embrace, a score of pugs and poodles yelled their protest, in which trustees and aunts and uncles joined,

> "'What, with him!
> Go' (shrill'd the cotton-spinning chorus); 'him!'
> I choked. Again they shriek'd the burthen—'Him!'
> Again with hands of wild rejection 'Go!—
> Girl, get you in!' She went—and in one month
> They wedded her to sixty thousand pounds."

The character of the artist was not questioned by the merchant, nor did he take exception to his profession; he may have been good and clever, but he was poor, and that fact alone justified his being set upon by yelping poodles and vulgar snobbery. Nor did the purse-proud man consider the natural feelings of Letty, nor the wounded life of the artist. With him love and peace and art compared with wealth were mere dross.

The story has its comic side, but is none the less serious as a protest against pride of wealth.

The Northern Farmer (New Style). BUT the poet, not content with these examples of the degradation of love in the higher strata of society, traces it to the lower in the "Northern Farmer" (New Style). Here we have a humorous illustration of the value of emotion compared with property. The farmer's son is in love with a poor curate's daughter whom he would marry, but his parents are of opinion that he is an ass.

"Luvv? what's luvv?. thou can luvv thy lass an' 'er munny too,
    Maakin' 'em goä togither as they've good right to do.
    Could'n I luvv thy muther by cause o' 'er munny laaïd by?
    Naäy—fur I luvv'd 'er a vast sight moor fur it: reäson why."

It is clear from the repeated application of the classic word ass to his son that, while he regards love as a pleasing sentiment, he reverences "pro-putty" as a permanent substance

Thus, veiled by humour, we have the story of a sordid soul crushing out the tenderest flower of the human heart.

"The Sisters," "Guinevere," and "The Wreck" form another trio showing the poet's passion when dealing with fleshly loves; his moral indignation is here a furnace at white heat, whose flames leap upon the betrayer. Tennyson is always in a rage when writing of the degradation of love; he sees clearly that pure love is the inspiration of noble deeds, but when weakened by ignoble passion its strength is gone. Love must be kept spiritual if life is to be kept noble; when love is carnalised, life is debased.

The Sisters. IN "The Sisters" the nemesis is terrible. The sinning sister goes to meet her doom in "burning flame," and the living one becomes an avenging angel. She conceives a plot in which feelings of fiendish hate and loving admiration mingle, giving pathos to the tragedy.

> "I hated him with the hate of hell,
> But I loved his beauty passing well.
> O the Earl was fair to see!"

She wins his love to slake her vengeance. Unconscious of the tragic fate hovering over him, the earl sleeps. She sharpens the dagger and the winds rage. The deed is done! The despoiler of love pays his penalty. How careful she is of the murdered body! Was not there a touch of irony in the combing of his comely head? Was not it his beauty that had charmed her sister to her shame? Yes, and so shall he be carried and laid at his mother's feet, that she may look upon the lovely face that killed another. The vengeance is exquisitely refined!

How sympathetically, too, nature is made to express the mood of the avenger! When the gleaming dagger is in her hand, the wind is "raving," but when the tragedy is over the wind falls with her falling passion.

> "The wind is blowing in turret and tree."

əvere. WE saw how Guinevere was responsible for the degradation of love and the resulting evils. In dealing with fleshly loves the poet points out not so much the cause as the effect. The cause is lightly touched, but the effect is vividly coloured. Through carnal loves he makes us see the spiritual evils. When the Queen lay prostrate at the feet of the King and he, more like a god, stood passing judgment on the sin he dare not justify, it was with the spiritual results rather than with the sensual sin that he dealt.

> "The children born of thee are sword and fire,
> Red ruin and the breaking up of laws."

Again, when later he spoke of the high aims of the fair order he had established, it was only to give force to the terrible charge that her sin had wrecked the goodly realm.

> "'Then came thy shameful sin with Lancelot;
> Then came the sin of Tristram and Isolt;
> Then others . . .
>
> .   .   .   .   .   .
> And all thro' thee. . . .'"

That stream of impurity issuing from the highest source in the court of the Queen crept on and grew until it became a torrent sweeping away the realm of chivalry and purity. Thus the results of degraded love are vividly portrayed in the wreckage of spiritual character and sublime ideals.

The   " THE Wreck " is powerfully dramatic.   It
Wreck.*   is a story of seduction with the inevitable
result of retribution.   In the wailing of the woman
at the convent gate we hear the cry of an outraged
conscience.   While her position creates pity, her
conduct calls for blame.   She is a woman of fine
poetic feeling, who reads Shelley and loves art, but
she is bound to a husband who is sordid, without
culture and tenderness.   She is met with a kiss
chill as a snowflake, and their only child is scorned
for being a girl.   The mother's heart dies, and she
flings herself on the stage and into the dance.   She
meets a man of wealth, almost a dwarf and de-
formed, but he is highly cultured and can talk
wisely, with face all aglow.   She has found her
affinity and, kissing her babe, they sail together
for the Orient in calm and summer and sin.

But the calm is broken, the storm broods o'er the
deep, and we have another illustration of the poet's
use of nature in delineating emotion.   In the shriek
of the growing wind the fugitive mother hears the
cry of her absent child, and in the crash of the
thunder she hears the judgment of Heaven.   In
the cataract of water flung from the deck and in
the roar of the storm she hears only voices of doom.

" In the rigging, voices of hell—then came the crash
of the mast.
'The wages of sin is death.' . . ."

* For the origin of " The Wreck " vide *A Memoir* ii., p. 319.

The guilty lovers are now in the torments of an avenging conscience ; the woman is consumed with grief at the thought of her sickly, forsaken child, and, as the man strives to comfort her with false platitudes, the storm without voices itself in the terror within. They are reconciled at the moment when the ship shivers beneath an avalanche of water, and all, except the woman and a man lashed to the helm, are swept into the deep. She is rescued by the boat of a passing vessel, but her grief is great, and takes the mood of the storm.

When the wind-swept sea rises again in fury, her thoughts are with the drowned man ; but when the sea falls into the peace of a sleeping child, her mood changes and her heart cries :

". . . 'O child, I am coming to thee."

On landing she writes to the nurse, and a reply comes from her husband enclosing a notice of the child's death.

"And gone—that day of the storm—O Mother, she came to me there."

The poem is a protest against the moral laxity that would break the marriage bond on the ground of non-affinity. The free-thinker urges that persons, legally united, are justified in separating and forming a new alliance when affinities are lacking. Such is the situation in the poem. Husband and wife lack mutual sympathy. He is coarse and

sordid, she is sensitive and cultured, with the result
that he kills her love. The question arises, Was
she justified in leaving her husband and child and
eloping with Stephen whom she loved and who
was her intellectual affinity ? In other words: Is
a legal marriage morally binding ? Tennyson gives
his answer in the storm which sweeps upon the
fugitives, tears them asunder, and leaves her in
lonely exile tormented by the thought that her sin
had drowned the man and killed the child. The
marriage bond is inviolable, though no love may
exist. If the bond could be broken on the plea
of no affinity, the fabric of society would fall.
Marriages ought to be the result of affinities ; when
these are lacking the contracting parties have only
themselves to thank, and must suffer patiently the
penalty of marrying in haste.

In " Mariana," " Mariana in the South," " The
Ballad of Oriana " and " Edward Gray," we have
illustrations of the degradation of love under a
special aspect. They are all true to life, but
to a side of life that needs correcting. In each
case love is disappointed, and in each case love
is degraded into passionate regret that wastes in
wailing the noblest energy.

Mariana.   THIS is a picture of utter desolation and
    unredeemed sorrow. The passion of grief never

changes except when the wish for death becomes a
prayer. The dirge sobs through day and night.

> "She only said, 'My life is dreary,
>   He cometh not,' she said.
> She said, 'I am aweary, aweary,
>   I would that I were dead!'"

The power of the poem lies in the skill with
which familiar objects are laid under contribution.
They are all stricken with the wailing of Mariana,
and wear the same funereal look. The whole poem
is pre-Raphaelite in the finish of its detail, and
affords one of the earliest examples of the poet's
use of nature as a magic mirror reflecting the moods
of the soul. In the first lines the flower-pots and
the rusted nails and the broken sheds are all apparently in sympathy with her grief, and look as if
they were suffering from unrequited affection. The
following is a realistic picture of death and desolation in nature, expressing the waste and loneliness
of the grief-stricken soul—

> "About a stone-cast from the wall
>   A sluice with blacken'd waters slept,
> And o'er it many, round and small,
>   The cluster'd marish-mosses crept.
> Hard by a poplar shook alway,
>   All silver-green with gnarled bark:
>   For leagues no other tree did mark
> The level waste, the rounding gray."

Blackened waters, a dreary waste, one poplar
casting its shadow, when the moon was low, upon
her bed. What a picture of desolation!

Mariana in the South. HERE we have a portrait of an Italian woman disappointed in love. The difference in the two Marianas is apparent. Mariana of the Moated Grange lacks the sensuousness of the Italian. The Italian is more self-conscious; she is fond of looking at "her melancholy eyes divine" in the mirror. She pities her own sense of loneliness, and prays to the Virgin out of passion rather than piety.

It is impossible to feel that her love is anything like so deep and genuine as the love of the other Mariana, and yet she is saved from the hopeless despair of the other by her pure, sensuous feeling. She is sensitive to the sights and sounds of nature. The deep peace of the Italian night and the sweet music of the sea save her.

> "There all in spaces rosy-bright
> Large Hesper glitter'd on her tears,
> And deepening thro' the silent spheres
> Heaven over Heaven rose the night.
> And weeping then she made her moan,
> 'The night comes on that knows not morn,
> When I shall cease to be all alone,
> To live forgotten, and to love forlorn.'"

The Ballad of Oriana. GRIEF, as in the two Marianas, saps "the wine of life" in the ballad of Oriana. It is full of tender, passionate feeling, and yet it is a tragedy of pathos, for no pure flame of noble deed leaps out of the ashes of vain regret to illumine and cheer the darkened life.

We hear the man plight his troth. We see him ride boldly from the castle into the fight. We see Oriana standing on the wall, her lovely face all aglow, as she watches her lover. At that moment a foeman intervenes, when her lover draws his bow, and the winged arrow, missing its mark, quivers in the heart of Oriana.

The battle rages as if in sympathy with the passion of his grief, and he falls upon his face and cries for death.

> "They should have stabb'd me where I lay,
>   Oriana!"

His life is spared ; but what is life without her ! Ever a pulsing pain with dreams of her pale face, and, deepest pain of all, heaven is eclipsed. The darkness of love's remorse blots out the stars of God.

> "Thou comest a-tween me and the skies."

He cannot forgive himself, and sinks into a ceaseless moan, as of a wild, ever-restless sea, sobbing through all his wasted life.

> "Thou liest beneath the greenwood tree,
> I dare not die and come to thee,
>   Oriana.
> I hear the roaring of the sea,
>   Oriana.

In all three poems the passion of grief disappointed in love is natural but fatal to the best and noblest uses of life.   When grief, through love, paralyses action, love is degraded and life is broken.

Edward Gray.   " EDWARD GRAY " affords another illustration of the waste of life through hopeless love. He is engaged to Ellen Adair, contrary to the wish of her parents, but fails to understand the silent deep of her nature.

> " 'Shy she was, and I thought her cold ;
>   Thought her proud, and fled over the sea ;
>   Fill'd I was with folly and spite,
>   When Ellen Adair was dying for me.' "

On his return home he finds that death has taken her, and now only a grave on a lonely hill and a memory in a lonely heart remain.

He was the victim of his vanity ; he had cherished the poison of suspicion until it killed the flowers of his life ; and though, at last, by the side of her grave, he bitterly repents, still—the flowers are dead.

> " ' "There lies the body of Ellen Adair
>   And there the heart of Edward Gray ! "
>   .   .   .   .   .   .
>   But I will love no more, no more,
>   Till Ellen Adair come back to me.' "

Thus far he feels the sanctity of love, but degrades it in the lack of sensibility to the redeeming power of a great sorrow.   It does not inspire

him to build over the ashes of ruined hopes a
character of chastened beauty and enduring strength.
Grief has frozen him into passivity when it ought
to have quickened the energy of noble action. Life
is redeemed, not by wailing for the dead, but by
working for the living.

THE RELIGIOUS POEMS

GOD: HIS DIVINE IMMANENCE.

The Higher Pantheism. Flower in the Crannied Wall.
The Human Cry. De Profundis. God and the Universe.

TENNYSON is much more than an artist. Art that contains no moral value is defective. A poet may have a perfect instrument of expression but if the moral idea be lacking the instrument must suffer. The attempt to divorce the ethical from the artistic must result in the decadence of art. Its standard is of necessity determined by its moral idea. " It is easy enough to babble of the beauty of things considered apart from their meaning, it is easy enough to dilate on the satisfaction of art in itself, but all these phrases are merely collocations of terms, empty and meaningless. A thing can only be artistic by virtue of the idea it suggests to us ; when the idea is coarse, ungainly, unspeakable, the object that suggests it is coarse, ungainly, unspeakable ; art and ethics must always be allied in that the merit of the art is dependent on the merit of the idea it prompts." *

And, supposing the art form to be infused with

* " Reticence in Literature."—ARTHUR WAUGH.

the moral idea, must not the form itself, as the instrument of expression, be enriched ? The relation of ethics to art is not unlike the relation of soul to body. The body as a mere form may be faultless, but does it not gain or lose according to the soul it holds ? If tenanted by the pure soul, the soul will flash its own peculiar beauty through the veil of flesh, but if tenanted by the impure soul the body, even as a form, must suffer. Without an ethical soul it becomes carnal, and so art divorced from the moral idea is apt to be " fleshly."

Tennyson gives us the body of beauty, and rarely omits the tenant of the moral idea. While therefore he is such an artist he is also a teacher. But it must be remembered that no great artist sits down with the avowed object to teach. Being what he is, he unconsciously expresses *himself*, his deepest feeling and highest thought, in his work.

As a teacher we shall find him impatient of the rigid forms of faith.

> "And what are forms ?
> Fair garments, plain or rich, and fitting close
> Or flying looselier, warm'd but by the heart
> Within them, moved but by the living limb,
> And cast aside, when old, for newer,—form"
>
> (" Akbar's Dream").

Faith is the soul and forms are but the dress. The soul of faith is ever growing and the dress must be changed to fit the growth.

Truth, the object of faith, is infinite. Why

strangle the infinite in the dress of the finite ? The danger lies in fixity of form, and so the poet seldom clothes his teaching with doctrinal dress. The result is that, while much is gained, something is lost. A swifter movement of spirit and a wider sweep of vision are won, but clearness is lost. He draws great outlines and leaves us to fill them in, or he gives us a mystic flash and tells us to follow the gleam, or he sings some broken chord and sends us in search of the rhythmic whole.

Further, the poet is an idealist in philosophy, and a realist in art. His philosophy is the philosophy of Kant and Hegel and Coleridge and Wordsworth ; he is the last of the Lake School in his sympathy with and interpretation of nature. Nature to him is the visible garment of God through which the divine glory gleams. Behind the veil of the world there is the Making Soul. He is not a scientific agnostic nor a poetical pantheist, but he is a Christian theist, accentuating the truth of the divine immanence. He does not identify nature with God, but he sees so clearly in nature the working of the mystic life that he is convinced, were the physical veil withdrawn, the spiritual Power would be revealed.

The Higher Pantheism. "THE HIGHER PANTHEISM" gives clear expression to this truth and affords an illustration of pure idealism. God is in nature and in man. The living power which cannot be seen evolves the things that are seen, and so, through the finite many, we may draw near to the infinite One.

> "The sun, the moon, the stars, the seas, the hills, and the plains—
> Are not these, O Soul, the Vision of Him who reigns?
>
> Is not the Vision He? tho' He be not that which He seems?
> Dreams are true while they last, and do we not live in dreams?"

And should the world be dark to us and the vision veiled it is because God in nature is not realised as God in consciousness. To have the divine within is to find divinity without, but to be destitute of the feeling of God is to be blind to the vision of God.

> "Glory about thee, without thee; and thou fulfillest thy doom
> Making Him broken gleams, and a stifled splendour and gloom."

To the spiritual man nature is the shrine of deity, and all phenomena are symbols of His presence and working, and the pure heart will find Him. God, the ever-present Spirit, answers the cry of the spirit of man.

> "Speak to Him, thou, for He hears, nd Spirit with Spirit can meet,
> Closer is He than breathing, and nearer than hands and feet."

The physical is the barrier between God and the soul, but if the barrier were removed the soul would see God.

"And the ear of man cannot hear, and the eye of man
cannot see ;
But if we could see and hear, this Vision,—were it not
He?"

Flower in the Crannied Wall. AND so with the "Flower in the Crannied Wall." If man could see into the meaning of the glory that lies on land and sea, flashing from the wing of the meanest insect and flushing the leaf of the lowliest flower, he would see the divine reality. To know all that makes the flower is to know God.

"Little flower—but *if* I could understand
What you are, root and all, and all in all,
I should know what God and man is."

The same truth finds expression in "De Profundis," with its welcome to the little child that came

" From that true world within the world we see,
Whereof our world is but the bounding shore,
Out of the deep Spirit, out of the deep."

The child-spirit is an emanation of God, of that real world in relation to which what we see is but the " bounding shore."

The Human Cry. MORE clearly is the truth of the divine immanence voiced in "The Human Cry." Man is imperfect, but he is folded in God until the fulness of God flows around him   Now

he feels that he is nothing and that God is everything ; now he is something, for God is moving in
him, but God is the something and not the man.

> "We know we are nothing, but Thou wilt help us to be.
> Hallowed be Thy name, Hallelujah ! "

In the same poem man's highest thinking is
powerfully condensed in three lines. In the relation
of the human soul to God this sublime trinity of
thought emerges,

> " Infinite Ideality !
> Immeasurable Reality !
> Infinite Personality ! "

It would be difficult for the constructive theologian
to match this formula expressive of what God is
in the concept of man.

God and the FURTHER in the restful poem " God and the
Universe. Universe," amid all its sublime and majestic
forces the soul is told to look upon the universe
as the "shadow " of God, and not to fear.

> "Spirit, nearing yon dark portal at the limit of thy human
>   state,
> Fear not thou the hidden purpose of that Power which alone
>   is great,
> Nor the myriad world, His shadow, nor the silent Opener of
>   the Gate."

We may thus claim the poet as teaching the
truth of the divine immanence, a truth held by the

Greek Fathers but obscured by the Latins. God is near, and the spirit of man in reverent search may find within the veil of sense "the vision of Him who reigns."

Hegel, whose disciple Tennyson was, declared that matter cannot be conceived apart from thought; that it is permeated with thought, hence, as thought presupposes mind, and mind permeates matter, God must be immanent in the universe.

Wordsworth sings the same truth:

> "I have felt
> A presence that disturbs me with the joy
> Of elevated thoughts; a sense sublime
> Of something far more deeply interfused,
> Whose dwelling is the light of setting suns,
> And the round ocean, and the living air,
> And the blue sky, and in the mind of man,
> A motion and a spirit that impels
> All thinking things, all objects of all thought,
> And rolls through all things."

Goethe also speaks of nature as the garment of God, when in "Faust" he makes the earth-spirit say :—

> "Thus at the roaring loom of time I ply,
> And weave for God the garment thou seest Him by."

Carlyle again breaks into rapture as the vision of the divine immanence flashes upon him from the meanest to the sublimest object in creation. "This fair universe, even in the meanest province, is in very deed the star-domed city of God. Through every star, through every grass-blade, the glory of a present God still beams."

Thus, along with our best and greatest minds Tennyson has recovered for us the almost lost truth of the indwelling God.   Nature is not a mechanical body, but its phenomenal energy is the result of the activity of the immanent deity.   Its out-raying splendour is not the glory of impersonal life, but of a Great Intelligence and an Eternal Will.   The poet's faith is not pantheistic but Christian, which faith is also the highest philosophy.   His faith in the personality of God is thus expressed :

> "Eternal form shall still divide
> The Eternal soul from all beside,
> And I shall know Him when we meet."

CHRIST: HIS DIVINE PERSON-
ALITY.

In Memoriam. Harold. Supposed Confession. Locksley Hall Sixty Years After. Aylmer's Field. Crossing the Bar.

THE divinity of Christ is never dogmatically formulated, but it is always assumed. It is clearly expressed in some poems and involved **The Incar-** in others. What penetration into the mean-
nation. ing of the Incarnation is found in the sugges-
tive lines of the " In Memoriam " !

> "For Wisdom dealt with mortal powers,
>   Where truth in closest words shall fail,
>   When truth embodied in a tale
> Shall enter in at lowly doors.

> "And so the Word had breath, and wrought
>   With human hands the creed of creeds
>   In loveliness of perfect deeds,
> More strong than all poetic thought."
>
> <div align="right">(<i>Ode xxxvi.</i>)</div>

We could have no clearer exposition of St. John's declaration, " The Word became flesh and dwelt among us." A word is the expression of a thought.

If the word be unuttered the thought lies in silence.
What word is to thought Christ is to God, the
divine articulation. Further, deeds reveal character.
God must robe Himself in the mantle of our
humanity and, through it, shine " in loveliness of
perfect deeds," if we are to know what is most
vital to man—the character of God. The " Word "
must come into the " flesh " before the flesh can
apprehend the Word, is a truth the poet firmly
held.

**The
Divinity
of Christ.** IN the *prelude* the divinity of the personality of Christ is clearly affirmed.
  In the first stanza He is not only
addressed as the

> "Strong Son of God, immortal Love,"

but He is recognised as the object of Christian faith.
The poet always finds the focus of faith, not in
Church nor creed nor ceremony, but in Christ.

He further attributes creatorship to Christ in
the lines :

> "Thine are these orbs of light and shade ;
> Thou madest Life in man and brute—"

in which we seem to hear an echo of the Scripture—
" the world was made by Him."

In the fourth stanza we have the mingling of
the human and divine natures in the mystery of
the Incarnation.

"Thou seemest human and divine,
    The highest, holiest manhood, thou."

And we find the secret of the spiritual life in the surrender of the human will to the making will of Christ.

" Our wills are ours, we know not how;
    Our wills are ours, to make them thine."

In the fifth stanza we have the relation of creeds. to Christ. They are only broken lights of the sun. They change, for they are fallible opinions of infallible truths—

"They are but broken lights of Thee,
    And Thou, O Lord, art more than they."

The · poem concludes by acknowledging the Son of God as the source of spiritual knowledge, and prays for more of reverence and asks forgiveness for the grief that would not be consoled. Thus he leaves his friend hidden in the life of Christ.

"I trust he lives in Thee and there
    I find him worthier to be loved."

The whole of this sublime Ode, now sung in our churches as a hymn of praise, is a strong affirmation of the divinity of Christ and a clear echo of the primitive truth, " Thou art the Christ, the son of the living God."

There are other scattered references which

acknowledge the Christian teaching relating to the great facts of the life and death of Christ. The **References to Christ.** poet's reverence for the Holy Scriptures is apparent in the fact that there are no less, than 450 quotations from and references to the Bible in his works.

We have a reference to the birth of Christ in the line—

> "The time draws near the birth of Christ."
> (*Ode xxviii.*)

His birth is noted as the dawn of hope, and of a great gladness to the weary heart of man.

> "O Father, touch the east, and light
> The light that shone when Hope was born."
> (*Ode xxx.*)

And in "Harold" we find the significant line :

> "The Lord was God and came as man."

In the same drama, true to the old legend that there were oxen in the place of His birth, we read,

> "Like the great King of all
> A light among the oxen."

The birth of Christ is also beautifully touched on in the "Supposed Confession"—

> "That happy morn
> When angels spake to men aloud,
> And Thou and peace to earth were born."

In the "In Memoriam" we find the miracle of the raising of Lazarus,

> "Behold a man raised up by Christ!"
> (*Ode xxxi.*)

And further, in the lovely lines in which Mary turns from the face of the risen Lazarus to look upon the Christ, the poet touches a vital truth of the Christian consciousness—that Christ is the secret and the source of its deepest life.

> "Her ardent gaze
> Roves from the living brother's face,
> And rests upon the Life indeed."

The highest place is given to the unique personality of our Lord in "Locksley Hall, Sixty Years After."

> "Love your enemies, bless your haters, said
> The Greatest of the Great."

But more explicitly does he give expression to His moral perfection in two exquisite lines of the "In Memoriam."

> "The sinless years,
> That breathed beneath the Syrian blue."

It may be affirmed that the poet is merely an artistic mirror reflecting current orthodoxy, but the whole of this sublime epic attests the personal faith of the poet. It is impossible that any one, not Christian, could have written such a poem.

His Character and Ministry AGAIN the character of Christ, with His tender ministry, is finely fixed in " Aylmer's Field " in the three words " Lord of Love."

> "Wearing the light yoke of that Lord of Love,
> Who stilled the rolling wave of Galilee."

In the same poem we have a reference to the sufferings of the Man of Sorrows in the lines—

> "As cried
> Christ in His agony to those that swore
> Not by the temple but the gold."

Further, in the " Idylls of the King," we find an allusion to the Resurrection. The knights who do not wander from the field of duty may find the deepest realities.

> "Nor the high God a vision, nor that one who rose again."

And " In Memoriam " is musical with the sweet tones of the bells that chime away the griefs and feuds of men and ring in the crowning of the Christ,—

> "Ring out the darkness of the land
> Ring in the Christ that is to be."
> *(Ode cxi.)*

Lastly, in " Crossing the Bar," we have, clearly and sweetly sung, the poet's own faith and hope.

> "For tho' from out our bourne of time and place
> The flood may bear me far,
> I hope to see my Pilot face to face
> When I have crost the bar."

He is not passing into the chilling shadows of materialism, nor into the starless darkness of agnosticism, but into the peaceful night of death, with the Christian hope of seeing his Pilot in the morning.

These scattered references contain the central facts of the Christian Gospel. We do not expect to find a doctrine of the Incarnation, and it is possible that the poet could not express himself in the formula of the Nicene creed,* but it is evident that he grasped and taught the truth of the incarnation and the necessary truth of the divine personality of Christ.

* His creed, he always said, he would not formulate, for people would not understand him if he did ; but he considered that his poems expressed the principles at the foundation of his faith."—*A Memoir*, i., p. 307.

CHRIST: HIS DIVINE SUFFI-
CIENCY.

In the Children's Hospital. The May Queen. Sea Dreams.

I N "The Children's Hospital" we have pathetically
expressed the inspiration for noble service, along
The In- with the glow of a tender hope in death on
spiration the face of a little child, as the result of
for Service. practical faith in Christ.

The coarse materialist from the schools of France
mutters:

"'All very well—but the good Lord Jesus has had His day.'"

To which the patient nurse replies:

"'Had? has it come? It has only dawn'd. It will come
by and by.
O how could I serve in the wards if the hope of the
world were a lie?'"

And little Emmie, who has overheard the kindly
old doctor speak of the pending operation to the
nurse, and express his fear that "she'll never live
thro' it," is greatly concerned, and turns to her
friend Annie, crying, "What shall I do?"

"Annie consider'd.   'If I,' said the wise little Annie, 'was
    you,
I should cry to the dear Lord Jesus to help me.'

.   .   .   .

'Yes, and I will,' said Emmie ; 'but then if I call to the
    Lord,
How should he know that it's me? such a lot of beds in
    the ward!'
That was a puzzle for Annie.   Again she consider'd and
    said:
'Emmie, you put out your arms, and you leave 'em outside
    on the bed—
The Lord has so *much* to see to! but, Emmie, you tell it
    Him plain,
It's the little girl with her arms lying out on the counter-
    pane.' "

Emmie, in the dawn, with her white face and
her thin arms stretched out to the infinite goodness,
is the mute expression of the faith of the human
heart in the all-sufficiency of Christ.

"Say that His day is done! Ah why should we care what
    they say ?
The Lord of the children had heard her, and Emmie had
    past away."

The Cry for EMMIE personifies humanity with its sins and
Emancipa- sufferings, with its ever-haunting mystery of
tion. death, crying to some power, not itself, for
emancipation, and Christ is God's infinite answer.
When the poet thus records the sufficiency of Christ
he reflects the Christian faith and consciousness, and
when he affirms that His day has only dawned and
that the future lies with Him, he utters a prophecy

in harmony with the facts of revelation and the slow processes of nature.   We are only in the dawn of His day.

> "It will come by and by."

The Work of Christ.   THEN in " The May Queen " we have the subjective work of the spirit of Christ, in the testimony of the once selfish little Alice, delicately touched in the line—

> "He taught me all the mercy, for he show'd me all the sin."

And in " Sea Dreams " we have a reference to the sufficiency of Christ to soothe the anguish of the city clerk who had been robbed by the canting hypocrite, along with a scathing denunciation of the heated pulpiteer who spends his strength in barren polemics.

> "Not preaching simple Christ to simple men,
> Announced the coming doom and fulminated
> Against the scarlet woman and her creed."

Thus, in his religious teaching, the poet does not speculate on the personality of Christ, but at once sees that He is the King of truth, and crowns Him.   In the " Idylls of the King " he condenses the ethics of Christ and the essence of Christianity, as the rule of life, in three lines :

> "'Follow the Christ, the King,
> Live pure, speak true, right wrong, follow the King—
> Else, wherefore born?"

MAN : HIS EVOLUTION.

Idylls of the King. In Memoriam. Will. Timbuctoo.
By an Evolutionist. The Dawn. The Play. The Making
of. Man. The Dreamer. Locksley Hall Sixty Years After.
Merlin and the Gleam. Faith. Silent Voices.

THESE poems contain the teaching of the poet
relative to the evolution of man. God is the
unfolding cause within nature and man. He is
immanent for a specific and moral purpose. Divine
immanence apart from beneficent purpose and
activity, is incredible ; but to conceive the activity
and purpose, to make always for righteousness in
man and order in the world and ultimate perfection,
is to conceive what is worthy of deity. The poet
believes in evolution, but he sees clearly that evolution is a modal and not a causal theory. It offers
an intelligible explanation of the *modus operandi*
of nature, but it does not profess to account for
the genesis of life. There is always that vexed
problem of "origins." As no life exists apart
from "antecedent life" there is room left for
God in the scientific theory of development, and
the poet, with his pure idealism, sees God at the

root of all things and beings, as the initial cause. The materialist would affirm that the development of life is the result of natural selection, of purely physical causes, but Tennyson traces the order and evolution of nature and man to the divine immanence. God at the root determines the design and gives bias to. the whole series. He believes that the Almighty works through law ; he sees law, universal and uniform, working in the rounding of a dew-drop and the sweep of a planet. "Growth under the conditions of law he sees everywhere, and the progress that will in the remote future make real that which the poet now sees in the ideal. The slowness of this advancement of the world is a kind of nemesis in some of his poems. He expects no radical overturning of the world, such as Shelley believed in, and to ardent natures this snail pace of progress is a cause of chafing and sadness. Tennyson is content with the slow advance which comes of growth, through conditions of law, because his mind rests satisfied with the law itself as the basis of human good."

God and Law. IN the slow evolution of man, then, he accepts God and Law. There can be no final making of man without the recognition of the supernatural and obedience to law. He has no sympathy with the phase of agnosticism that would calmly dismiss the Almighty from the universe. He burns hot

with indignation against the materialism that would
resolve all of being into protoplasm. He protests
with scorn against the pure and noble things, the
victories of right and achievements of genius, being
buried, at last, in our own "corpse-coffins." He
sees the ultimate man made by God, through processes of law, finished and crowned.

> "One God, one law, one element,
> And one far-off divine event,
> To which the whole creation moves."

But while the poet is not a scientific agnostic
in the sense of eliminating God from the universe,
he may be called a spiritual agnostic, in the sense
that he clearly recognises that the Almighty cannot
The   be known nor His existence demonstrated by
Supremacy intellect alone. Throughout the " In Memo-
of Emotion. riam " he asserts the supremacy of emotion
over reason. He teaches that love is greater than
knowledge, and may feel God when the reason
staggers with doubt. He believes in faith as the
point of contact between God and the soul. By
faith he does not mean, necessarily, the acceptance
of historic traditions, but the testimony of the soul,
in its instincts and intuitions and aspirations, to the
existence of a supreme being, along with the evidence
that lies in the order and beauty and wonder of the
universe, to the fact of the divine immanence.
Turning now to the poems we have grouped

under the evolution of man, we shall find an
illustration of these propositions.

The   THE first great fact which the poet accentuates
Existence   is the existence of evil.   Evil is recognised as
of Evil.   a terrible factor in the problem of human life.
M. Renan on being asked, " What do you do with
sin in your philosophy ? " replied, " I suppress it " !
But no philosophy is complete or moral that does
not take into account the existence of evil.   The
poet or philosopher who would suppress sin fails
to interpret a most glaring fact of human life.
Tennyson has never been guilty of the *suppressio
veri*, but has expressed himself clearly.   The temptation to suppress must have been great in a poet
with such pure and delicate sensibility.   When
he draws a character like Vivien, his moral loathing is apparent, and his very repulsion, as Mr.
Swinburne thinks, makes the character defective.
Evil is the ugliest thing on earth, and he sees it
not only with the calm, critical eye of the true
artist, but with the sensitive shrinking of the pure
soul ; his hand is steady as he draws the divine in
man, but it trembles with the hot pulse of indignation when he delineates the diabolical.   Not by the
cynical method of Renan has he sought to eliminate
evil.

Note how he points the prophet's finger of revelation and of warning as he conceives evil under

the aspect of animalism, the "beast" or "brute"
or "ape and tiger" in man. Illustrations abound
in the "Idylls of the King."

In "The Coming of Arthur" the realm is thus
described :

> "Wherein the beast was ever more and more,
> But man was less and less, till Arthur came."

Again :

> "Arise, and help us thou !
> For here between the man and beast we die."

The Fleshly Nature of Evil. AND in the cause of the opposition to Arthur,
as assigned by Bedivere, we have the fleshly
nature of evil :—

> "For there be those who hate him in their hearts,
> Call him baseborn, and since his ways are sweet,
> And theirs are bestial, hold him less than man."

Further, in "Gareth and Lynette" the lawless
knight overthrown by Sir Gareth personifies the
carnal forces with their enslaving power :

> "He seem'd as one
> That all in later, sadder age begins
> To war against ill uses of a life,
> But these from all his life arise and cry,
> 'Thou hast made us lords, and canst not put us down.'"

In "Balin and Balan" the same conception of
evil prevails :

> "'Let not thy moods prevail, when I am gone
> Who used to lay them! hold them outer fiends
> Who leap at thee and tear thee, shake them aside.'"

And in "The Last Tournament" when the King almost despairs of the purity of his realm, we find the "beast" again:

> "'Or whence the fear lest this my realm, uprear'd,
> By noble deeds at one with noble vows,
> From flat confusion and brute violences,
> Reel back into the beast, and be no more?'"

And in "The Passing of Arthur" in that pathetic lament of Bedivere:

> "'And all my realm
> Reels back into the beast and is no more.'"

In "Merlin and Vivien," as the magician becomes dimly conscious of the carnal spell that lures him to his doom, evil, as the war of Sense, is thus portrayed:

> "World-war of dying flesh against the life,
> Death in all life and lying in all love."

And "In Memoriam" fixes in two lines the conception of evil which dominates the poet throughout.

> "Move upward, working out the beast,
> And let the ape and tiger die."
> (*Ode cxviii.*)

These passages sufficiently indicate the character which evil assumes—they suggest a strong prejudice in favour of making the flesh rather than the will the vehicle of evil ; the conception merges on manichæism—it is always under the symbol of the animal in man that he speaks of evil. The "beast" within has to be chained or crushed or wrought out. Sin is the result of the power of the flesh over the ethical will, and is always the violation of law, physical or moral. What then is the remedy ? The remedy lies in strengthening the ethical will by communion with God— until it is strong enough to grapple with the "beast" within. The poet believes in the sufficiency of the will, divinely conditioned, to destroy the evil.

The Remedy for Sin.

If evil is immanent in man, so also is God, and the will, linked to the indwelling God, is strong enough to rule. By will he seems to mean conscience, for which he claims implicit obedience. His remedy for evil is thus finely expressed in the poem " Will " :

> "O well for him whose will is strong!
> He suffers, but he will not suffer long ;
> He suffers, but he cannot suffer wrong."

And now, because evil is to be wrought out by the process of obedience to law, ethical and physical, the poet sees clearly that the process must be a slow one, and may involve ages. It is interesting to note how, in one of his early poems, he grasped the slow but sure moral evolution of man, which he expresses with such emphasis and ever growing gladness in his later writings. In the

poem "Timbuctoo" we find the keynote to the
slow ascending scale in the lines :

> "There is no mightier spirit than I to sway
> The heart of man, and teach him to attain,
> By shadowing forth the unattainable,
> And step by step to scale the mighty stair
> Whose landing place is wrapped about with clouds
> Of glory of Heaven."

**The
Slow
Progress.**   IN his later poems he still sings of the slow
progress, but he sees more clearly the ultimate
man, and his songs are like clear pealing bells
of gladness over the finished work. The poet is an
optimist who sees afar off the last unfolding of
spiritual evolution; he sees man as he lives in the
divine ideal, the pure reflection of the perfect image.

The slow progress and the final consummation
in the finished humanity, is the theme of the
following poems—"By an Evolutionist," "The
Dawn," "The Play," "The Making of Man."

In "By an Evolutionist," the body is supposed
to be the product of matter when the soul of the
man asks of God, "Am I your debtor ? "

> "And the Lord 'not yet but make it as clean as you can,
> And then I will let you a better.'"

But if the soul be identical with matter then
why seek to be nobler ?

> "Why not bask amid the senses, while the sun
> Of morning shines?"

The poet sees no room for lofty ideals and moral

aims in materialism.   If God and immortality are fictions why not live a life of mere sensations ?   If soul is matter there is no moral reason why it should not live in the " stable " of being, with the " hounds " ! But old age affirms that it has starved the " beast " within, and gives the secret of the process :

> " Hold the sceptre, human Soul, and rule thy
> Province of the brute."

Thus the evil may be coerced and expelled. Conscience must be crowned and obeyed, and the final result appears in the partly spiritual man :

> " But I hear no yelp of the beast, and the Man is quiet at
> last
> As he stands on the heights of his life with a glimpse of a
> height that is higher."

The Promise of Day. AGAIN in " The Dawn " the progress is slow. As the poet catalogues the evils of our social life, he sees clearly that we are only in the dawn—

> " Dawn not Day—"

with just enough light to reveal the many in the dens of being.   But are not the escaped few prophets of the imprisoned many ?   Is not dawn the promise of day ?   So the poet thinks there is time for the race to grow, and lay the ghost of the brute that haunts us.

> "In a hundred, a thousand winters? Ah, what
> Will *our* children be?"

"The Play" gives an answer to the question with which "The Dawn" closed, as well as an answer to the series of questions in the poem "Vastness."

> "Our Playwright may show
> In some fifth Act what this wild Drama means."

The Playwright at Work. THEN in "The Making of Man" he draws the curtain and we seem to see the Playwright at work, shaping the last act in the human drama. Ages have passed and generations have played their part. Very slow is the great law of progress. We see vast forces of the supernatural annexing the results of human experience and moulding man into rhythmic order.

> "Shall not æon after æon pass and touch him into shape?"

Then slowly, grandly, in the far-away time the ultimate man emerges crowned in the midst of creation, a symmetrical soul.

> "Hallelujah to the Maker 'It is finished' Man is made."

This assurance of the final triumph of good over evil, in the evolution of the perfect man, rises again in clear ringing cadence in all the later poems. But observe there is for man a condition of attainment which the poet enforces in "The Dreamer," and "Locksley Hall Sixty Years After," and

"Merlin and the Gleam," and "Faith," and in "Silent Voices." The condition lies in the *persistence* expressed in the poem "Will" and here repeated in "The Dreamer."

The dreamer, haunted by the sacred text "The meek shall inherit the earth," falls asleep, when the earth-spirit creeps by wailing her lost youth, and faded vision, and clashing battles, and contending classes, and gloomy doubts, and hollow graves, in a very dirge of pessimism; but the dreamer answers the wail with a song of the coming triumph and seizes the refrain of the earth-spirit and sets it to the music of hope:

"Whirl, and follow the Sun!"

The Lesson of Persistence. IT is the lesson of persistence; stagnation is death, but motion is life. The law of progress is slow but sure, and man must work with the law if he would come to his best. Behind all the brooding darkness there is a sun, flashing his beams into the shivering night. The man must not doubt his destiny, but in the orbit of duty

"Whirl, and follow the Sun."

Again in "Locksley Hall Sixty Years After," when that passionate outburst of pessimism, which denounces the social evils of the times and betrays the mistrust of old age in Demos subsides, the poet returns to his normal meliorism and the unclouded vision of the splendid destiny of man. The bells ring out again across the stormy scenes of the vast struggle glad peals of hope, with the ever-changing chimes of will and resolution and persistence.

> "Follow light and do the right, for man can half control his doom,
> Till you find the deathless angel seated in the vacant tomb."

The Poet's Youth. AND again in "Merlin and the Gleam," the pure idealism of the poet is expressed and the lesson of persistencies repeated. The interest of the poem, however, lies in its autobiograpy. It is a series of pictures of the life-work of the poet. It portrays his changing moods, and marks his persistence and gives his peaceful outlook when on the border of boundless ocean. As the grey Magician the poet addresses the young Mariner to whom he tells the story of his life. He tells how in youth, when his soul was sleeping, the wizard, the spirit of poetry, found him and "learned me magic" and set before him a pure and lofty ideal which he strove to realise. At first the way was light, but soon it was darkened by the critics.

> "A demon vext me,
> The light retreated."

But he obeyed the whispered voice and followed the "gleam" when it led him on through fairy scenes of nature with her many-voiced music into the region of human life, with its varied interests, until it brought him to the world of romance when it inspired the " Idylls of the King." Then the shadow fell again.

> " Arthur had vanish'd
> I knew not whither,
> The king who loved me,
> And cannot die."

The Shadow of Sorrow. THE reference is to Arthur Hallam and is skilfully woven into the passing of the Arthur of romance. His sorrow had caused the gleam to wane " to a wintry glimmer," but it gave a new meaning to life, and touched its finest chords and voiced the tender song of the " In Memoriam." Then the shadow passed into the gleam and was clothed with it.

As he grew older the gleam grew " broader and brighter " and his songs were filled with light and with music of hope.

Old age creeps upon him, yet still he follows the gleam, and the grave blooms with flowers, and he can die rejoicing.

> "And all but in Heaven,
> Hovers The Gleam."

He concludes with a message to the young Mariner of a restless age, face to face with the sea of life, to be persistent and not to trust the material lights, but to follow the pure idealism of the soul.

> "After it, follow it,
> Follow The Gleam."

The Victory of Faith. THE lesson is repeated in the glowing poem "Faith," as it takes up the glad note of progress and sings of the golden age. "Faith" rebukes the agnosticism that hugs its doubts and the pessimism that darkens life with the shadow of the tragedy wrought by the resistless energy of nature. In the midst of its wild forces and in the glare of human passion we are not to forget that we are being evolved, that the work is unfinished and there is a gleam of what is higher.

It is fitting that "Silent Voices" should conclude the series on the evolution of man. It is a glad song sung by the shore of the deep from under the falling shadow of death, in which we hear the clear, swelling notes of the complete triumph of the spiritual over the material.

The human soul has wrought out the evil of the flesh and now stands by the silent sea waiting for the calling of the voices to the wider vision and the richer life of a more glorious day.

> "Glimmering up the heights beyond me
> On, and always on!"

MAN: HIS CREEDS.
MYSTICISM.

St. Agnes' Eve.   Sir Galahad.   St. Simeon Stylites.

WE have in this trio the delineation of three sides of mediæval life. There is a mysticism that sublimates the soul into pure and heavenly rapture, and there is a mysticism that degrades. "St. Agnes' Eve," with its delicate touch and perfect colouring, is a charming picture of passive, contemplative mysticism. Mr. Swinburne regards it as "the poem of the deepest charm and fullest delight of pathos and melody ever written by Mr. Tennyson," and as a portraiture of what was best and purest in that old conventual life it may be said to be unsurpassed. If it be true that the mediæval type of faith produced the greatest saints along with the greatest sinners, then the portraitures are correct. St. Agnes and Sir Galahad are the saints, and St. Simeon is the sinner.

The Ideal Woman-Saint. IN St. Agnes we have the saintliness of pure spiritual womanhood with no trace of self-consciousness. Her spiritual *abandon* to the heavenly bridegroom is not only the secret of her

303

charm, but transfigures the art form. The beautiful soul, longing for the whiteness of the snow and exultant with hope, is clearly portrayed. For simplicity of art and rapture of mysticism it would be difficult to match the lines beginning—

> "He lifts me to the golden doors;
> The flashes come and go;
> All heaven bursts her starry floors,
> And strows her lights below."

She is the ideal woman-saint of mediævalism; she is dead to the world, and the world is dead to her. She is alive to Christ and under His spell. He fills her vision, and she would welcome death. Such was the effect of conventual mysticism on a certain type of nervous organism and spiritual sensibility. The soul was absorbed in pure emotionalism and spiritual rapture.

The Ideal Man Saint. "SIR GALAHAD" gives us the ideal man, or warrior-saint, of mediævalism, who goes in search of the Holy Grail. Galahad is pure and spiritual and visionary. St. Agnes seems to be in heaven, but Galahad is a heavenly man on earth, with a little of the earth-spirit clinging to him. A thin vein threads his pure heroic soul—a vein of self-consciousness. He is a man and, as self-esteem is not easily wrought out of the man, he is not so spiritual as St. Agnes. His vision is not filled with that Other Self; but his own self creeps in and seems to say, " Some of Christ and some of self,"

> "Then move the trees, the copses nod,
> Wings flutter, voices hover clear :
> 'O just and faithful knight of God!
> Ride on! the prize is near.'"

The poet does not wholly condemn the contemplative aspect of monastic life, with its absorbing mysticism. For some it may be the only way of redemption from self and the world, and yet it is clear, in the later poem of the " Holy Grail," that he has little sympathy with the mysticism that neglects the duties of daily life. On the contrary, he thinks that in the faithful discharge of these duties the highest vision may be won. Should the mysticism of St. Agnes become the ideal of religious life it might degenerate into a virulent form of selfishness. George Eliot, with keen insight, saw that "other worldliness" may be as immoral as what is called worldliness. As in the case of Ambrosius, asceticism generated naught but the exhalations of earth in an earthy cell. In these two poems, then, we have the portraits of the best religious types formed by mediævalism. The portraiture, however, is not complete without a contrasted picture, and this we have vividly delineated in " St. Simeon Stylites."

St. Simeon is a type of abused monasticism in

20

which the soul is degraded by egoism and selfishness. He is hoisted on his pedantic pillar by the lever of his own self-righteousness; while his eyes are turned towards heaven his soul cleaves, with secret longing, to sensuous pleasures. He calls himself a great sinner; but the sense of sin, in its moral repulsion, never flashes in flame through his soul. He strives to make an arrangement with Heaven on the principle of *quid pro quo*. He has made sacrifices and suffered practical inconvenience on his pillar by being blistered by the sun and stung by the frost and punctured by disease. These he would offer to Heaven as so much merit by which to cancel his moral obligations.

The Abuse of Monastic Life.

> "Who may be made a saint, if I fail here?
> Show me the man hath suffer'd more than I."

The *quid pro quo* of the monastic life was the virus that poisoned the soul and darkened its vision of God. It had no clear conception of the nature of sin. When St. Simeon thinks of sin he finds refuge in heredity and shifts the whole responsibility on to his ancestors.

> "A sinful man, conceived and born in sin:
> 'Tis their own doing: this is none of mine;
> Lay it not to me!"

Self is never absent from his thought and wraps him round like hardened skin; he feels that he is indispensable to the Almighty, and that the glory of the Highest finds a prop in the pillar of St. Simeon.

> "Ah, hark! they shout,
> 'St. Simeon Stylites' why, if so,
> God reaps a harvest in me. O my Soul."

The portrait is a painful delineation of an actual type of the old monastic life. His humiliation is the cant of self-consciousness, and his religious aspirations are veiled forms of selfishness. His body might have been kept in subjection without destruction. That beautiful complex organism was designed as a shrine to be purified and tenanted by the spirit of holiness.*

* "Among these examples of religious fatuity, none acquired greater veneration and applause than those who were called Pillar Saints (*Sancti Columnares*), or in Greek *Stylitæ*, persons of a singular spirit and genius, who stood motionless on the tops of lofty columns during many years and to the end of life, and to the great astonishment of the ignorant multitude. The author of this institution in the present century (the fifth) was Simeon of Sysan, a Syrian, who was first a shepherd and then a monk and who, in order to be nearer heaven, spent thirty-seven years in the most uncomfortable manner on the tops of five different pillars, of six, twelve, twenty-two, thirty-six and forty cubits' elevation, and in this way procured for himself immense fame and veneration. This stupid form of religion continued in the East quite down to the twelfth century, when it was entirely abolished."—MOSHEIM, *Ecclesiastical History*, p. 194.

CALVINISM.

Despair. Rizpah.

IN "Despair," which is a dramatic monologue, we have a powerful delineation of the effect of hyper-calvinism upon certain sensitive souls. A glance at the creed will throw light on the poem. The germs of Calvinism are to be found in the teaching of Augustine, which is thus summarised. "God had chosen a limited portion of the race to be for ever blessed ; chose them before they were born ; chose them from all eternity and without regard to any future foreseen merit on their part ; chose them of His own free grace, undetermined by any quality in the object or by any consideration out of Himself ; chose them by an act of irresponsible absolute will—and His will was irresistible. No one who was pre-ordained to eternal life could fail of his destination, or forfeit the blessedness in store for him through any step or fault of his own. He might sin as other men sin, but his sin would do him no mortal harm. His "effectual calling" would triumph over all the defects of his nature and all the evils of his life and carry him to heaven in spite of himself by the " final perseverance of divine grace."

Augustine, while affirming that the elect were predestined by the sovereignty of God, did not commit himself to saying that the rest of mankind were predestined to endless misery ; but he held that they were " left to sink by the natural gravitation of their sins to perdition."   Where Augustine paused Calvin advanced and formulated the doctrine of reprobation.   He argued that "many so present election as to deny that any is reprobate, but very ignorantly and childishly, since election itself would not stand unless opposed to reprobation."   Further, he made the amazing statement that "God actually caused the sins which He afterwards forbids ; that this is not a contradiction in Him, for His nature is different from ours ; and that God created all solely for His own glory, as also He did sinners to glorify His justice " !

The Hopelessness of Calvinism.   Now the poem " Despair " portrays the fatal effect of Calvinism upon a man and woman who lose faith in God and determine on suicide. The woman is drowned, but the man is saved by " a minister of the sect he had abandoned."   Man and wife had knelt in the little chapel by the sea, but now despair broods over them.   God, to them, is only a mocking phantom of human desire.

"He is only a cloud and a smoke who was once a pillar of fire."

Suicide offers the only escape from their misery. But what is the cause of their despair ? It lies in two suggestive lines,

"See, we were nursed in the drear nightfold of your fatalist creed."

But why should Calvinism generate despair ? Why call it a "fatalist creed"? Calvin himself supplies the answer, " I again ask how it is that the fall of Adam involves so many nations, with their infant children, in eternal death, without remedy, unless that it so seemed meet to God ? *The decree, I admit, is horrible.*"

The fallacy is in the assumption that the Almighty did decree to eternal death these nations and children ; but for our purpose we note the fact that Calvin could only believe in the decree by violating the truest and deepest instincts of his nature, nor does he cloak his moral repugnance, but calls it "horrible ! " If such were the effect of his own theology upon himself we cannot be surprised at its effect upon the man and wife in "Despair." When, too, Luther was so far in accord with Calvin that he could write, " When God says to men, "Do this and live," it is merely irony on His part, as though He had said, "See if you can do it, try it "—what shall be said of the morality and the effect of such teaching ? When, further, Jonathan Edwards, driving the creed to its hard logical issues, affirmed that it made God the author of sin, we feel that the poet was justified in the use of the words "fatalist creed" and in naming it

"The dark side of your faith and a God of eternal rage."

The fatalism of Calvinism is the cause of the hopeless misery of the two characters. They belong to the "reprobates," and the poem traces the results. They are driven, first, into materialism.

They not only break from Calvinism but from Christianity—

"And we broke away from the Christ, our human brother and friend"—

because they were taught, as an article of the faith of Christ, to believe in an endless, hopeless hell.

They turn to materialism with the hope born of advancing science, only to find that materialism, with its dry light of intellectualism, leaves the moral nature unsatisfied.

"We had passed from a cheerless night to the glare of a drearier day."

Nor does agnosticism satisfy them, and they drift into atheism.

"We had read their know-nothing books and we lean'd to the darker side."

The sequel shows with what results,

The poem is thus far not only a protest against Calvinism, but against the scientific scepticism that would give us a body without a soul, a universe without a God. A true poet is a seer; he may not be a theologian or philosopher or logician, but he is a born seer. His intuition is such that he can see with pure insight the trend of thought and the final result. Thus Tennyson sees clearly that the reign of a daring negation, deriding faith and resolving great deeds and noble ideals into mere wave-emotions of nerve changes or molecular vibrations, would end in blank despair. He sees the heart of humanity bursting with grief and dying in the darkness of pessimism. He sees all the flashing lights of suns and systems as luminous lies quivering, like gleaming arrows, in the heart of darkness.

> "Flashing with fires as of God, but we knew that their light was a lie."

The Laureate has struck the keynote once again of that old melody of spiritual assurance which is the antithesis of infidelity and hell. A great poet sees with the vision, which is his special panorama, the darkness of fatal and unretrieved doubt such as the common mind may but feel. He but voices more eloquently than timid Christian apologists the disgust of insulted souls with the pig-stye ethics of materialism. When the great singer tells us that—

> " Doubt is the lord of this dunghill
> And crows to the sun and the moon
> Till the sun and the moon of our science
> Are both of them turned into blood "—

the scope and tendency of infidel teaching are grandly focussed in two lines of passionate verse."

But there is another result of the " fatalist creed " in the hopeless despair of the suicides.

We hear the piercing wail of it in the confession of the man.

> " Of a life without sun, without health, without hope."

We feel the heart-ache in the pulsing lines :

> " O, we poor orphans of nothing—alone on that lonely shore.
>
> .   .   .   .   .   .
>
> Come from the brute, poor souls—no souls—and—to die with the brute."

While Calvinism made them shudder before an infinite Tyranny that destroyed their faith, materialism led them through mocking lights that revealed only the corpse of a universe. The poem leads up to the final result.

Terrified by a caricature of the Christian gospel and mocked by a soulless science, they seek to cool the hot pulse of their pain by suicide. Lightly they pass over the sands, hearing the call of the sea, she with her hand in his, until the foam gleams about their feet and they wait the coming of death. The thought of God still haunts them. It is so lonely! Perhaps in the deep silence of their ocean grave they may find Him, for in life He was not! Then a blind wave steals upon them and sweeps the woman into the hungry deep and flings the man upon the barren shore, where he is rescued by the minister, and blasphemes, for he hates life and longs for death.

Such is the fine monologue in which the poet has uttered his protest against Calvinism and materialism and an everlasting hell.

We see now more clearly, in the light of ever-growing truth, how fatal Calvinism was to a just conception of the character of God. It not only assumed that He was the author of sin, but the creator of the " reprobates," without possibility of reclamation and predestined to doom. For them no pulse of love throbbed in the eternal heart, no voice on Calvary cried, " It is finished." They might wail their penitence through the darkness and, with remorse, seek to break the bonds of destiny, but it was of no avail since it was decreed! It is easy enough now to see that this was not a Christian photograph of God, but a painful caricature. The features of the August Majesty were drawn in hard lines of severity, unsoftened by the tender grace of Divine Fatherhood. But further, the creed was fatal to a true estimate of man.

It taught him that he was morally corrupt, it denied efficacy to his will and destroyed any motive to virtue by affirming that it could not affect the decree. It had therefore, a fatal influence on morals and drove the despairing into reckless sin and daring blasphemy. Maddened with the horror of despair and with the hatred of such a being, they wallowed in the slough of sensualism or wandered in the desert of materialism. It was a great intellectual system, and a marvellous logical structure, but it was based on false premises. Guizot truly said, " In spite of its imperfections it is on the whole one of the noblest evidences ever erected by the mind of man, and one of the mightiest codes of moral law which ever guided him." But he also recognised the defect of the system. " When Calvin proclaimed the absolute infallibility and universal authority of the Holy Scriptures, he failed to recognise the true object and meaning of the divine revelation which they contain."

On the whole the protest of the poem is justified but we must not regard it as absolute. Calvinism contained great and vital truths when it accentuated the malignity of sin and the grandeur of Divine Sovereignty. In spiritual minds it wrought out noble and stately characters, it moved them with mighty impulses and produced some of the strongest saints. We find them among Huguenots, and Waldenses, and Covenanters, and Puritans. But while some were made great by its truths, many were wrecked by its errors. The creed controlled the mind of Europe for three centuries, but it is now exhausted and can never be revitalised. We should do well, however, to revive its spirit of august reverence in the presence of the holiness of Deity and its vivid conception of the heinousness of sin.

Another aspect of Calvinism is portrayed in " Rizpah."

Love's   IN " Rizpah " a dying mother tells her tragic
Revolt.   story of grief to a kindly vis..or. She relates how once she had a boy whose crimes were those of reckless daring, rather than of actual depravity. He was challenged to rob the mail, and did it out of sheer bravado, flinging down the purse he took ; but he was arrested and tried and condemned to death. The mother tells how she went to his cell for the last time, heard his pathetic cry, " Mother," and would have returned but for the jailer. Through the years and the darkness that cry had wailed in her soul until it shook her brain and she was treated for imbecility and then released. But ever the cry, " O mother, come out to me," had haunted her, and through the storm she crept to the gibbet, " led by the creak of the chain." There she had groped, and gathered his bones and buried them in the old churchyard.

Her story is interrupted by the visitor who makes some reference to sin, with the suggestion that her son did not repent, and with the implication that he was finally lost; he was not of the elect, but of the reprobate.

She exclaims, with righteous indignation and mingled love,

"Election, Election and Reprobation—it's all very well.
  But I go to-night to my boy, and I shall not find him in hell.
  For I cared so much for my boy that the Lord has look'd into my care."

Then the dying woman draws near the calling voice, no longer out of a bright sky, over the white snow.

"Willy,—the moon's in a cloud—Good-night. I am going. He calls."

Calvinism, with its decrees of election and reprobation, would have extinguished the last ray of hope in the mother's heart. To suggest that her boy, who, for a stolen purse, had paid the penalty of his life, was sent to an endless hell was to suggest a caricature of Divine justice and to violate the deeper instincts of the human heart.

It is the old question of heart *versus* creed. Which is safer in determining the divine character and His justice, a creed expressing the hard thinking of the doctors of a hard theology, or the human heart with its best instincts and intuitions and aspirations? The poet is in favour of the heart. Here and always he makes love a swifter, surer guide to divine realities than the intellect.

Reason and Faith are near the throne, but Love is crowned. He teaches "that knowledge severed from love and faith is a child and vain," and that she should know her place, which is the second and not the first."

It was intellect divorced from heart, knowledge from love, that created Calvinism with its reprobates. Against the appalling injustice of consigning her son to an endless hell for the sins of impulsive youth the mother's heart cries in passionate protest.

> "But I go to-night to my boy, and I shall not find him in hell."

In other words she sees in her own heart a dim reflection of God who made it and taught it how to love. To think of God pre-ordaining her son to endless punishment was to think of Him as mocking the heart He made, and rolling across its tenderest aspiration the cast-iron creed of inexorable decrees. But her own heart tells her that behind the august sovereignty beats the pulse of loving fatherhood. If not, she will go to her boy and sacrifice her own soul.

> "Do you think that I care for *my* soul if my boy be gone to the fire?"

She would rather be with him than with such a God; but God is not like that creed, and the mother's heart saves her from hopeless despair—

> "I have been with God in the dark"—

and she knows better.   She had felt the hand that comes through darkness and knew by the pulse that it was not unlike a mother's heart.

But now the question arises, Was she right in making her own emotions symbols of the love and justice of God ?   In other words—may we interpret the Divine character from the best human instinct of right and wrong ?   The answer seems simple— The soul is a vehicle of revelation ; but if love and justice in us be opposed to love and justice in God the revelation is impossible ; it is precluded by the constitution of our being.   Calvinism was thus defective on its human side.   It formulated an intellectual creed of Divine sovereignty without reference to the human heart.   It never heard the undertone of the restless deep : "Show us the Father."   The result was a creed in which human will was so paralysed and moral inability so accentuated that vast numbers were driven into hopeless despair and spiritual death.

LATITUDINARIANISM.

Akbar's Dream. The Higher Pantheism. In Memoriam.
Despair.

THE Broad Church School, whose foundations
were laid in the philosophy of Samuel Taylor
Coleridge and broadened by the noble freedom and
charity of Arnold of Rugby, whose walls were
reared by the chaste theology of F. D. Maurice, and
whose edifice was crowned by the brilliant scholar-
ship of Dean Stanley, found for itself a singer in
the voice of Tennyson. It is easy enough now to
speak in terms of derision of the "Gospel of
Tennyson" who, through the charm of his muse,
has probably exerted a greater influence than the
theologian in saving not a few from the despair of
scientific negation and the sensualism of practical
infidelity. Those who are born into the wider
vision of the later theology are scarcely able to
appreciate the difficulties of a poet-seer who, fifty
years ago, predicted the breaking up of the old
paths and affirmed that

"God fulfils Himself in many ways."

320

There is a penalty exacted for clearer vision in
the timid suspicion of the orthodox and in the
enforced isolation of the soaring soul.   The great
lives that go far up the heights and see deeper and
wider are lonely lives.   Bereft of human sympathy,
they wait in the cave of Horeb for "the voice of
gentle stillness."

In the first place the poet had to battle with a
theological conception of nature morally repellent.

Wordsworth had entered the arena and had
fought bravely against the mechanical theory of
Pope ; but when Tennyson came men still believed,
with the majority of the Latin Fathers, that the
Almighty, through Adam's sin, had withdrawn from
the world and cursed the world in withdrawing.
It was evident that a poet, who came teaching the
doctrine of the Divine immanence and singing of
a larger hope than the dogmas held, would have
to battle with theological prejudice.   He found the
prevailing conception of the relation of God to man
hostile to the new theology.   Divine Sovereignty
had dwarfed Divine Fatherhood, and election and
reprobation had fettered men's minds.   A sovereignty divorced from apparent justice had resulted
in unbridled license.   The teaching of Calvin held
sway.   Further, the poet soon discovered that
certain formulæ of the creeds were too narrow for
the expression of the larger thought of the *renais-
sauce* in which Faith had taken to herself a flowing

garment, and they who knew her only by the outward form, now failed to recognise her inward spirit. But he continued to ring out fearlessly the music of the larger truth, with the result that weary hearts listening from their beds of pain were soothed to peace, souls swept on stormy seas of doubt were saved by a song, lives wrecked on burning shores of sin were lured by the "larger hope" back to the Infinite Love, mourners sitting over against their sepulchres weeping, heard the strain and, looking up from empty graves, saw the light. It is not too much to say that Tennyson, singing of a hope, large with the compassion of God, has brought the peace of a tender dawn upon the wild waters of many a heart.

It may be well to state here the nature and scope of the Broad Evangelical School, with the view of fixing the theological position of the poet. "It does not propose to do without a theology. It seeks no such transformation of method or form that it can no longer claim the name of a science. It. does not resolve itself into a sentiment, nor etherealise into mysticism, nor lower into mere altruism ; yet it does not deny an element of sentiment it acknowledges an element of mysticism, and it insists on a firm basis in ethics. It is the determined foe of agnosticism, yet it recognises a limitation of human knowledge. While it insists that theology is a science, and that therefore its

parts should be co-ordinate and mutually supporting
and an induction from all the facts known to it,
it realises that it deals with eternal realities that
cannot be wholly compassed, and also with the
mysteries and contradictions of a world involved
in mystery and beset by contradictory forces. If
it find itself driven into impenetrable mystery, as
it inevitably must, it prefers to take counsel of the
higher sentiments and better hopes of our nature,
rather than project into it the framework of a
formal logic and insist on its conclusion. It does
not abjure logic, but it refuses to be held by what
is often deemed logic. While it believes in a
harmony of doctrines, it regards with suspicion what
have been known as systems of theology, on the
ground that it rejects the methods by which they
are constructed. It will not shape a doctrine in
order that it may fit another which has been shaped
in the same fashion—a merely mechanical interplay
and seeking a mechanical harmony. Instead, it
regards theology as an induction from the revelations of God—in the Bible, in history, in the nation,
in the family, in the material creation and in the
whole length and breadth of human life. It will
have, therefore, all the definiteness and harmony it
can find in these revelations, but it will have no
more, since it regards these revelations as under
a process still enacting, and not as under a finality."*

* Munger, *Freedom of Thought*, p. 7.

This clear-cut outline of the Broad School fairly expresses the relation of the poet to theology, and indicates the general ground taken by Maurice and himself when assailing the prevailing view of nature in the mechanical theory of Pope, and of theology, in the hard teaching of Calvin. Maurice was thus the theologian and Tennyson was the poet of the *renaissance.* He not only voiced the "higher sentiments" with their silent protest against the "fatalist creed," but he believed that their unuttered hopes and aspirations were derived from the "likest God within the soul." He believed in truth and followed the gleam wherever it shone. It would seem as if, in later life, he became more suspicious of systems of theology and made his inductions from *all* the revelations. One of his latest poems, "Akbar's Dream," is purely latitudinarian.

Eclecticism of Akbar. THE eclectic system of Akbar gave the poet scope for the expression of his theological attitude. We not only hear the ring of the Tennysonian rhyme, but the chime of the bells that are to ring in "the Christ that is to be."

The impatience of the Broad School with narrow sectarianism breathes in the lines :

> "For every splinter'd fraction of a sect
> Will clamour 'I am on the perfect way,
> All else is to perdition.'"

Again :

"I hate the rancour of their castes and creeds."

The truth of the Divine indwelling, which makes the universe one of the organs of the "revelations," is thus finely expressed :

"I can but lift the torch
Of reason in the dusky cave of life,
And gaze on this great miracle, the world."

The value of religious forms, in revealing the ever-growing life of spiritual faith, is clearly expressed in the lines :

"And what are forms ?
Fair garments, plain or rich and fitting close
Or flying looselier."

And the specific object of the Broad School finds voice in two lines giving the avowed purpose of Akbar :

"To spread the divine faith
Like calming oil on all their stormy creeds."

The whole poem, as a self-revelation of the mind of the poet, and as showing his attitude towards Oriental philosophy, deserves careful study.

The Larger Hope. IT is, however, the poet's sympathy with the "larger hope" of Maurice that fixes his theological position. The following letter, in which Maurice dedicated his "Essays" to Tennyson, reveals the mind of the poet on the then burning question of future punishment.

"I have maintained in these Essays that a theology which does not correspond to the deepest thoughts and feelings of human beings cannot be a true theology. Your writings have taught me to enter into many of these thoughts and feelings. Will you forgive me the presumption of offering you a book which, at least, acknowledges them and does them homage? As the hopes which I have expressed in this volume are more likely to be fulfilled to our children than to ourselves, I might perhaps ask you to accept it as a present to one of your name."

Comparing the "Essays" with the poems, the reflex of thought is apparent. Maurice based the "larger hope" upon the Scriptures, and showed it to be in harmony with reason and the voices of the soul. The word eternal, which was the crux of the question, must, he maintained, "be considered in reference to God. Its use, when it is applied to Him, must determine all its other uses." This is the key put into the lock of mystery. Orthodoxy argued that if the word "eternity" applied to the Almighty, means everlasting, then, the same word applied to the finally impenitent must carry a similar meaning. Maurice replied that the word in its application to God stood in relation not to time but to being, to His substance and to the eternal things, *e.g.,* His righteousness, truth, love, and that for man the knowledge of God, who is love, is eternal life. It follows from this that the loss of that life is "eternal death." Of those who cling to the popular meaning of the word eternal and say that it is endless and salvation impossible he asks, "What is the consequence ? Simply this. I believe the whole Gospel of God is set aside. The state of eternal life and eternal death is not one we can refer only to the future, or that we can in any wise identify with the future. Every man who knows what it is to have been in a state of sin, knows what it is to have been in a state of death. He cannot connect that death with time, he must say that Christ has brought him out of the bonds of eternal death. Throw that idea into the future and you deprive it of all its reality, of all its power." * Thus the essayist impressed the awful fact that hell is in the conscience of the man who will not love God. Eternal death is here and now, in the soul that refuses to know God. This death is not the result of any arbitrary Divine decree, but the soul's deliberate refusal to know and love the revealed God. It makes its own character and shapes its own destiny. "The undying worm is preying in thousands of hearts whose faces are merry. The unquenchable fire is burning within them. What is any talk of the future compared with the actual

* Maurice, *Theological Essays,* page 475.

present experience?   If you dare tell men and
women of One who has come to deliver them from
this worm, to raise them out of this fire, they may
welcome you as heavenly messengers, for are you
not announcing that there is an escape from sin and
the devil to righteousness and God ?   But if all you
can say to these men and women is, ' Unless you
believe what we tell you, God will keep you in hell
for ever and ever,' they must understand the words
to mean, ' God will keep you in sin for ever and
ever.'   Can these tidings have been brought from
the region of purity ?   Must they not have ascended
from the bottomless pit ? "   Such was the ground

The Soul of the "larger hope," taken by Maurice.
the Source Turning now to Tennyson we find these ideas
of its own poetically clothed in various poems.   The
Misery. soul's misery is traced to itself, not to any
arbitrary decree, as in " The Higher Pantheism."

> "Dark is the world to thee: thyself art the reason why;
>   For is He not all but thou, that hast power to feel 'I,
>   am I'?
>
>   Glory about thee, without thee, and thou fulfillest thy
>   doom
>   Making Him broken gleams, and a stifled splendour and
>   gloom."

Again, Maurice appealed to the instinctive, silent
hope of the human heart, which the poet had
voiced in the lines of the " In Memoriam."

> " The wish, that of the living whole
>   No life may fail beyond the grave,

Derives it not from what we have
The likest God within the soul?"

To which the essayist replied, "I do indeed accept with all my heart and soul the belief that it is what is 'likest God within the soul' which cherishes the poet's amazing expectation."

Maurice's estimate of the intrinsic value of the individual soul was thus expressed : "It would seem the idlest of all fancies either that mankind does form 'a living whole' or that each life has a preciousness and sanctity which he will acknow-ledge."

The poet had uttered the thought in the noble lines :

> "That nothing walks with aimless feet,
> That not one life shall be destroy'd,
> Or cast as rubbish to the void,
> When God hath made the pile complete."

Maurice could not tolerate the thought of a hell for the majority of men, when a few predestined souls were enjoying heaven. " If God has shown no care for my race, if He has left it to perish, we must sink together."

Again : " If you take from me the belief that God is always righteous, always maintaining a fight with evil, always seeking to bring His creatures out of it, you take everything from me, all hope now, all hope in the world to come."

Tennyson voices the same conviction, when, in

the poem "Despair," he puts into the lips of the rescued suicide the words :

The Deepest Thing in God.
"What! I should call on that Infinite Love that has
    served us so well ?
Infinite cruelty rather that made everlasting hell,
Made us, foreknew us, foredoom'd us."

Further, Maurice in his essay affirmed the deepest thing in God to be love, and that such love cannot be limited by finite creeds. With him it was an intuition that life is greater than death and will abolish death, and that love is deeper than hell and will destroy hell. The propositions "God is love" and "Hell is everlasting" appeared to him mutually destructive. "I am obliged to believe in an abyss of love which is deeper than the abyss of death. I dare not lose faith in that love. I must feel that this love is compassing the universe."

The poet echoes these memorable words, with their vast meaning, in the expressive lines :

"Ah yet—I have had some glimmer, at times, in my
    gloomiest woe,
Of a God behind all—after all—the great God for
    aught that I know ;
But the God of love and of hell together, they cannot
    be thought."

The essayist clung to the larger hope because he believed in the revelations of God in Christ, in redemption and in reconciliation. If it were not for this great evangel he affirmed, "The fact of sin and misery which I witness around me—which I feel within me—would be far too mighty for any dream of a restoration which may sometimes visit me." But clinging to that deepest love of the Father he could cherish " the poet's amazing expectation " expressed in the tender lines :

> " Oh yet we trust that somehow good
> Will be the final good of ill."

Thus in Maurice and Tennyson theology and poetry celebrate their union and take their place among the regenerating forces of the world.   They reveal a Faith that finds God in all the revelations, a Faith that sings of eternal hope for the race, a hope that flashes a heavenly ray into the mists that swathe the future.

And yet we may not dogmatise.   We can but pray, out of the tragedy of sin, to the perfect Goodness and throw our arms about the cross of Christ, which is ever the symbol in time of the dateless and deathless love of God.

SPIRITISM.

Enoch Arden. Aylmer's Field. Maud. The Ancient Sage. In Memoriam. The Holy Grail. Locksley Hall Sixty Years After.

WHAT has Tennyson to say on this subject of profound interest ? Was he a spiritualist ? Is there anything to show that he was conscious of spirit influence ? If spirit communion is possible we may look for some evidence in the writings of a poet with such intuition. We shall find fragmentary references which suggest that he was a pure spiritualist, and that he was conscious of spirit influence. There are two kinds of supernaturalism, the physical and the spiritual. By the physical is meant an impression of actual or future events conveyed to the mind through the neurotic system, when unduly excited. By the spiritual is meant pure contact of spirit with spirit when the nerves of sense are practically numbed. The following are examples of physical supernaturalism.

Physical
Super-
naturalism.
IN " Enoch Arden," when the lonely man, in his lonely isle, hears the ringing of the bells on Annie's wedding day, we have an illustration.

> "Though faintly, merrily, far and far away
> He heard the pealing of his parish bells,"

or when Annie, looking in her Bible for a sign that her husband was living or dead, dreamed she saw him

> "Sitting on a height
> Under a palm-tree, over him the Sun."

In " Aylmer's Field," when Edith, far away from Leolin, dies of fever, calling upon him, and when he, at the moment of her calling, leaps wildly from his bed, we have another example of an impression received through a highly wrought nervous system. The passage is the following :

> "Star to star vibrates light: may soul to soul
> Strike thro' a finer element of her own ?
> So, from afar, touch as at once ? or why
> That night, that moment, when she named his name,
> Did the keen shriek 'Yes love, yes, Edith, yes,'
> Shrill." . . .

And " Maud " affords illustrations of this kind of spiritism.   After the murder the lover of Maud is terrified by her apparition.

> " Then glided out of the joyous wood
> The ghastly Wraith of one that I know ;
> And there rang on a sudden a passionate cry,
> A cry for a brother's blood:
> It will ring in my heart and my ears, till I die, till
> I die."

And when he had made his escape over the sea he is still haunted with the phantom of Maud.

> "A shadow flits before me,
>   Not thou, but like to thee :
>   .   .   .   .
>   It leads me forth at evening,
>   It lightly winds and steals
>   In a cold white robe before me,
>   When all my spirit reels
>   At the shouts, the leagues of lights,
>   And the roaring of the wheels."

Thus the over-wrought man is distressed with the apparition of Maud, now her own lovely self, singing as of old, and now the avenging angel of a brother's blood.

> "By the curtains of my bed
>   That abiding phantom cold."

Spiritual Super-naturalism. BUT spiritual supernaturalism differs from physical supernaturalism in that, while the nervous system is supposed to be perfectly quiescent, the spiritual nature is intensely active and receives, by pure contact with spirit, knowledge not discernible by the senses.

There is evidence that the poet was something of a spiritual or trance-medium. In replying to a letter from one who communicated some singular experience, under the influence of anæsthetics, he wrote the following remarkable letter :—

"I never had any revelations through anæsthetics,

but a kind of waking trance—this for lack of a better name—I have frequently had, quite up from boyhood, when I have been all alone. This has often come upon me through repeating my own name to myself silently till, all at once as it were out of the intensity of the consciousness of individuality, the individuality itself seemed to dissolve and fade away into boundless being, and this not a confused state, but the clearest of the clearest, the surest of surest, utterly beyond words, where death was an almost laughable impossibility, the loss of personality—if so it were—seeming no extinction, but the only true life. I am ashamed of my feeble description. Have I not said the state is utterly beyond words?"

Doubtless this is the experience we find related in "The Ancient Sage." *

> "And more, my son! for more than once when I
> Sat all alone, revolving in myself
> The word that is the symbol of myself,
> The mortal limit of the self was loosed,
> And passed into the nameless, as a cloud
> Melts into heaven."

The poem goes on to describe how all physical sensation was numbed; he touched his limbs and they did not appear to be his, and at the same time consciousness was keenly alive and the intensity of life was inexpressible.

Again in the "In Memoriam," we have a similar

* Vide *A Memoir*, ii., p. 319.

experience. The poet doubts whether it is possible
for a spirit to reappear in corporeal form.

> "I shall not see thee. Dare I say
> No spirit ever brake the band
> That stays him. . ."
>
> (*Ode xciii.*)

But he thinks perhaps the spirit "may come"
when all the nerves are at rest, with sensation
numbed, and hold communion with him.

> "Where all the nerve of sense is numb;
> Spirit to Spirit, Ghost to Ghost."

Then comes the inarticulate yearning for fellowship with the spirit of his friend

> "Descend, and touch, . . .
> .   .   .   .   .
> That in this blindness of the frame
> My ghost may feel that thine is near."

He states the conditions of spirit communion.
There must be the pure heart and the sound head,
and the spirit must be at peace. Imagination and
memory and conscience must be calm and cloudless.
The spirits cannot enter where discord and doubt
prevail.

> "They can but listen at the gates,
> And hear the household jar within."
>
> (*Ode xciv.*

He further relates a trance experience in which
it would appear that the spirit of the poet was in
direct communion with the spirit of his friend, and

in which he struggles to express the inexpressible
When all had gone to rest and the poet was left
alone, he read the "noble letters of the dead," and
as he read he fell into a trance of vivid consciousness, with thrilling experience.

> "And all at once it seem'd at last
> The living soul was flash'd on mine,
>
> And mine in this was wound, and whirl'd
>   About empyreal heights of thought,
>   And came on that which is, and caught
> The deep pulsations of the world"
>   (*Ode xcv.*)

The trance, with its wonderful sights and sounds,
lasted until the dawn.

Again, in the "Holy Grail," we have a reference
to those visions that distinctly belong to trance
experiences and which, according to the *Spectator*,
are a transcript of the poet's own experience.

> "Let visions of the night or of the day
> Come, as they will; and many a time they come,
> Until this earth he walks on seems not earth,
> This light that strikes his eyeball is not light,
> This air that smites his forehead is not air
> But vision."

If the experiences, related in the "Ancient Sage,"
and "In Memoriam" and "The Holy Grail," were
personal, it is clear that the poet was a trance
medium and in sympathy with pure spiritism.

As to whether in waking moments he was
conscious of the presence and the inter-action of

22

intelligences not of earth, we have little direct evidence. "It is understood that he, the poet, believed that he wrote many of the best and truest things he ever published under the direct influence of higher intelligences, of whose presence he was distinctly conscious. He felt them near him, and his mind was impressed with their ideas. He was, to use the technical term, a clairaudient and an in-spirational medium. He was not clairvoyant. These mystic influences came to him in the night season. They were heard in the voices of the wind. They made him write what he sometimes imperfectly understood, when in a state of mind that was not always distinguishable from trance."

In "Locksley Hall, Sixty Years After," the possible influence of spirits upon the destiny of the world is touched in the lines :—

> "Ere she gain her heavenly-best, a God must mingle
> with the game :
> Nay, there may be those about us whom we neither
> see nor name."

MAN : HIS IMMORTALITY.

WE have already seen in the analysis of some of the poems that the poet decides for the "Everlasting Yea," but it is interesting to find the ground on which he bases his faith. This becomes clear as we bring together the scattered poems which contain intimations of immortality. The intimations become arguments and may be clearly deduced from the poems and formulated.

The Pure Justice of God. *First*—He finds an argument for immortality ✓ in the pure justice of God.

> "Thou will not leave us in the dust:
> Thou madest man, he knows not why:
> He thinks he was not made to die;
> And Thou hast made him: Thou art just."

The justice of God is involved in the immortality of man. Man has the thought, and cherishes it with pathetic persistence, that he " was not made to die." Whence comes the thought that leaps the

339

bound of time and sense and thinks itself part of
a larger order—beyond the limits of the finite?
Who but the infinite One could inspire an infinite
thought in a finite mind?   The thought of immortality is imbedded in the consciousness of the race.
" My mind can take no hold of the present world,
nor rest in it for a moment, but my whole nature
rushes on with irresistible force towards a future
and better state of things."   What was thus philosophically expressed by Fichte is poetically voiced by
Tennyson, in the lines :

> " My own dim life should teach me this,
>   That life shall live for evermore,
>   Else earth is darkness at the core,
> And dust and ashes all that is."

If God be just He will not crush the seedling
thought sown broadcast in the human mind.   The
very thought is a prophecy and a promise.

The Inward *Second*—He finds an argument for immor-
Evidence tality in the inward evidence of being, to
of Being. which he gives expression in " The Two
Voices."

> " Who forged that other influence,
>   That heat of inward evidence,
>   By which he doubts against the sense ?

> " He owns the fatal gift of eyes,
>   That read his spirit blindly wise,
>   Not simple as a thing that dies.

" Here sits he shaping wings to fly :
His heart forebodes a mystery:
He names the name Eternity."

What is this " inward evidence " ?   It is the
sense of eternity.   The soul is ever haunted with
the mystery of death and with the feeling that
death does not end life.   As the sky bends over
the earth and is its complement, so eternity domes
the soul and completes the unfinished life of man.
Strike out immortality and a whole host of human
powers and aspirations, and intuitions, would find no
explanation either of their origin or persistence.
But the poet, along with Emerson, infers that
" when the Master of the universe has points to
carry in his government, he impresses his will in
the structure of minds."   God has built into the
structure of the human soul this sense of eternity,
and it is incredible that he should place it there
without a moral purpose.   Having implanted an
infinite desire He will surely satisfy it with an
infinite reality.   The poet sees in the human soul
heights and depths beyond all material limits.
This thought finds speech in " The Voice and the
Peak," where the things within the soul are larger
than all without.   In its instincts and intuitions
and aspirations the soul is keyed to the spiritual
and eternal.   The voice of the Peak tells of constant
change, the flux of nature.   The physical heights
are drawn down into the depths of ocean.

> "They leave the heights and are troubled,
>   And moan and sink to their rest,"

but only to be reared again—and yet not for long.
The cycle of change must end and the material
forms will

> "Pass, and are found no more."

But the soul is greater. It has heights beyond
the mountain—its aspirations soar to God. It has
depths deeper than the sea—it carries within a
spiritual world, with endless tides of feeling.

> "A deep below the deep,
>   And a height beyond the height!"

And so, in the "inward evidence," the poet finds
an intimation of immortality.

The Persistence of Human Love. *Third*—He finds an argument in the persistence of human love.

How delicately touched in that poem of
deep human feeling, "The Grandmother," is
this persistence of love!

The pathos of the poem lies in its naturalness.
It is the voice of the human heart crying for those
"within the veil." The white-haired grandmother
sits and prattles of the husband of her youth and
of the children who had come and gone—of the
babe whose little face was troubled with pain as
he fought in vain for life. Annie and Charlie and

Harry are dead, and yet she will have it that they are all alive.

> "They come and sit by my chair, they hover about my
> bed,
> I am not always certain if they be alive or dead."

Now that she is told of the death of her Willy there are the same tender recollections with the persistence of love in believing that there is a dawn to death.

> "For Willy I cannot weep. I shall see him another
> morn."

She is old and tired and wants to rest, but her love is young as the morning. She talks of death as if it merely meant going into another room. She will go soon and find her dear ones waiting there !

> "Gone for a minute, my son, from this room into the
> next ;
> I, too, shall go in a minute. . . ."

The poem, in its simplicity and pathos and naturalness, voices the pure instinct of the universal heart, that death does not end life. Whatever reason may say, when haunted with the mystery of the future, the heart is always ready with its protest and supplies its own proof of immortality.

> "And like a man in wrath the heart
> Stood up and answered, 'I have felt.'"

The larger part of "In Memoriam," as we have

seen, is a noble affirmation of man's immortality, but the persistence of love is finely focussed in Ode xxxv. The poet shows that immortality is involved in the existence of love. If some trust-worthy voice declared that death ends all in his narrow house the poet would still want to keep love alive, but he would be reminded by the disintegration of nature of the final death of love itself. In that case love would lose its sweetness and become a pain.

"Half dead to know that I shall die."

But the case is impossible. If love were linked to death and not to life it never could have been.

"If death were seen
At first as death, love had not been,
Or been in narrowest working shut."

It would have remained animal and instinctive love instead of becoming spiritual and perceptive. Thus the existence of love, which ever craves the object "loved and lost awhile," is to the poet an intimation of immortality.

The Incom-
pleteness
of present
life.
Fourth—He finds an argument in our un-finished lives and unrealised aspirations.
The argument is powerfully condensed in "Vastness," where he sums up the utter failure of nature and human life apart from immortality.

> "What is it all, if we all of us end but in being our
> own corpse-coffins at last,
> Swallowed in vastness, lost in silence, drown'd in
> the deeps of a meaningless past?"

What if our philosophies and arts and sciences and human loves and noble deeds pass into eternal silence? Then God has surely mocked us, and human life, with its pathetic cry for fuller, richer being, is but "a murmur of gnats in the gloom." The poet falls back on love, and rests in it, as the deepest thing in the soul demanding immortality. Death cannot kill love nor the loved one and, as he recalls the memory of his friend, he sings once again in the shrine of love the song of immortal life.

> "Peace, let it be! for I loved him and love him for
> ever: the dead are not dead but alive."

The Human Spirit Distinct from Matter. *Fifth*—He finds an argument in the human spirit as an entity distinct from matter.

In the " Ancient Sage " the mystic dreamer tells how his self or spirit became separated from the body and in its separation entered into life unspeakable.

> "I touch'd my limbs, the limbs
> Were strange not mine and yet no shade of doubt,
> But utter clearness, and thro' loss of self
> The gain of such large life as match'd with ours
> Were sun to spark—unshadowable in words,
> Themselves but shadows of a shadow-world."

In such experiences, more common among the dreamers of the Orient, the poet finds a mystic hint of immortality. Indeed, the letter, penned by himself and already quoted, shows that in this passage he was relating his own experience as a trance medium. Whatever may be said of the experience, doubtless the fact that we do not think of spirit in the terms of matter becomes an argument for existence apart from matter and is expressed in the passage.

Thus in all his works the poet protests, with glowing indignation, against the crass materialism that would resolve all of man into dust. It is incredible that the mighty forces of nature and of civilisation should have spent themselves on the making of man, only, at last, as he rises to higher life, to use the hidden hands that made him, to thrust him back into the grave of eternal silence and sleep.

> "What then were God to such as I?
>
> .   .   .   .
>
> 'Twere best at once to sink to peace,
> Like birds the charming serpent draws
> To drop head-foremost in the jaws
> Of vacant darkness, and to cease."

INDEX.

347

FOURTH EDITION.

Cr. 8vo. art canvas, gilt, 2s. 6d.

The House of Dreams

An Allegory

By W. J. Dawson.

Author of " London Idylls," &c.

"'The House of Dreams' belongs to the same class as Mrs Oliphant's 'A Pilgrim in the Unseen,' and may rival the great popularity of that striking fancy. . . . A book of signal literary beauty, of profound tenderness, and deeply reverent throughout; the work of a man who finds in earth and heaven alike the sign and token of the Cross."— *The British Weekly.*

" A very beautiful allegory. . . . The author's deep reverence and exalted phantasy never ring false, and his work cannot fail to inspire the reader with reverence for ideals undreamed of in worldly philosophy."—*The Pall Mall Gazette.*

Crown 8vo, buckram, 3s. 6d.

The Sorrow of God

And Other Sermons
By Rev. John Oates.

" For the contents of 'The Sorrow of God' we have nothing but praise, and we could wish for nothing more than that the book might be widely circulated. Spiritual insight, large culture, with its consequent breadth of sympathy and eloquent expression, are the distinguishing features of what is, without exaggeration, a collection of notable sermons. . . . Those of our readers who value a fresh utterance on the great problems of religion will lose no time in getting acquainted with a book we have been able to notice all too briefly."— *The Sunday School Chronicle.*

"There are many noble utterances in these sermons. . . . It is because the author helps us to feel purer and better that we so heartily commend his book."—*The New Age.*

London : 10 Henrietta Street, Covent Garden, W.C.